SIRENN

By Nelle W., Illustrated by
RosyMollet

<u>Warning!</u>
There are mentions of Abuse,
Drugs, Sex, Violence, and Suicide.

Contents

Chapter 1

'Rhiannon'

In mythology, sirens were captivating, human-like beings known for their irresistibly, enchanting voices, and seductive charm. In my case, my main focus was survival. I moved through the streets with the stealth and precision of a predator, seeking opportunities to offer various services in exchange for compensation. My services ranged from providing a listening ear for fifty dollars to more intimate encounters for a hundred to three hundred dollars, always placing safety and protection as my top priority. Some may label me as a dangerous temptation—a figure often associated with the terms like hooker, prostitute, or whore. On the streets, I embody an homage to those mythical beings who ensnared and captivated pirate men, seizing their very essence.

You might think I'd be the queen of the fucking world because of it, but no, I am a victim. Not a slave but a victim to the life I had to endure. I've always had a rough life, decent, but still rough. My household felt like a nightmare. My father was absent for most of my life, and my mother was the most narcissistic person imaginable. Being an only child made life even worse—no one to play with or lean on for support. I never had friends because others simply didn't interest me. They were mostly bullies, followers, or just plain ignorant. I'm not rich, but I'm not wealthy either. I'm not ecstatic about life, but I'm realistic, never hopeful. I'm not religious, yet I believe someone must be hovering above this cesspool we call the "world." I'm not loving but somewhat charismatic. I'm seen as a whore, yet never destined to be recognized as a human being by others. I'm not pure but rather tainted.

I only saw the world in black and white. It could never be gray—complex, but not gray. It was too evil and pessimistic to be anything in between. I tended to see the darkness in everything, even the most innocent. I liked to think it was a curse I bore—to condemn others as I had been. No one gave me a chance, so why should I give the world one? Everything I consumed or came into contact with felt filthy and dark. That was all I could see and nothing else. I wished to see the light and pretend the darkness didn't exist, but it haunted me everywhere. It perched upon my shoulders, heavy as a burden I couldn't shake off, staining me for the rest of my life. But what could I do? I was just as unclean as the next person—nothing anyone, any man, couldn't see.

My life had always been challenging since I had run away from home at nineteen. It hadn't been to seek attention or to get my mother to express her undying love for me, but to be free. As free as anyone could be, so I thought. This path led me to the city, which was ironic because I had been a Southern girl born and raised. All I had known were crops, dirt roads, and nothingness for miles, but in the city, there had been bright lights, sidewalks, people, sin, money, and even worse, fun. My mother would have smiled at the outcome of my decisions. She would have said, "I always knew you were a whore. Anybody could see you were a fast thing from a mile away." A harsh truth I hadn't liked to think about back then, but had come to terms with. At least I was needed in the city, and she had still been stuck in that vastness of a town.

I would admit that the small towns were more hospitable than the city and less of a dump—well, at least where I lived was. I stayed in the city's poorest area, in a small, old, damp, and cold apartment—a place only a runaway could find. I wasn't alone, which I found somewhat comforting. Most of my peers here were runaways, drug addicts, mentally ill, trafficked, and just homeless. Nothing that most of the public or tricks didn't already know. It was disheartening at first, but as time went on, you learned to adapt and became numb to your situation, especially regarding others around you. It felt like a prison, but you had to get by with slim pickings and only a few hours of fresh air while living in the poorest area. It was pretty drab for someone of the utmost demand.

I lived with a roommate named Moe (aka Bambi), who took me in when I needed her. Although the apartment belonged to her, I paid most of the bills, which made it feel more like mine. She didn't like it when I said that because she believed she contributed just as much as I did, but she barely stayed here and didn't earn nearly as much as I did. Most of the time, she was high on low-quality cocaine. I didn't know how she managed to get it since she couldn't afford it. She was like my sister—we had been through a lot together. We supported each other through dealing with pimps, tricks, drug overdoses, and hospital visits. She was the closest thing to family in that terrible place. She was as thin as a tree branch, with small breasts, a fawn-like face, big ears, and short, wolf-cut hair.

The only thing that unsettled me about her was her hollow, slate-gray eyes. The color was eerie, especially coupled with her tendency to slur her words. If an average person came into contact with her, they would have thought she was half-dead and starved. But that was Bambi, high on life yet dead inside. There was nothing inside her small head except the whistling of air. I'm surprised she survived this long on her own. When I first met her, she had a pimp named Rio, whom I found to be less intimidating than a rat in the city sewers. He always carried a gun that didn't even have bullets, just for show to scare his girls. He walked with an almost erratic drag of his right leg, and his teeth were chipped and yellow. But she loved him. She took me in, which he thought meant he owned me.

I was new to the scene and a kid who came from an abusive household, so I wasn't too open-minded about authority or someone owning me again. I gave him a run for his money, even though he introduced me to the nightlife. I mean, I was young with little to no education, money, and hungry, so I did everything he said to do. Of course, with his girls, the first lesson was to pleasure the trick - a lesson that led to me having sex with him. It was hell to have let such a creep touch me, but I did what I had to do to survive. I felt repulsed after that encounter; it made my skin crawl. I couldn't sleep for nights because of it, and I even lost my mind for a short time, crying after every transaction. Bambi said it would become easier as time passed, but that only made me hate myself more each day.

I know what you're thinking. Why didn't I get a job like everyone else? It wasn't as easy as you might think to be a runaway in a new place. I didn't exactly have a resume, little to no money or a functioning phone. But, I did manage to get two jobs: one in waitressing and one in fast food. I moved from motel to motel, but there was so little money that I couldn't earn enough. Still, I survived for a while until I lost both jobs due to unfortunate circumstances. I don't want to go into too much detail about it. Let's just say I was better off, not that this new occupation was any better. I am the product of a troubled life and a hopeless soul. I never had a chance. It was even harder because I wanted to call my mother and beg her to let me come back home, but I knew I would end up in the same situation. I couldn't return to that town and hear the screaming of such a cursed woman like her. I know for certain it would have led to bad outcomes, and I wanted everyone to keep their lives for as long as possible. Bambi was my answer for the time being.

Anyway, I wanted to get rid of Rio and didn't have to do much. He was a heavy drinker, and I planned to slip something into his favorite bottle one night, but it turned out he owed money to some important people. He hid from them by having a decoy place and a real place where he stayed. Somehow, they found him and confronted him in his dingy apartment, which wasn't too far down the hall from us. One bullet to the head. One silent bullet. Bambi was devastated, but I was numb to it. We were free, and I didn't have to fuck whoever he wanted or have him exist in this life. It was freedom, baby! Besides my role in ratting him out, which demonstrated resilience on my part, we could sleep in, choose when to find a trick, and spend our money on guilty pleasures like clothes, food, and hygiene—well, what little we could afford in such an expensive, big city.

He was a cliché. Nobody liked him, not even his so-called "friends" or "business partners." He was buried in a box at thirty-five with nothing to show for it, and no one except Bambi and me attended. The other girls found another pimp or madame or resorted to self-service. She cried for forty days and nights over that asshole as if he were so special. If you let her tell it, he took "care" of her and "loved" her. But who beats and treats someone they care about like property? She knew how I felt about the late Rio but would always say, "He was a good pimp. If you listened, there wouldn't be any problems, and half the time, it was just the drugs and alcohol talking." Sometimes, I would tune her out because she was a slave to her circumstances. She didn't know anything better than the life shown to her, but I chose this life. I decided to be a predator looking for prey, hoping to gain some pay in such a short lifespan.

I liked to think of myself as a cat—not just any cat, but a black cat—beautiful and mysterious. I tend to be alone, searching through life for meaning, but in the end, I am left disappointed. An eternity of roaming the streets at night, hoping to find freedom from the insanity of my life through some hopeful plea. Ask anyone around. I was like a protector, an animal marking my territory as no one dared to cross or stand where I stood on the block. I'm not innocent, nor do I want to be saved. I would help myself and find somewhere I could call home.

That's the only thing I truly wanted in life: to have a place I could call home. Materialistic to others but crucial to me. There was nothing I wanted more.

I wouldn't consider myself the prettiest of the bunch. I was average, or so others said. I weighed a solid 185 pounds and had an hourglass figure with double D-cup breasts. I had a baby face with oval-shaped, coffee-brown eyes, high cheekbones, and bushy eyebrows. My lips and nose were rather ordinary. My hair was thick, long, curly, shoulder-length, and as black as my heart. I found that my hair was the only good thing about me. It was the prettiest thing I possessed, and sometimes, as a little girl, it would hurt when my mother trimmed my hair or when I over-dyed it. It meant my best feature no longer held me in the running, and I would confront the fact that I wasn't all that pretty.

Not that the men cared. As long as you were a good fuck and gave a good blowjob, money would be the reward. People hated to admit it, but money was a reward for everything, and everyone was a whore to obtain it. Except for a woman, you were a slut before you ever became a fetus. It was a given right to be a whore because of the one thing between your legs. It was a profession created solely for the pleasure of others and the torment of some—woman, child, or man. A tale that was as old as time. I found Bambi much more beautiful, but the drugs changed her drastically. She would be a knockout like she once was if she had stayed away from that poisonous powder.

An ugly duckling like me got by with outfits, makeup, and hair, but take those away, and I was very average. Well, at least that's how I felt. Before I could walk, my mother would call me fat, ugly, and unloved. Not that she was gorgeous herself. I never knew if it was true or if those exact words embedded in me made me think that way. I always felt hideous, no matter how much others called me "pretty." It was my job to be sexy and confident, but inside, I knew that same darkness would never let me be happy. I could never truly think positively about myself.

I despised my large pores, uneven shoulders, and hip dips. I longed for perfection. I seemed perfect to some extent, but in reality, I wasn't. I tempted men for a living with my kind and affectionate words and the comforting embrace of my body. There was nothing more valuable that I could offer. Love and family were not an option because a prostitute couldn't become a housewife unless her husband was manic or abusive. I was a Greek myth that lured men with a façade of purity and perfection, only for them to approach and discover the horrid and dark beast within. I came offering my wet and voluptuous body for the promise of coins. A fate worse than begging on the streets for an ounce of compassion. I would receive no sympathy, even if I were someone's daughter, sibling, or companion — not that I had to be. I felt like a creature trapped on a rock with waves crashing against the surface, hoping to find a way back to my humanity and a place in the world.

The apartment building was in disrepair, featuring crumbling walls, vines growing out of the cracks, broken windows, empty apartments, and garbage scattered on the sidewalks. The hallways were covered in graffiti, with broken doors and aging stairwells that failed to meet inspection standards. The lobby had old, dented metal mailboxes with torn-off doors and a tangle of wires hanging from the ceiling. Mold and half-torn flyers decorated the walls. Only tenants who had paid their rent could enter the building. Our landlord, Amy, was solely focused on collecting rent. If you couldn't pay, you couldn't stay. Because of Amy, I had to work like a dog in heat. Bambi didn't help, as she irresponsibly spent money on drugs, forcing me to cover her share of the rent. At $200 a month, it was a reasonable place to live. It could have been more appealing, but at least it provided a roof over our heads.

Regardless of the age of the apartment—built in the 1950s—we surprisingly didn't experience any bug or rodent issues, which was a relief. However, the decaying walls, with peeling paint and plaster, affected our peace of mind. It was evident that there was mold somewhere, possibly hidden within the walls, which drove us crazy, but we couldn't afford to be picky due to the limited housing options in the area. Despite the shortcomings, we were content with what we had and didn't complain. The kitchen, although small, had a quaint charm with its white refrigerator and stove, a round wooden table adorned with a white plastic tablecloth, and a window that, unfortunately, wouldn't open, limiting ventilation. The inadequate lighting in our apartment was also a challenge, with only three lights: one for the bathroom, one for the kitchen, and one for the combined living room and bedroom, leaving some areas poorly lit.

The walls of our apartment were stark white, but they bore the marks of time, showing faded grey sweat spots and peeling plaster. Two oversized paintings adorned the walls, presumably left behind by the previous artistic tenants. One of the paintings depicted a figure that defied gender identification, while the other was an intriguing arrangement of squares in various radiant colors. A discarded wool carpet, salvaged from the trash, covered the blue-tiled floor, adding a touch of warmth to the otherwise bare space. The living room was sparsely furnished with only two separate dressers, and CDs were meticulously lined across the floor. We had to share a bed because we could only afford one. It was a makeshift bed supported by boxes filled with bricks. It looked like a full-sized bed with orange and white floral pillows, white sheets, and an oversized floral comforter we bought for a low price.

The bathroom tub, cabinets, and walls were a ghastly shade of yellow that seemed to have been plucked straight from a 1950s time capsule.

Once dull brown, the tiles were cracked and chipped, with several missing, leaving unsightly gaps. Unhinged and dysfunctional, the door remained permanently ajar, offering little privacy. There was no window, and an old-school sink, along with a dingy mirror, occupied the space. The room was stripped of any character or charm, and we made no effort to change that. It wasn't that we didn't want to; after being surrounded by such a depressing atmosphere with no money for so long, you tend to ignore decorating your space for a while.

Unlike the Upper East Side, where I lived felt like a gutter, lacking resources, Christmas carols, elegant apartments, and mansions. It was the absolute worst. Bambi and I got by most days because people recognized us and knew what we did, but that didn't ensure our safety. Sometimes, we had to fight with our bare hands to survive. I've lost count of how many times I've heard girls tell stories about being taken advantage of, especially without pay. It was brutal. Even Bambi had her own stories, which kept me awake at night. I took precautions with a gun and a knife. We never walked alone, always in groups; those were the rules. It kept us safe and alive. The streets were dangerous, particularly at night. The world thought it owned us. We were prostitutes, but we were human beings with beating hearts. We weren't cattle or prey to be slaughtered for others' enjoyment. We had dreams, hopes, and lives before becoming enslaved to what we do. Whether by choice or not, it was never a real choice given the cards we were dealt. Each of us carried a darkness inside and a light that never dimmed. We all wanted to break free from whatever haunted us, but most importantly, we yearned for a life beyond this. It wasn't fair, but it was all we had to make it day after day. We were lost children; that's what we were: lost souls.

I followed three rules regarding potential customers: no kissing, no orgies, and always using protection. Girls like me had to be strict, especially since we were easy targets for perverts, police, and freaks. Fending for ourselves daily was exhausting, but everybody had to follow the rules, or anarchy would arise. If I had known better when I arrived in the city, I would have become a dancer or escort; at least they obtained men with more money, but a man with a fetish or a dick was a potential paying customer. I came in contact with some weirdos, mainly the type that had a foot fetish or liked being pissed on.

I made $300 most nights, but it wasn't nearly enough to live on. We often had to choose between food and clothing, and trust me, our clothes were old. Honestly, nine times out of ten, the money went towards rent. Sometimes, I got lucky and made an extra $50 to $100 to save for emergencies or treat myself. It was a gloomy existence, but really, what could we do? Bambi and I would take on two potential customers together if it meant more cash. We haven't come away too hungry or crazy during the past few holidays. She was often so coked out of her mind that she could only make around $100 or less per night, and that was only if she didn't run into a trick who bolted with her money or beat her senseless. And that's why I choose customers for her now and keep her close by my side.

I couldn't judge her, though; I wasn't inexperienced when it came to drugs, and I'm not talking about weed. She seemed to handle cocaine easily, but I preferred taking pills courtesy of my divorced mother. Old habits never die hard; they're just passed on to the next person who suffers. Diazepam was my mother's favorite for her anxiety, and for some reason, one day, I snuck into her room and stole some. That day was a trip because she was outraged, but I was higher than Bugs Bunny. It made me feel more alive than any experience I had in life, and I didn't stop. I made sure to be controlled in indulging my own guilty pleasure. I can say I overdosed only once on my habit, while Bambi had overdosed a total of six times. I was surprised that her body still functioned for such a small person.

I kept my little habit hidden from Bambi, not because she would disapprove, but because I didn't want her to see me as equally lost. While her current lifestyle and work were her sole passion and focus, I felt the need for change, but saving up was challenging with her constant presence. I longed to build a foundation that would let me live life on my terms. It was exhilarating to imagine living in a spacious white farmhouse surrounded by open land and experiencing peace. I cherished the independence of having my thoughts separate from Bambi. Even though we were inseparable, there were times when she would disappear for days at a time. It weighed heavily on my conscience to feel any hint of joy as I worried about who would take care of her and ensure she was properly nourished and rested. I couldn't bear to leave her behind. She wouldn't survive this time.

We were both a mess before we found each other, but we've been looking out for one another ever since. But who was I fooling? I was caught in the same destructive cycle as her – a junkie and a prostitute. No matter how hard I tried to break free from this nightmarish existence, I always found myself entangled again. It felt like I was trapped in a bottomless pit filled with demons, forgotten souls, and fallen angels. I wanted to be different, to escape this life, but I realized I was no more special than anyone else – just a simple runaway with nowhere to go and little hope for change. Bitterness towards life consumed me. It didn't seem fair that some people had it so much better than the rest of us. I often wondered what might have been if I hadn't left home. I could picture myself working at the local diner, perhaps pregnant, or even mistakenly believing I was in love with a small-town boy. It would have been a bleak existence, but it seemed preferable to my current reality. I would have been just Rhiannon, the small-town girl in that life.

Chapter 2

'Irish Twins'

Woven together like Siamese twins, we lay stark-naked in the bathroom tub—two lost children cradling each other for affection, sisters with different mothers and fathers. The coldness of the room hit our exposed bodies as we lay behind the sheer shower curtain. I felt pressed against her, her pale, soft skin suffocating me. The light shining through the curtain transformed into a disco ball, casting dancing shadows over us. The roughness of the chipped paint on the tub scraped my leg as it grew numb under Bambi's weight. Frustration settled in as I tried to move, with only my head, left arm, and leg being mobile. The poor quality of our blue wigs created uncomfortable friction against my scalp.

As I leaned back against the tub's edge, I noticed her heavily made-up face and the natural color of her hair peeking out from under her wig. The morning felt hazy as I stared at the bare wall. Bambi was still asleep next to me, and the previous night was a blur. I knew we enjoyed partying, but not to the point of amnesia. I felt sluggish, wondering what time it was in the morning. It couldn't be too early or too late because if it were early, my eyes tended to be dry, but if it were late, my nipples would be rock hard. It was my body's way of keeping track of time, and although I didn't believe in superstition, I had faith in my body. I couldn't stay in the bathroom indefinitely and knew I had to wake her up, but I wanted to take a few minutes for myself before I did.

My mouth was dry, and we both smelled strongly of alcohol and sex. I noticed the grime on our feet at the end of the tub from who knows what. Our bodies felt filthy as we tangled together. I wanted to get out of the tub. It was claustrophobic, and I didn't like being in closed spaces too much. The apartment was already small, but had enough open space for me not to lose my mind. How did we even manage to end up in this position with so little room? We must have been completely out of our minds to do this, especially in that state. Knowing me, it was probably my idea, and she went along with it. When I'm drunk, I tend to do the most idiotic things, like accepting a dare to walk on top of people's cars. That led to me being intoxicated, arrested, and held for 36 hours without a shower, surviving on vending machine food.

I traced circles on her shoulder with my finger as she slept, my eyes outlining the shape of her petite nose and long, false lashes. I wondered what she was dreaming about as she moaned in her sleep. Bambi rarely talked about her past, even if she had dreams. It made me sad for her. Life had broken her before she could grow into her own person. However, I appreciated how she spoke her mind, especially when expressing her love and admiration for something or someone. It was bittersweet. I placed my forehead next to hers and smiled. She seemed lifeless and cold next to me. My peachy, tanned skin created a stark contrast between us.

As much as I loved her, I gently caressed her face as she lay beside me, hoping she would wake up. I made another attempt by poking her face and saying, "Bambi, wake up." But she just moaned in annoyance. I said in a soft but encouraging voice, "It's morning; time to get up," while rocking her shoulder. I could hear the birds singing outside and the bustle of the busy streets. My stomach was ravaged with hunger, and my body felt weak, so I did what I had to do. I straightened my hand and positioned it over her face, and with the firmness of my palm, I smacked her hard and said, "Wake the fuck up and get off me!"

It was as if a shockwave had jolted her awake as she sat up quickly. She was disoriented, but at least it meant I would have free rein of my body. I pushed the shower curtain back with my free hand as Bambi somehow managed to stretch and regain her senses. She rubbed her face, revealing a bright red spot where I had smacked her, and asked, "Did you really have to smack me so hard?"

I nodded. "Yes, because you wouldn't wake up."

"Are you at least going to say sorry?" she said in a husky voice.

"No!" I replied, annoyed. "Now get off me!"

We took a moment, but we eventually untangled ourselves and freed ourselves from the tub. I stumbled back onto the floor as I sat up, my hands gripping the rim of the tub, while Bambi wobbled to the bedroom, completely naked and drowsy. I snatched my wig off, feeling relief as my hair was able to breathe. My ass was attached to the cold tile floor, and I could hear Bambi puking. I rolled my eyes and said, "Don't puke on the bed, please!" This was one of the reasons I hated it when we partied too hard: because of cleaning up behind each other, but more so, I was behind her.

I ran my hands through my hair as I listened to Bambi retch into the kitchen sink. She could never handle her liquor. She was always so delicate and needed saving, even from herself. Although she was older than me, I cared for her, but that was nothing new. She reminded me of my mother, except she was likable and had a kind heart. In less than a minute, the apartment fell silent, and all I could hear was the drip of the bathroom faucet and the whistle of the wind outside. I frowned and leaned forward to gaze out the door, waiting to see if she was okay.

We had a pink, tattered curtain separating the kitchen from the living room, so I could only see the edge of our bed and two closed curtains. Worry began to set in, so I asked, "Are you okay?" But she didn't respond. I mustered my strength to get up and walk to the bathroom doorway. "Moe! Are you okay? Don't make me come in there because, I swear, if you're dead, I'm going to kill you!" I yelled in concern.

"I'm—I'm okay," she said wearily, breathing heavily.

I walked swiftly into the living room and saw her lying on the bed, hungover. I let out a sigh of relief and laughed at the sight.

"You scared the shit out of me, you know that?" I said as I pulled the cover over her.

"I didn't mean to. I forgot how shitty it feels to be hungover," she said as she tossed her wig onto the floor and cradled her stomach.

"You want me to make you something?" I asked while freezing my ass off.

She whined weakly. "No. Let me lie here. I'll eat later."

I shrugged. "Okay, suit yourself." I strolled over to the vintage wooden vanity dresser we both use and carefully selected a fresh set of clothes, neatly folded and waiting for me. I decided to freshen up, so I returned to the bathroom and turned on the shower. As the water warmed up, I tested it by placing my hand in the stream, ensuring it was scalding hot, just the way I liked it. I then reached up, pulled off my hair tie, and let my long hair cascade down my back, gently separating the strands with my hands. I checked on Bambi again and found her asleep, allowing me to complete my routine. Not that I had much to contribute to my limited beauty. I stepped into the shower headfirst and let the water wash over me, cleansing myself of the previous day's energy and people. My muscles relaxed as I washed away the makeup from my face. I held my neck as I breathed in the hot steam filling the apartment, bringing warmth and the lingering scent of soap in the air. I carefully washed my body, contemplating whether I wanted to go out at night with Bambi, but everything in me protested. I wanted to stay in and indulge in whatever little food we had in the apartment, then maybe later find some new tricks. It went against my better judgment to make less money than necessary because the rent was due soon, and I knew Amy would come looking for it. Stressing while everyone else remained untroubled was my daily routine.

✹

I carefully tipped my bowl, letting the cereal cascade onto my spoon. Sitting at the kitchen table, I was engrossed in old Scooby-Doo reruns on our vintage TV perched atop the refrigerator. In the background, Bambi lounged on the bed, focused on flipping through model magazines while taking slow drags from her last cigarette. Next to her lay a partially eaten apple and a delicate rosary. Whenever she indulged in a smoke, she used the apple as an impromptu ashtray, insisting it balanced out the toll of her daily tobacco consumption. It seemed she had taken only a single bite from the apple, a symbolic gesture rather than a meal. Her minimal eating habits were unsurprising, considering her preference for cigarettes and Coke as her breakfast and dinner staples. The stark prominence of her ribcage suggested fragility, as if any impact could lead to a fracture.

She had heavy bags under her eyes, as if she had cried for days, but I knew it was from malnutrition. I could get her to eat some days, but she protested now more than ever. It wasn't like I was Mother Teresa when I approached people about their problems. I couldn't be gentle on some issues. It wasn't me, and I hated talking around in circles. I was blunter than the average person, and Bambi was fragile, broken, and confused about life. I wanted to help her like I wanted to help my mother and myself, but it was useless. She was just as stubborn as me.

I drank the milk from my bowl and set it on the table before turning off the TV.

"I was listening to that," she exclaimed, staring at the outdated fashion magazine.

I grabbed the bowl, put it in the sink, and turned to look at her. "Good for you," I said nonchalantly, then turned on the water and started washing the dish.

"What's up with you?" she asked. "You've been snappy since early this morning—more than usual."

I took a deep breath, turned off the faucet, and faced her. "When are you going to eat? I haven't seen you eat in three days, and frankly, I don't want to see you die on my watch."

Bambi chuckled and rolled her eyes. "Here you go again!" she whined.

I crossed my arms and leaned against the kitchen sink. "I worry about you. What can I say?" I said sarcastically. She smiled and replied, "Don't be! I'll eat when I get hungry."

"You haven't been hungry in three days," I pointed out.

"Yes!"

"Bullshit!"

"What do you want me to say?" She sat up on the bed.

"I don't want you to say anything. I want you to eat," I said, raising my voice.

"If I eat, will it shut your fat mouth up?"

I mockingly pondered and then said, "You said it, not me." My eyes were wide. We stared at each other for a minute before she got off the bed and headed into the kitchen.

"Fine!" she shouted, pulling ingredients for a sandwich from the fridge.

I grabbed the bowl from the sink and dried it off. "You are so stubborn, and I don't understand why. You need to eat to survive." Bambi sighed in frustration. "I get it. You're tired of hearing the same thing come out of my mouth, but I love and worry about you. It wouldn't make sense for me not to care."

"Okay," she said, making herself a sandwich.

"Don't make me out to be the villain when I'm the one who has to take you to the hospital or watch over you at night through your overdoses, hunger, and withdrawals," I said as I placed the bowl in the dish rack, then walked over to the bed and dropped down.

"Oh, please, you don't take care of me. I take care of myself. You're not my mother, okay?"

I chuckled at the audacity. "Sure, Moe. I'm just doing it for fun."

She stood beside the kitchen table and took a bite of her sandwich. "Happy?"

"Never better, baby." I winked and crossed my legs, leaning back on the bed.

"Don't forget, we're going out with Tigress and Jenny later."

I was hoping she wouldn't remind me. I didn't want to leave tonight. I wanted to stay in like a normal human being and be a sloth. It was a Saturday, and they wanted to go out instead of relaxing. I liked Jenny and Tigress. They were nice but had a knack for causing trouble. They were the closest thing to friends we had. They reminded me of Lindsay Lohan in The Parent Trap. They were mischievous and twins, unlike us, even though we were sisters, not by blood. They both had red, luscious, flowing hair and pale, dark eyes and occasionally wore cheetah print clothing with fur coats. They had this witchy laughter and strange intuition regarding money and men, two things they never gambled with. It wasn't hard to tell them apart, given that one was skinny and the other chubby but not fat. They were very welcoming, like Bambi, when I was new to the city and its lifestyle. They were there for us in rough, happy, and sad times. I couldn't depend on anyone else like them. I loved them just as much as I loved Bambi—they were my sisters, bonded no matter what.

We had planned to hang out a few weeks ago and grab some pumpkins to carve. We hadn't hung out in a while, and I wanted to make it up to them. However, that was weeks ago, and I'm stuck on a decision I made while being social. I had been working nonstop for the past two weeks without a break. I didn't think I had the energy for an outing with the girls. I knew I couldn't make up an excuse because I was terrible at lying, and it was out of the question to have Moe lie for me. I didn't know what to do, but I would try to get out of it. I didn't want to see anyone right now. I wanted to be alone, especially on a foggy, cold night like this.

"Can I take a rain check? I just don't feel like it tonight."

She stared at me, dumbfounded. "You do this all the time," she said, her mouth full of bread.

"I hang out with you guys all the time. Just go without me."

She grabbed a cup from the cabinet, turned on the faucet, and filled it with water.

"No, you haven't lately. And they miss you."

I rolled my eyes. "Unlike some people, I've been working nonstop, so let's just say I'm tired, okay?"

She sipped some water and said, "We all are tired from fucking, including me, before you made it on the scene, so please stop acting like a martyr. We need a normal night, and I miss them."

"Then go! I don't want to," I said, facing her.

"You're going. As your elder, I demand that you go."

I smirked. "Like that's going to happen."

She finished the last piece of her sandwich and placed the cup on the table. "If you go, I promise to eat for a full two months without you having to remind me." She smiled.

I was in disbelief that she would pawn her health to get me to leave the apartment. Smart move? No. Better move? Yes. I had no counter-move, but that didn't mean I would go. I wished she hadn't said that because I wanted to level the playing field and get ahead by one. I knew she had been in the game long before me and was tired of being a thirty-three-year-old prostitute. I never meant to throw my efforts in her face, but that's what I ended up doing. I gave her leeway for a long time, but it's been seven years since I moved to the city, and I was tired of being one too. If she demanded—no, required—me to leave the comfort of our home, then it would be on my terms. I bit my lip and smiled mischievously. "Okay, I'll leave, but I'll tweak what you offered and double it," I said as I crossed my feet.

She lifted her chin and asked, "What will it be? How much will it cost me?"

I gave a hesitant smile and said, "If you eat and quit cold turkey for six months, making more than fifty dollars a night, then yes, I will go."

Bambi seemed hurt, which I had anticipated. She understood that suggesting such a thing would lead to my taking the matter seriously. I could sense her desire to destroy me. I recognized I was a hypocrite who took a pill now and then, but I wasn't addicted to the point of resembling a skeleton. She yearned to escape the abyss of her life through drugs, and with me around, she felt unable to do that. She reminded me so much of my mother—hopeless and scarred by wounds inflicted without consent. But so was half the world, and that wasn't an excuse. I propped myself up on my elbow as she fell silent. She didn't even want to meet my gaze, and that twisted my stomach. The expression on her face shattered me. My words hurt her. It made me feel regretful, but I didn't dare take back what I said because I meant every word. It was a yes or no situation. It was straightforward math. If I dared to speak the truth, she could set off down a better path and leave this place for good. Sadly, life doesn't work that way, and some people can't be saved. It was up to her to escape the black hole she reveled in without me.

"Never mind. Forget it."

Indisputably, she responded, "No. We won't forget it."

"Okay."

"Yes, to everything you said."

I smiled quickly and sat up. "You're not fucking with me, are you?"

She winked and replied, "Do we have a deal?"

I nodded. "Deal."

She picked up the TV remote and turned Scooby Doo back on. "Now let me watch my shit."

We both laughed.

"I'm going to rest my eyes for a bit. Wake me when it's almost time to leave."

Bambi shrugged as she settled into the chair, focused on the show, and said, "Sure."

We had very few clothes. Bambi and I often had to share because our wardrobe consisted of only about twenty clothing items and three pairs of shoes. Although we never shared undergarments, there was a time during a struggle when we both chose not to wear any under our clothes instead of sharing. It was challenging for us because we had such different tastes in clothing, but through small expressions of individuality, we managed to make it work so well that sometimes people didn't even notice. When dealing with clients, we didn't care to wear too much clothing since we needed to grab attention and quickly move on to the next customer afterward.

Bambi was more of a free spirit. She loved wearing tight dresses, skimpy skirts, tall platform boots, oversized fancy coats, and plenty of jewelry. On the other hand, I preferred oversized shirts, sweaters, crop tops, jeans, sneakers, boots, and kitten heels. I had little to no jewelry or a coat to keep me warm at night while going about my day on the streets. We made do with what we had, which wasn't much, but we were grateful to have clothes.

I wore a white, short-sleeved mini-dress with slight rips, small silver hoop earrings, knee-high boots, and a worn brown leather jacket. Bambi took forever to get dressed, as if she had plenty of time, but I knew she was applying her heavy, dark clown makeup. We planned to meet Jenny and Tigress outside.

"Come on!"

"Wait a second! I'm just adding the final touches."

I stood against the wall next to the front door, feeling annoyed and ready to leave. "Bambi, I'm sure you look stunning, so let's go! I'm starving."

She peeked her head out of the bathroom. "Then eat a snack," she said, her voice husky.

My big, bold curls hung in front of my face as I stared at her, unamused, with my hands in my pockets. "You know we hardly have any food, especially damn snacks."

She giggled. "I know," she said as she returned to the bathroom.

"I can't stand you," I murmured through clenched teeth. "Come on! Grandma!" I exclaimed, hoping to provoke a reaction.

Bambi turned off the bathroom light, walked into the living room, stared at me, and then took a deep breath. "I'm not that old, bitch," she said, throwing a pillow at me, and I laughed.

"I know, but at least it got you to leave the bathroom."

She rolled her eyes. "Whatever. As if you know me so well."

I scoffed. "We've lived together for how long?" I asked cynically.

She moved toward the door. "Exactly."

She opened the door and paused in the hallway. "Rhiannon?"

"Yeah," I said, locking the door and turning to her. "Try to have fun tonight. You need it, okay?" Her ash-brown hair contrasted with her pale gray eyes.

I gave her a genuine smile. "I'll try," I said, gently caressing her arm.

The hallway was a dead end, forming an endless circle. It was water-damaged and moldy, with dusty, old, broken doors that creaked at the slightest touch. The dim, flickering lighting cast an eerie green tint over the space, creating long, ominous shadows on the walls. An abandoned glass table, shrouded in a thick layer of dust, appeared to have sunk into the grimy floor. The black-and-white patterned flooring, worn and weathered, featured a large hole to our left, emitting a foul stench that churned our stomachs. We cautiously descended the creaky stairs, the sound echoing through the desolate hallway, reminiscent of a scene from a horror film. Living on the fifth floor made reaching the lobby daunting, especially with weariness weighing us down, turning the journey into an eternity.

As soon as the tips of our shoes touched the lobby floor, we spotted Jenny and Tigress on the front steps of the building. I quickly rushed through the door and bent down to hug them while joyfully rattling. Their cold hands clutched my arms as they embraced me back. It was wonderful to see them again. It felt like ages, which was one thing Bambi was right about. The sweet scent of their floral perfume warmed my heart, and I nearly cried at the sight of our best friends.

"Okay, okay, don't squash them, Rhiannon," Bambi laughed.

"Sorry," I said, teary-eyed as I released them.

Both twins smiled and chuckled. "We missed you, you know," they both said. "We understand you're a working girl, but that doesn't mean you can forget about us." They winked and blew kisses.

I wiped away my tears and said, "Sorry. I've just been wrapped up with my own bullshit, you know."

"Mm-hm," Jenny said. "But I'm here now."

"I practically had to negotiate with her to get her to leave the apartment."

"Oh, really!" Tigress laughed with her sister.

They both stared at us and asked, "Bargained with what?"

I smirked and motioned for Bambi to respond. She rolled her eyes, pulled out a cigarette, took a drag, and exhaled smoke into the air.

"Please don't keep us waiting," I said jokingly.

"Yeah, Bambi, what did you do?" Jenny smirked.

She buttoned her feathery white coat and said, "I promised to eat and make more money."

"That's it?" They laughed.

"No," I said, poking the bear. "What's the biggest offer you made me?"

Bambi looked at me, irritated, then hesitantly said, "I said I would stay clean! Okay!"

"Oh shit!"

"Wow!"

I rolled my eyes and walked to the bottom of the steps. I leaned against the railing and said, "That's what I said, all to get me to come outside." I smirked.

"Shut up." She winked.

Jenny slapped her thigh. "Who would have thought?"

"We'll see how long it lasts."

"I can do it!"

"You've said that the last thousand times," Tigress joked.

"Fuck all of you, okay." Bambi pointed at all of us.

I took in a breath of cold, fresh air. "What have you girls been up to?"

"Same shit as you: working, partying, and nothing."

I tilted my head. "Yeah." I let out a sigh.

Bambi tossed her cigarette onto the ground and stamped it out with her heel. I glanced at the passing traffic and the empty streets, noticing girls working the corners. "Where are we going to eat tonight?" Jenny and Tigress looked at us as if they were hiding something. "It's a surprise."

Bambi and I exchanged suspicious glances. "What does that mean?" I chuckled.

"You'll see, and I trust you will love it!"

"You know I hate surprises," Bambi said, shivering in the cold.

I balled my hands into fists inside my coat pockets. "Okay," I replied as the cold outside seeped into my breath.

After hopping out of the cab, we followed the twins as they led the way along the sidewalk, wondering where they were taking us. It was cold in mid-October. I had always enjoyed the fall; it was spooky and melancholic, and I liked Halloween. The scent of the crisp, cool air made me somewhat happy as I counted the cracks in the concrete. The streetlights made everything more visible, more real around us. Nothing seemed as it was anymore. There was nothing new amid everything appearing the same outside my sad little life in the apartment: same cars, same stores, same faces, same everything.

We didn't have cars, so we either rode the train, took the bus, or a cab, or walked. I enjoyed walking the most. It was peaceful and allowed me to sort through my melancholy thoughts about life. It made me feel like I had some control over whatever happened. In a sense, I did, but not to the extent of snapping my fingers and making everything good. Even the nagging thoughts in my head were the same: rent, money, Bambi, and escape. I needed to experience something beyond my circumstances. I want to feel free and joyful to the fullest, but I can only do that for so long. I never even dared to leave the Lower East Side. It was pathetic. I found everyone around me, including myself, lonely and pathetic.

I wasn't the most open-minded, but if one of us made it out of here, it would give me an ounce of hope that I could, too. It would reinforce that this life wasn't meant for me, and there was a mix-up that, in reality, I should be somewhere drinking mimosas on a farm somewhere with money and tranquility. It was a far-fetched goal, but what could I do but dream? That's all you could do as a working girl in these parts. We all deserve better. I loved my girls more than anyone I knew, and I could give a shit about anyone else in the world. I was kind and used to having a big heart, but things changed. We had to be selfish, just as others had been toward us. We could die tomorrow, and the world would go on. We have to live life to the fullest, especially in our profession.

My neck felt stiff, so I rubbed it as we walked hand in hand. I noticed Bambi and the girls staring, making me look around at them, confused.

"What?" I smiled, feeling uncertain.

Bambi shrugged. "Nothing. I just happened to look at you."

I glanced at the twins. "And you?"

Jenny laughed and replied, "Is your neck okay?"

Tigress chimed in, piggybacking off Jenny. "Yeah, are you?"

"I like to think I'm alright. I've just been stressed lately, and my neck sometimes hurts."

"I know a great masseuse who could help for cheap."

"Yeah. How much will that cost me?"

"A blow job." She chuckled.

I simply laughed. "Of course, no thanks."

Tigress smiled. "I'm kidding! She'll ask for around thirty dollars for it."

My eyes widened. "That's for the low end."

"Don't be a cheapskate, okay?"

I rolled my eyes and let go of Bambi's hand. "Easy for you to say."

Jenny frowned and asked, "What does that mean?"

I sighed, feeling the cold creeping in on me. "It means you have regulars with big Mulla, unlike us."

Bambi walked ahead, gazing into the shop windows.

"I mean, we can't control that," she said, flipping her auburn hair.

"I know that. It's just that things are tight at home."

"Like always, and you know why."

I looked hurt. "It's not like I can throw her out. She has her ways, but she's family."

"We're not saying that. We've known her longer than you, but it has to be taking a toll."

"Definitely!" I chuckled nervously. "Look, just don't, okay? Moe is going to get better."

"Okay!" Jenny said doubtfully.

Tigress nudged me and smiled, playfully flicking one of my curls.

"I'm starving. How much farther?"

"Not too far, just a block away. You guys are going to love it. High quality, and it's on me."

"Oh wow, wait until Moe hears; she'll be ecstatic."

"We know!" they laughed.

I smirked and shook my head. "You really had a great week."

"The high seas blessed me," Jenny winked.

"I wish it were me." I shifted my shoulders as we walked up the block, getting closer to the restaurant.

"You will, Rhiannon," Tigress said, caressing my chin.

As we stopped in front of the restaurant called The Little Window, I was pretty against that. The place was known for being expensive, and where most of the wealthy went, so it was intimidating to realize that Jenny and Tigress took us there. Bambi and I looked at each other, confused. We knew the twins had regular johns and sound money, but not that much. It was a restaurant nestled between two others, with tall, mostly dark wood on the outside, at least at the door, surrounded by concrete walls. "Jenny, I'm not sure if it's just me, but don't our pockets seem a little too funny to eat here?"

She confidently said, "No," shrugged her shoulders, and opened the door. Tigress swiftly walked into the establishment before we could even question her.

"Sweetie, I know I'm not the best candidate to say this, but what the hell!"

Jenny smiled warmly. "I'll explain inside, okay?"

Bambi nodded. "I hope so because I'm not going to jail or washing dishes just because we can't afford this place," she whispered sternly, a concerned look in her eye.

I smirked. "The high seas blessed you indeed."

Jenny winked and whispered in my ear, "It did very much." Bambi was ahead of us as we walked into the restaurant together.

I quickened my pace, pulling my hands out of my pockets as I walked to our table. The tall booth was made of gleaming mahogany wood, with soft leather seats and a pristine white cloth draped over it. A gentle glow emanated from a delicate lamp positioned on the table, illuminating the carefully arranged dishes. The restaurant's interior resembled a grand cathedral, with a striking mix of sturdy concrete walls and an intricate wooden structure adorned with elaborate floral designs and patterns that extended to the ceiling. Through the large wall opening beside our table, we caught a glimpse of the spotless, white-tiled kitchen of the bustling restaurant. The stainless-steel appliances sparkled under the bright fluorescent lights, and the chefs were seen skillfully maneuvering through the organized chaos, creating culinary masterpieces.

I sat next to Bambi, with Jenny and Tigress seated across from us. I looked around and smiled at the beautiful architecture. It was a place unlike any I had ever visited, and I felt like a kid experiencing it for the first time. We got comfortable by taking off our jackets and waiting for the waiter to arrive. Dining at a place with real food made me feel fancy and joyful. It was wonderful not to have canned weenies or fast food for dinner. Who would have guessed that the customers of the twins were introducing them to this?

Biting my bottom lip, I smiled and said, "Just tell us already." I leaned on the table, nudging the extravagant wine glass aside.

Bambi smirked and pulled out a cigarette. "You can't smoke in here," Jenny cautioned.

She shrugged and tossed it back into her purse. "It's not like they don't have insurance."

The twins chuckled. "Still, let's play it safe, okay?" Tigress said calmly.

I rolled my eyes. "Don't keep us waiting. What's the 4-1-1?"

Jenny sighed. "Maybe we should eat first." Everyone at the table groaned in discontent.

"Just tell them," Tigress said with impatience.

"I will! I'm getting there."

"Okay," she replied, waving her hands.

"What's wrong?" I asked anxiously, touching Jenny's hand.

"Yeah, what's going on? You two are acting like someone just died," Bambi remarked, leaning back in her seat.

Jenny wore a pained expression as if she were bearing the weight of a terrible deed. I sensed a slight unease in my mind, indicating something was wrong. Her demeanor seemed different when I saw her, yet the reason escaped me. The seriousness with which they treated this secret suggested its significance. For the first time, my concern for my friends overshadowed my worries about Bambi. I struggled to determine whether my anxiety came from instinct or an overactive mind.

Unwavering and smiling, she said, "We've known each other for years, and I'm grateful for your friendship."

"Jenny?"

"Let her talk," Tigress protested.

"Okay, sorry."

She looked around at us, blushing and contemplating her words. "I remember when I first saw Bambi when I was new. She was high out of her mind, but it didn't stop her from taking me under her wing and teaching me how to make money and survive." She choked. "And Rhiannon, you were different than anyone I had met!"

Everyone at the table laughed. "You were so young and bullheaded. You still are, but a good friend who assured Tigress and me were okay. You even take care of Bambi."

I smiled at her compliment, and Bambi remained quiet. "You are both a mother figure and a sister to me and Tigress."

"Yeah." Jenny began to cry and said, "I thought this dinner would be a great opportunity to share some good news and celebrate the bond we've developed over the years as friends — no, as sisters." She fidgeted with the tablecloth.

We nodded. "What's the good news?"

"Let me guess, you bought us a penthouse," Bambi joked, causing everyone to chuckle.

"No." Jenny smiled. The waiter approached the table, surprising us all.

"Sorry, ladies," the waiter said. We all laughed.

"It's okay."

"Yeah, you're fine."

"What will it be tonight?" I placed my hand on my chest, rubbed it, and opened the menu. The waiter poured water into our glasses, waiting for our decision. As I opened the menu, my eyes quickly landed on the prices of the food. I immediately looked up at the twins, shocked, and then at the waiter.

"Can you give us a minute?" I chuckled nervously.

"Sure, of course. Would you like any drinks while you wait?"

"I'm good with water," I said, swallowing hard.

"I'll have white wine."

"Me too."

"Red for me."

"Alright, I'll be right back."

The bustling restaurant fell silent as the waiter walked away, leaving us in an expectant hush. Jenny's eyes sparkled as she glanced over at her sister, unable to contain her excitement. With a nervous smile, she turned to face us, her cheeks flushing with emotion. She took a deep breath and extended her hand, revealing a stunning ring glistening under the soft ambient light. "I'm engaged!" she exclaimed, her voice filled with joy as she waved her hand, showcasing the magnificent ring. My breath caught in my throat as I gazed at the breathtaking sight before me—a lustrous golden band set with a vibrant blue sapphire at its center, encircled by delicate small diamonds that seemed to shimmer with every movement.

It felt as if the back of my head had exploded, and my heart had stopped. Not to sound skeptical, but who would propose to a prostitute? Either she found the one, or she had lucked out with a psychotic man who wanted to control someone, because there was no way in hell a man would marry a working girl. I was losing both a friend and a sister. I knew that one of us would make it out of here one day, but I didn't expect it to be Jenny. She and her sister, Tigress, had always expressed their enjoyment and longevity in this life, so the clarity took me by surprise. I looked over at Bambi; the announcement overjoyed her, but I wouldn't expect anything less. She always wanted a prince on a white horse to save her. It just happens that I'm that prince.

Everyone was excited and jumping for joy, except for me. I didn't know how to react or what to say. It might sound terrible, but I felt jealous—no, heartbroken—that it wasn't me leaving this dreadful place. I wanted to be the champion of this obstacle. I could taste the bitterness in my mouth, so I drank some water, but it wouldn't calm my envious heart. However, I wouldn't ruin her moment, so I kept smiling to let her know I was "happy" for her. It made me feel like a terrible friend to have these thoughts, but I'm only human at the end of the day. Bambi held her hand for dear life, staring at the engagement ring and asking about its value. My ears began to ring as the room felt stuffy. I hated how I burned inside, wishing it could be me. Why not me? I couldn't help but stare at Jenny. It's no wonder she's engaged. She is stunning with her vibrant, gorgeous red hair and lovely figure. Her face was plain, but in a way, it was so captivating that it could become an obsession, especially when paired with her sweet personality. I looked away, hoping no one could sense my disdain for the subject. My appetite had vanished as the urge to leave arose within me. I don't know why I felt entitled to a blessing that wasn't meant for me; maybe it was because I'd been here less time than them, but she truly deserved it. Their whole lives, they have been symbols of pleasure, mere toys for men's whims. It was time for most of the people at the table to find their own version of happiness.

I felt a tear roll down my face, and with a gentle touch, I wiped it away. As I stared at my finger, I realized, "The high seas did not bless me." I don't hope, never have, but at this moment, I truly wish that I were next to leave. If I don't, I might end up like most of the girls: dead or forever a prostitute.

Tigress touched my hand and whispered, "Are you okay?"

I just nodded, my tongue blocking my words.

"Who is the lucky guy?" Bambi asked.

"It's a trick I've been seeing," she said with a fond smile.

"Is he handsome or rich? Is he nice or an asshole?"

Tigress opened her menu again.

"He's not the most handsome, but I like him. He's as kind as anyone can be, and he's loaded, okay?" She giggled. She genuinely seemed happy, so why couldn't I be happy for her?

"What's his name?" I asked, opening the menu.

She glanced up at the ceiling, bit her lip, and said, "His name is John Devo."

Everyone at the table snickered.

"A John who is a John." I smiled, feeling a sense of guilt.

"Well, he sounds lovely."

"Thank you."

"Welcome," Bambi winked at Jenny. "Does he know how to fuck?"

I instinctively slapped her arm, and she flinched. "You don't have to answer that."

"He is," Tigress replied casually.

We both giggled. "How would you know that?"

Jenny looked down, and Tigress sighed. "Because he fucked us both but decided only to marry one." Jenny took a sip of her water and smiled. "Yeah, we met in unfortunate circumstances, but I'm happy."

"Where's that waiter with our drinks? I'm ready to order," Tigress said, expressing annoyance.

"Are you leaving?"

"Yes, she is. She'll be moving away with her new husband." She pinched Jenny's cheeks.

"We'll be sad to see you go, and we hope to get an invitation," I said indifferently.

"You will, and Tigress will be coming with me."

"I haven't decided on that yet," Tigress shrugged.

"Right."

The tension between them was apparent, and I didn't realize it until now. But her sister would be crazy to pass up the chance to leave this neighborhood. I would love to escape this lifestyle. The waiter approached us with the drinks we had ordered. "Why do you need to think about it?" I asked, feeling confused.

He placed the drinks on the table. "Are you ready to order?"

"Yes, we are," Jenny said, happy to ease the tension and start the conversation. "I'll have a Caesar salad and a side of avocado dip with chips."

The waiter nodded as he wrote on his notepad, "I'll have a well-done burger with a side of fries, but no ketchup, please."

"Would you like to choose another dipping sauce?"

Everyone at the table felt tense.

"Yes—uh, ranch."

"Yes, ma'am."

"Chicken parmesan for me."

"I'll have what my sister is having: a Caesar salad with a side of avocado and chips, but please add chicken to the salad." The waiter took all our menus and repeated our orders before leaving.

"Look, guys, I love my sister and hate that she's leaving, but I still have my own life, and I don't want to depend on her."

"I'd be happy for you, too."

"That wouldn't feel right."

Bambi laughed mockingly and sipped on some of her wine. "You would be dumb not to take your sisters' invitation."

"I said I would think about it."

"Think harder!" I placed my hand on her shoulder.

"You have an opportunity to leave all this. Take it, or you will be waking up as a thirty-three old prostitute with nothing going for her but cheap fucks and drug addiction."

She said, gripping her wine glass with a crooked mouth.

"Moe, leave it," Jenny said, feeling hurt.

"No," I said, annoyed. "Tigress, take the offer. It's dumb to stay here. You can always visit, or we can visit you."

"He lives in New England." Our expressions fell.

"Oh," I replied, leaning back in my seat with my arms crossed. "That far."

"Yeah."

"Beats being around here," Bambi said with a tight-lipped smile.

I cracked my neck and said, "At the end of the day, it's up to the two of you, so can we move on to lighter things to talk about? You're making Moe and me depressed." I whispered playfully.

Everyone agreed, and the room felt less heavy. I clapped to get everyone's attention and said, "Now, catch us up on how you met and the wedding plans." I smiled.

We had been enjoying our dinner for about an hour. The aroma of sizzling steaks and the clinking of cutlery created a warm and inviting atmosphere. I casually dipped a crispy fry into the creamy ranch dressing as we discussed the details of marriage and the possibility of living in England. The idea of our friend Jenny marrying an Englishman named "John" sparked waves of amusement around the table. We envisioned her across the sea, surrounded by lush green grass, embracing the rainy seasons, becoming part of quaint villages, and perhaps even living in a charming castle. It was a whimsical thought to imagine her as an actual princess, not in solitude, but with family — a true fairytale.

It saddened me to think about how moments like this wouldn't last. Our friendship wouldn't endure because we would eventually go our separate ways. Jenny and her sister would be far away and happy while we remained stuck in this cramped city. I was unsure if Bambi and I could escape like they could. It felt as though our lives were ending, and we had nowhere to run or hide. We would have to face reality quickly. I took another bite of my fries as my mind became overwhelmed with the weight of my life, ending in misery. I didn't want to be an old woman in this situation.

I'm not saying I want to leave this life by getting married. I want to have my own life and independence and live on my own terms. I didn't need a man or love for that. I just had to grapple with the idea of leaving Bambi behind, which I wouldn't do. But if she couldn't get clean or eat, what could I do? I'm not a doctor or a savior, but I have felt like one a million times for her. It wasn't my responsibility, but she wasn't mine either. It weighed heavily on my heart because I didn't want them to leave us, nor did I want to leave them. They were the closest thing to family I had.

It was like a cycle of life. I didn't know how to explain it, but nothing in life was permanent. Their friendship was a small glimmer of a home for me, and I pleaded with myself daily to gather the courage to create an authentic, loving, and accepting home. I needed it, whether I was deserving of it or not.

I used the knife to cut my burger in half. "Does this mean you'll meet the royal family?" I joked.

"I might!" she shrugged, then playfully added, "You think so?"

"I don't know," I chuckled.

"I'm stuffed," Bambi said, rubbing her belly.

I rolled my eyes and took a bite of my burger.

"You eat so slowly," she laughed.

I turned my head and said with my mouth full, "Excuse me for not being greedy."

"Yeah, Moe, you eat like a man," Tigress scrunched her nose at her.

"How do you even eat like a man?" she raised her hand. "Don't even answer that."

"It's just an observation," Tigress shrugged, giggling.

I wiped my mouth with a napkin and took a sip of water.

"I need a smoke," Bambi whined.

I set my glass down on the table. "When do you not need a cigarette?"

"Until I no longer need them."

Jenny cleared her throat to get our attention. "I have presents for you, and then, Bambi, you can smoke as much as you want."

"Finally! I've been dying for the last hour," she replied.

Jenny looked at her sister and pulled a white plastic bag from under the table. Nothing remarkable about it except for its fullness. She untied the bag and handed us a small box of genuine snakeskin, cold and rough to the touch.

"Open it!" she said with anticipation.

Everyone glanced at each other and opened the boxes at the same time. They were matching gold friendship bracelets, and the day we met was engraved on the inside with the words

"May the sea bless you." The moment's significance hung in the air as we each fastened the bracelets around our wrists.

"Thanks, Jenny," I said, standing up to hug her across the table. The embrace lasted for a moment. "I'm going to miss you the most." She whispered kindly in my ear.

I smiled and hugged her tighter before Bambi smacked me across the ass hard. I flinched and released Jenny, exclaiming, "What!" Everyone in the restaurant turned to stare. "Sorry," I said quietly, my face flushed with embarrassment.

"What is it?" I sat back down in my seat.

"I need you to let me outside so I can smoke."

I looked at Bambi, crossed my arms, and stood up, letting her out of the booth. "Thanks." She winked, and I flipped her off as she spun around, heading for the exit.

Tigress sighed. "Alone at last." She chuckled, and I nodded as I picked up my burger.

"You were starving when we got here. Now, you don't seem so hungry."

I leaned back in the seat and placed my hands in my lap. "No. I think the news of your engagement excited me more than I realized."

"Mm-hm. That's it."

"I'll miss you," Tigress said sadly. "We didn't think it would happen so soon."

"Neither did I." I picked at my nail beds.

The room suddenly felt chilly, so I put my jacket back on.

"Would you like to see a picture of him?"

"What about Bambi?"

She shook her head. "I won't show her. All she'll do is talk about his looks."

I smirked. "Yeah, she will, but maybe later, okay?"

"All right." She ran her fingers through her hair. "I might join her for a smoke."

Jenny was let out of the booth. I sipped more water before realizing I had to pee, so I excused myself to the restroom. Tigress grabbed my wrist before I placed my foot on the floor.

She leaned forward and said, "Take this." She placed two rolls of money in my hand.

I jerked my hand back. "I can't take this," I said, stunned.

You will because you need it, and I want you to be taken care of when we leave."

"So, you're leaving?"

She nodded. "I wanted to deny it so badly, but I can't leave my sister."

"Okay," I looked at her longingly. "But as for the money —"

"Take it, please," she said with pleading eyes.

I closed my eyes and sighed deeply. "Okay." I placed the money in the inside pocket of my jacket, kissed her longingly on the cheek, and then headed toward the bathroom.

I quietly pushed open the door, and my boots echoed across the bathroom floor as I made my way to the first stall. When I sat on the toilet, I heard laughter coming from the nearby stalls as the doors opened and closed. It was idle chatter from women who appeared to be friends discussing their troubles in life, specifically their jobs and partners. They didn't seem happy, just upset about it. I furrowed my brows as I listened, trying to remain quiet. I could hear one of them crying about her supposed "boyfriend" not providing her with the emotional support she needed. Naturally, her friend offered the typical advice about self-empowerment and leaving him. I found it intriguing how my troubles came to me as a distinct problem compared to others.

But I did wish the most fundamental problems I faced didn't involve going to college, learning to drive, or crying over a man who wouldn't dare try to beat me or cheat me out of my money. I wish my life were as simple as coming up with a creative business idea or having a broken Chanel heel. However, my issue was unfulfilled life, just like hers, except life wasn't a man; it was a giant wheel of time that outlasted you. I didn't realize the average person could be just as miserable as I was.

I flushed the toilet to let them know I was in the restroom, and they abruptly stopped talking. I slowly exited the stall, and their eyes glared at me like a knife cutting through the skin. The woman had dried mascara on her face, yet she was dressed elegantly as if she were heading to a cocktail party. I acknowledged them and began to wash my hands. Then, her friend started to fix her makeup, even applying lipstick. I noticed they were still watching me, which made me visibly upset.

"Is there a problem?" I asked sharply.

"No," they both replied.

I turned off the faucet and dried my hands. "Then why are you staring?" I asked as I faced them.

The woman smiled hesitantly and said, "You have beautiful hair." My defenses lowered a bit, and I blushed. "Um—thanks." I glanced into the mirror, craving a moment alone, hoping they would leave so I could enjoy true silence. Her friend finished up and exited the restroom, smiling at me, but the woman stayed. She stood beside me, dabbing the lipstick on her lips with a paper towel.

"What's your name?"

I side-eyed her and sighed. "Rhiannon," I said, adjusting my curls.

She tossed the paper towel into the trash can by the door and said, "You are as beautiful as your name. I just wanted to say—"

"What?" I gawked.

"I wanted to say never to let anyone steal your beauty or joy."

"Okay," I said, feeling uncomfortable as I forced a smile.

"It happened to me," the lady shrugged, smiled, and walked away, leaving behind an unmistakable sadness that any broken-hearted person would feel.

I was accustomed to strangers sharing their problems with me. It came with my position in life, but it made me feel uneasy. I already carried a sadness within me; I didn't need anyone else's. All I longed for was stillness, just a moment of quiet, and then I would be okay. It amused me that she thought I still had joy or beauty because I was young — one I never had and the other I lost a long time ago. I put on a good front that made people assume I was optimistic, but I'd rather watch the room around me burn than let that happen. I've carried the dread in the room that people have tried to avoid since I was a kid, so I just pretended to be happy for the longest time; it was a skin I would slip on and off for entertainment.

Yet, there was no happiness and no reason for me to pretend in this place, city, and neighborhood. It was a feeling of release when I realized that other people were just as miserable as I was, worried about the burdens of life, both good and bad. I couldn't lie to myself any longer about how much I wanted to scream. I wanted to break the mirror and use the shattered pieces to scar myself, just like my circumstances. It struck me how heavy my emotions felt in my chest when I thought about Jenny and Tigress. I didn't want to show it, but I couldn't help but cry. Tears streamed down my face as my hands gripped the sink. I was losing friends and my sanity during such a dark time in my life. It was chaotic. It was about time for me to have a breakdown. I could feel it coming just from how the wind blew, and everything in life seemed too important.

I took slow, deep breaths, gripping the sink until my knuckles turned bright red.

And for old times' sake, I thought about an interesting fact about the twins: they weren't twins. They were born in the same month, on different days and years, but still managed to be the same age because of it. Tigress was older than Jenny by default, but still the same age. It's what society calls Irish twins. We used to tease them about it, leaving clovers in their hair for laughs when they weren't looking. They hated it, especially since their hair was red. I am not saying all Irish people had red hair, but it was ironic. It was remarkable that they were moving on in life, but it sucked that I wouldn't be a part of it. I would miss them greatly. It was a milestone to leave this place and find love. It never crossed my mind that women like us could find such a thing. We were the mistresses in the dark. Clearly, I was mistaken.

I stood tall, gazed into the mirror, and wiped away my tears. Curving my mouth into a smile, I wondered if I still had a purpose. I wasn't happy, but I was as content as anyone could be with life. Love, money, and happiness weren't things I possessed, yet I did have a family. I believed that happiness and money were attainable, but love felt limited. I've never experienced true maternal love; no man has ever captured my heart. It was strange to consider that someone could mean more to me than my family. A brother, a sister, or a friend represented love for me. As a child, marriage and love seemed ideal, but now, as an adult, I couldn't honestly say my views on marriage or destined love weren't affected. From what I understand, it might be nothing more than a transaction or a fetish for a prostitute, never something pure. It's what I've always known.

A secret of mine was that I hadn't felt worthy of it. I once did, but my mother scared it out of me. She was a vicious and cold woman. With her, it was always up and down or high and low. She made me feel so helpless that love seemed non-existent in humanity. It became a myth for me, as if it were an ancient power. It was painful to watch others possess it while I could not. I could love someone, but attaining love was a different matter. Grasping such a concept felt like pursuing an unreachable dream, so I strived for goals that I could achieve.

Besides, I didn't need to fall in love, get married, or worry about a man. I needed to be alone to discover who I truly was, not who I pretended to be. For most of my life, I experienced abuse and was left out in the cold, but now I'm a prostitute with nothing going for me except babysitting my friend. I feared leaving behind a shadow that I no longer needed, but who needed me. I longed for substance, as love wouldn't be enough. Love wouldn't bring me the peace I deserved; it would only bring pain and too much adrenaline to live the way I wanted. It felt like a death wish served on a gold platter, ice cold. And I preferred warm dishes.

I walked out of the restroom, tucked my hands into my jacket pockets, and kept my head down on the way back to the table. I wanted to be as invisible as possible. I didn't want to draw attention after the bathroom incident. I didn't talk much, but people seemed not to notice, as they mostly spoke for me or about me. I liked it that way because no one knew what I was thinking unless I believed it necessary. I was a loner at heart, and most of the time, I preferred to think in my head rather than use my energy to speak. Forcing myself into conversations felt like a chore. People deemed me rude, blunt, or a "bitch" whether I spoke or remained silent, often because I lacked social awareness. A stamp carved deep into my forehead suggested that people felt comfortable confiding their deepest, darkest secrets to me, to feel better inside.

I got lost in the translation of my thoughts and bumped into someone in the restaurant, which felt like two cars crashing in traffic. *It hurt like a bitch.* It was as if an alarm went off in my body.

"Sorry," I said, noticing the man had spilled his drink on his shirt.

He was of average height and wore a black turtleneck. His face looked agitated as he dabbed at his shirt.

"I'm so sorry." I grabbed a napkin from a nearby empty table and attempted to wipe his shirt, but he flinched in disgust, swatting my hand away like I was some peasant.

"I don't need your help," he said, frowning.

I ground my teeth as my anger rose, but I remained calm. "I said I was sorry. You don't need to be rude about it. It was an accident."

He scoffed. "I heard you the first time." He glared at me angrily.

"Well, sorry again," I said mockingly.

He stepped into the light, revealing his dirty blonde hair, piercing sepia eyes, and well-groomed full beard.

"Watch where you're going next time."

I licked my teeth and glared at him, rolling my eyes. "If I didn't see you, it must have been for a reason."

He didn't even look me in the eye. "You're not worth the argument. Just watch it next time."

I scowled. "And you do the same, even though there won't be a next time."

He offensively moved his wrist as he brushed off his shirt, as if dirt had touched it.

I wanted to take the high road, but the little devil on my shoulder couldn't resist. I flicked the napkin at him and walked away. "Asshole," I murmured.

He chuckled and said, "You litter, too. Great!"

I stopped walking, feeling my anger rise even more. But when I turned to say something, he was heading back to his table. To my surprise, the woman from the restroom was at the exact same table as him, which explained a lot. He was the cruel bastard she had lost her beauty and joy for. It was a shame because he certainly had his, even though he lacked manners.

His beauty was striking. I could see how she was obsessed with him, but I could only comment on what I could see from a distance. The restaurant had dim lighting, so he was mostly shrouded in darkness, but I knew from the shadow of his face and the niceness of his eyes that he was captivating. I was near my table but hid behind a brick wall to glimpse in his direction. He appeared no older than her, and he had a strength in his features that the shadows in the restaurant played around. His hair was medium-length and wavy. That was everything I could discern besides her crying at the table.

I tried to listen to their words, but I was too far away. He seemed so cold toward her, with an emotionless expression that suggested she meant nothing to him. She took his hand and placed it on her chest, where her heart would be. He remained unmoved. It made the ordeal even more difficult. She was pleading for mercy, but he wouldn't give it. It seemed her friend was nowhere nearby. She stood alone in the face of love, receiving nothing in return. I remained behind the wall, my heart beating rapidly and my feet growing tired. I could see everyone at my table enjoying themselves and laughing, but my eyes were fixated on the stranger and the lady for some reason. I wanted to know if he would say or do anything in response. He just sat there like a statue, as if she were being unreasonable. Nothing was happening except for her crying over and over.

I was about to walk away when he finally made a move. He kissed her cheek longingly and sweetly. Then, he whispered something in her ear as tears streamed down her face. Her hand held his close to her heart. A weight had lifted from her body as she relaxed, and he offered her a napkin to wipe away the tears. It wasn't a resolution but an ending, and I could see in her face how she confronted the facts of her reality. He was no longer hers. It was a shame because she was gorgeous for her age, with her long, dark hair, fairy-like features, and likable figure. She was taken for granted—a lonely soul. I could see myself in her, but I would never have been that weak. Not again, at least, and certainly not with a heartless man. My heart broke for her.

Love? What was it good for? Absolutely nothing.

He gave her one last kiss and said goodbye. As she looked ahead, she caught me eavesdropping. I was stunned and quickly hid behind the wall. I waited just a second before swiftly returning to the table with the girls. They weren't even curious about where I had been. I kept my head down and tried not to glance back in their direction, but I could see the rude man leaving out of the corner of my eye. His broad shoulders and long limbs moved through the door. The suaveness of his presence caught the attention of everyone in the restaurant, even us. He paused in the doorway and glanced back, but not at her. He put on a pair of sunglasses and his coat, then officially departed. Gargoyle—that's the word to describe someone like him. He was distant and cold like stone. Love must be an ancient power to endure and receive such cruel treatment from a man so easily despised.

Chapter 3

'Kerb Crawler'

I carved the pumpkin with a dull knife containing a semi-broken handle, worn down from years of use. I chose a giant pumpkin to decorate the window before it rotted. I was focused on the task at hand, trying to make the pumpkin more extraordinary than it was, like a reflection in a mirror. We had already gutted the pumpkin insides and planned to roast and eat them later. The sound of laughter filled the room as Tigress lay on our bed while Bambi stood in the kitchen, roasting leftover pumpkin.

It was the next day, bright and early. Jenny planned to spend the day with her fiancé, while Tigress wanted to hang out with us. The pain was evident in her entire demeanor as she joked with Bambi. You might think she would be happy to shed her old skin, but she wanted to cling to it instead. She was used to it, but being hurt by leaving this place was insane. I could gladly say I would be gone for good once I turned my back on this place. It had rotten, infested walls, and the people could stay and deteriorate along with it.

I set the knife down beside me on the floor and held the pumpkin in my hands. I examined it and smiled at how good it looked. It wasn't professional, but spooky enough for the season. I didn't want it to spoil before Halloween, so I placed it in the fridge under the false impression that it wouldn't. I briefly leaned over Bambi's shoulder to check on the progress of the pumpkin, and it smelled delicious. The aroma of steam and seasoning filled the kitchen.

Walking back into the living room, I sat down beside Tigress and lay back.

"You don't think the pumpkin will hold up in the fridge, do you?"

I turned my head to look at her and chuckled, "No."

"Brave, Rhiannon." She shook her head while laughing.

"Poor pumpkin," Bambi said teasingly. I rolled my eyes and gazed at the peeling ceiling above us, dreading the thought of walking the streets tonight.

Tigress poked my cheek and remarked, "You're quiet."

"I'm always quiet."

"Not like this," she said, concerned.

"I'm okay." I sat up, hunched over with my face in my hands.

"She is okay. She thinks about life, that's all. The usual." Bambi peered at me and smirked, smitten.

"Thank you for that observation, Moe," I yelled. She shrugged in response.

"Is it because you have to work tonight?"

"Yes." I sighed, and Tigress took off her coat and tossed it onto the chair in the kitchen.

She looked back and whispered, "What about the money I gave you?

Wasn't it enough for you not to work for a while?"

I chuckled. "Yeah, but when that runs out, then what?"

She sighed, her forehead creased. "Rhiannon."

I shrugged. "It's okay, but I'm not working tonight. Bambi is, and I wanted to make sure she was safe."

"Are you going to follow her around for the rest of your life?"

"I owe her that." I looked down.

"He deserved it. That doesn't make you evil or mean you owe her anything."

"I know." I avoided making eye contact.

"Then act like it!" Tigress said, gently caressing my shoulder. "You deserve better."

I whined as loudly as I could and then lay back on the bed. I had been exhausted for so long that it felt like I was on autopilot. I'd like to believe I kept an eye on Bambi because she was broken and couldn't care for herself, but in truth, I felt like I owed her because of what happened to Rio. Yes, she knew what I did. She hated me for it for a while, but then, out of nowhere, she acted like it never happened. This was also the reason she had barely eaten over the past seven years. It was as if she were punishing herself for something she had no control over: a love that was never love at all. I figured I could do the same if she still loved me, regardless of what I did. I thought about bringing her along for the ride, but didn't know if I could do it anymore. I never imagined she could secretly harbor negative feelings toward me, but you couldn't put anything past anyone in this world.

I looked over at Tigress and said, "She does too."

I heard the stove knob click. "Do you think it will be busy tonight?"

"We'll have to see," I said, rubbing my stomach.

"I'm wearing the heels tonight," Bambi declared loudly from the kitchen.

"Sure," I smiled.

"Are you coming tonight or hanging out with Jenny?"

Tigress looked out the window, resting her chin on her shoulder, then turned back to me. "Just for old times' sake. It'll be my last, but I'm planning to watch."

I giggled. "Duh! You're officially retired now, just like your sister."

"Retired!" Bambi shouted. "My baby is the youngest in the game to leave. I'm so proud!" she said, chewing on some pumpkin.

"I'm happy for you," I said, fluttering my eyelashes. "Really happy."

Tigress kissed me on the cheek and lay down beside me. I soaked in the last of her presence. It felt good to know that my friends would be taken care of and receive the lives they deserved, that we all deserved. One day, it will be me or us leaving this place. It was all I could think about. I felt the rattle in my bones, calling like no other. I must have been delusional, or I would lose my mind. Bambi placed the pumpkin scraps delicately on parchment paper in a pan and then put them in the freezer to become sweet treats. She strolled back into the bedroom and sat on the bed.

"I'm hungry and dying to get out of this place."

I rolled onto my stomach and buried my face in my hands. "Hungry for what?"

She played with her purple, polished toes. "I don't know, pancakes."

"Pancakes?"

"Yeah—I'm thinking IHOP," she sneered.

I glanced at Tigress and asked, "Craving pancakes?"

"I'm down." She winked.

"Okay." I sighed. "Pancakes are on me."

Bambi was happy. "Good! I can finally wear that new sundress I've been dying to wear."

I nodded. "As long as I can wear the sneakers today, I don't care what you wear."

She hopped off the bed and quickly ran to the dresser. I sat up on the bed and walked over to the window. The skies were clear and beautiful. It was a lovely day to be outside, but deep down, it didn't feel that way. For now, I won't think about it. I would pretend to be happy, Rhiannon, even if it was delusional. In my fantasies, I have dry cleaning to pick up, groceries to shop for, and a car that needs detailing. I am not a sex worker who plans to eat pumpkin snacks after finding tricks later tonight to pay my bills. I was an ordinary citizen who believed the saddest thing in life was having my drive-through order done wrong—nothing out of the ordinary. I was normal. I was just Rhiannon.

"I'm thinking about getting extra chocolate chips on my pancakes," I said as I bit the inside of my mouth. Tigress nodded, and Bambi smiled, saying, "That sounds great. I might get that, too."

"My treat," I said, looking back at them tenderly with sorrow behind my eyes.

*

I leaned against the weathered brick wall, basking in the warm glow of the streetlights, while Tigress had an animated conversation with Jenny on the phone. Meanwhile, Bambi confidently strutted up and down the bustling sidewalk, skillfully showcasing the latest merchandise and effortlessly capturing the attention of passersby. The night was darker than ever, with stars shining brightly in the sky. It felt like a dull night with no tricks out, and most girls had already gone home. This was expected due to the sports weekend and numerous parties happening. If Bambi wanted a trick, we would be out here until morning, which wasn't unlikely but could be a drag.

I didn't want Tigress's last night out here to be boring. Bambi was out of practice, and it didn't help that her clothes hung loosely on her body. She looked sickly, which likely turned away tricks. Watching her strut back and forth on the sidewalk as cars zipped by without stopping was tough. It was the third night in a row, but maybe that was a sign she should retire, too. But then again, we weren't young anymore either. I counted the cars that hustled through the streets as I nibbled on a pumpkin treat.

I whistled for her to come over. She looked my way and yelled, "What?"

I tilted my head and rolled my eyes. "I think we should go! No one is stopping, and we've been at it all night!" I said sympathetically.

She looked offended as she considered going home. "You can go home! I'll stay!" she said, irritated as she turned her back on me.

"Bambi!" I called faintly. "Moe!" I yelled loudly.

She turned back around, shocked, and then walked toward me. "Why would you call me by my damn government name!"

"You were ignoring me! You bitch!" I smirked.

She ran toward me and gently pushed me, then began to hit me, and I hit her back. We exchanged blows for a few minutes before I pushed her away. "Stop," I said, dumbfounded.

"You started it."

I rolled my eyes. "You're such a child," I chuckled. "It's a slow night. Let's go home; I'm exhausted from standing outside in the cold." I tossed the treat on the ground and put my hands in my pockets.

"I'm not ready. Give me another hour, then we can go." I glanced over at Tigress, who was still on the phone. "It's wrong to have her out here like this on her last night."

"And! What about me?"

I giggled and said, "What about you? You haven't pulled a trick in three days. At this point, you're going to piss me off." I flipped my hair out of my face.

"That's not my fault," she said, clearing her throat and closing her coat.

"I don't mean to, I mean." Her eyes were sad. "But you are welcome to give it a try." She pressed her lips together with a slight frown.

My eyes dropped. "I have for the past two months."

"Well—"

"What?" I frowned, confused.

"Nothing. Just give me another hour, and then we can do something else." She smiled and kissed me on the cheek before quickly running back toward the street.

"Boo!" I exclaimed as I wiped her kiss away.

I leaned back against the wall, trying to stay awake and avoid freezing. I could have been in our warm bed watching TV, but we were out here for her pride. I wanted to express my feelings so badly, but I knew it would only cause unnecessary chaos, so I kept quiet. My face and body felt stiff, like an icicle. Tigress seemed to be enjoying herself as she sat on the steps of an abandoned building. She blew a kiss while chatting on the phone, laughing and gossiping with her sister. I shook my head in disbelief and walked toward Bambi. As I did, a car quickly pulled up in front of her.

Excitement washed over me as she finally attracted a trick. I placed my cold hand over my red, swollen lips to keep from letting anyone know I was laughing. It seemed the tides began to turn, and I wouldn't be the sole provider anymore, but I couldn't get ahead of myself. It was just one trick; she needed at least five more to prove she didn't need my help anymore. She glanced at me as I approached the car and looked through the window. She nudged me on the arm, and I gave her a doe-eyed look, then saw the face of the trick, and it wasn't one. It was just Odyssey, her plug.

I leaned against the car and sighed. "What is she doing here?"

She shrugged. "She just popped up," she said with a smile.

"Nice to see you too, Rhiannon."

I gently moved Bambi out of the way and winked at Odyssey. "Hi— what brings you out here?" I blew my breath into my hands while I hovered by the window.

"I saw Bambi and wanted to see if she needed a kick, and you too."

Moe looked away, feeling guilty. "She doesn't, and neither do I. She's going cold turkey."

Odyssey seemed stunned. "Wow. Congratulations, Bambi."

"Mm-hm," she nodded.

"She will be fine. It was nice to see you again."

"Same—same! I guess I'll see you around."

Bambi said without hesitation, "NO!"

I felt disappointed when she pulled me aside and asked, "Can I do it just this once tonight? I'll go cold turkey tomorrow."

I looked at her, confused. "That's not how that works."

"I don't care. I need it badly tonight. I've been waking up in sweats and can barely eat."

I looked around us and then back at her. "It's because of that, if you haven't noticed."

"Please!" she pressed her hands together. "I really need this."

"No, you need to get clean," I said wearily.

She rolled her eyes. "I have my own money, so." She shrugged and went back to the car, leaving me in the cold. I felt stupid for thinking she could change, but she proved me wrong. I crossed my arms as she entered the car to do a line. I was all out of tears and patience. If I had left this place, I would have known the answer: whether to leave her behind or not. It was definite; she was holding me back. I wanted to grab her by the neck. She was the only person in my life who could make me more furious than my mother. Family, right?

I felt Tigress come up behind me and rest her chin on my shoulder.

"I see some things never change."

"I know," I sighed. "She makes it so hard for me not to hate her."

"You don't owe her anything."

I shot a sidelong glance at Tigress. "I heard you the first time."

"I wanted to make sure," she smiled. "How about we binge some TV reruns and have a girls' night after this?"

I stepped forward and turned to face her, wrinkling my nose. "Sounds like a plan to me." We shared a side hug and walked toward Odyssey's car.

"Hey!" Odyssey shouted to me. "I have some of your usual if you want."

I glanced at Bambi and Tigress, then shrugged and replied, "Fuck it! How much for three pills?"

"Three? That's it."

I laughed. "I'm responsible, sorry to say."

Odyssey chuckled. "Twenty-five."

I nodded and handed her twenty-five dollars, and she placed

three pills in my hand. I popped the pills into my mouth and swallowed. Tigress chuckled and remarked, "What a night."

"Who are you telling?" I looked over at Bambi; she was as high as a kite, her pupils dilated and speaking in tongues. I tried to pull her from the car, but she wouldn't budge. "Come on! Time to go."

She shook her head and resisted. "I want to sit here and talk to Odyssey." She giggled.

"See!" Tigress said, frustrated. "She is like a damn child. I don't know how you put up with this."

"I manage," I said, pulling at Bambi.

"She can stay until her high wears off, but it's taking time away from my other clients."

"And that means?"

She rubbed her fingers together. "Money! I fuck with you, but shit costs."

I licked my lips and stomped my boots. "I fucking hate you, Moe."

"It will be two hundred."

I coughed. "For her to sit here in your car!" I walked away and yelled into the air. It would have been most of the money we had received. I could feel Tigress judging me as I made my decision. I wanted to strangle Moe so badly. She would be the death of me. I saw her dancing to the radio in the car while Odyssey talked with her.

"I can spot you the two hundred." Tigress crossed her arms and smiled at me warmly.

"No. It's not your responsibility," I said, running my hands through my hair.

"I don't mind. My sister is loaded now, remember." I chuckled, feeling stressed. "Okay, thanks. I'll pay you back."

"No need," she said, placing the money affectionately in my hand. I hugged Tigress again and stared into the distance, imagining that I had mustered the courage to leave this place and Moe. She wouldn't have to keep promises or be my responsibility anymore. As much as I loved her, she was a terrible sister and friend. She relied on me too much, and I was exhausted from it. This life was already miserable, and I didn't need her to make it worse. I wanted peace. I wanted to go home. I wanted to be alone. I felt tears running down my face as I held onto Tigress. She caressed my back, making me feel seen. It was so difficult. It was like dealing with my mother all over again. It's been seven years, and I have gotten involved with another traumatizing pack with someone. I took a deep breath and let go of Tigress. She wiped away my tears, and I walked back to the car, handing Odyssey her money.

"Thank you!" she said, nodding. "Don't worry, I'll keep an eye on her."

"Don't give her anything else," I pointed out.

"Of course!"

I knelt by the car window and said, "When you sober up, we'll talk."

Bambi smiled, oblivious, her pupils huge. "Okay—sure," she said, licking her lips.

"She can't hear you; come on."
Tigress grabbed my wrist, but I didn't
move, afraid to leave Bambi.

"Maybe we should wait in the
car, too."

Tigress rolled her eyes. "I don't
want to wait out here all night for her
to sober up."

"I mean— I don't know. It
makes more sense."

Odyssey smiled. "It does."

"No one asked you," she said
defensively.

"Sorry!"

"I think we should," I said as I
noticed a car slowly approaching us.

She shrugged. "This is my last
night, and we have to chase after Moe.
It's ridiculous."

I pulled my wrist back.
"Welcome to my daily routine." From
the corner of my eye, I spotted the car
parked in front of us down the street.
Everyone went silent.

"Curb crawler!" Bambi laughed.

I shook my head. "Shut up."

"I think you might have one," Tigress said, intrigued.

I crossed my arms. "I doubt it. We barely get those around here, and Miss Thing is so high over here she can't even go see."

"Ooh! Do it for me."

I looked at her cross. "No!"

Bambi pleaded with me for the longest time as the car stayed parked at the end of the street. I resisted because I didn't intend to do anything involving a trick. I didn't even have the right outfit, and my hair was messy. I was neither equipped nor inclined to hook up with a trick tonight.

"No. Okay." I rolled my eyes. She tugged at my jacket.

"Please! You can keep the money," she sneered.

"Bam—"

"Let's go!" Tigress huffed and puffed. "I'm tired, and all this talk is pointless."

I sighed and replied, "You go. I'll wait here, okay?"

Bambi tugged at my jacket again. "At least say hi to the Kerb crawler." She covered her mouth and giggled. Tigress grabbed my wrist before I could say anything and dragged me along. I was shocked as I pleaded with her to let me go, but then I stood still.

"What are you doing?"

"It was idle chatter. Fuck her! We are cold and tired," she barked.

I looked back anxiously and gave Odyssey a thumbs up. She nodded and rolled the windows up.

"Good, now let's go."

The curb crawler car was still parked near where we were walking. When I observed it closely, I realized it was a BMW. At first, I thought I was just imagining things, but I wasn't. I was curious why such an expensive car would be parked in this part of the city. And no man of "status" would dare buy a cheap prostitute on the streets, openly. They usually preferred high-end escorts for variety, but as I mentioned, Jenny was the exception.

The car was all black and had purple headlights, which I found unique. I never owned a car and wouldn't even know where to start looking for one. I wasn't sure what my taste in cars was, but the BMW seemed nice — expensive.

As we walked, I nudged Tigress to show her the picturesque car. She didn't care, obviously, but I did. It was the most fascinating thing I had ever seen. The closest car I had come into contact with was a Honda or a Jeep. She walked ahead of me while I lingered behind. The driver appeared confused and kept pressing buttons in the car, making the windows go up and down. I stopped and watched in amusement as someone tried to operate a vehicle they didn't know how to drive. It was a quiet night, but it seemed to turn into a comedy. I smiled as I passed by, strolling. The driver seemed to notice me watching and paused.

I halted beside the car, Tigress far ahead, and bent down to see if they needed help. I waved my hand to get their attention. 'Hey!" I said tentatively.

Tigress heard me and turned to see me far behind. "What are you doing?"

"I'm checking to see if they need help," I said nervously.

She rolled her eyes. "Well, do they?"

I shrugged as the car window rolled down. I tilted my head and asked, "Do you need help?"

I could see a faint resemblance to a man with long, wavy hair. He turned on the car light, and to my surprise, it was him—the guy from the restaurant. I was at a loss for words. How did he end up downtown, especially in the roughest parts? He looked me up and down and then said, "I might need some help if you're offering?" His voice was raspy.

I wondered if he remembered me. I moved closer to the car and peeked through the window, flipping my hair out of my face. "It depends," I said teasingly.

He sighed heavily, "On what?"

I smirked. "What do you need help with?" I fluttered my eyelashes mischievously. I could feel the pills start to kick in as I felt giddy and sensual.

He squinted his eyes and licked his teeth. "I'm lost and do not know how to drive this car."

I tried not to laugh because my high was kicking in. "Um—why are you driving a car that you can't drive?" My body began to feel hot. I could see Tigress from a distance, waiting impatiently.

"You can call a cab if you're lost, can't you?"

"I could, but then I'd be leaving my friend's car here," he said sarcastically.

I raised my hands defensively. "Sorry," I sighed. "It's a BMW, right?"

"Yes."

"Are you lost or something? Calling your friend seems like the best bet."

"I did! But he's too drunk. He and his wife," he said harshly. I didn't know if he even remembered me. At least his attitude was still the same: blunt and rude.

"Look! You're the one who's lost, not me, so—" We stared at each other for a moment, and then I stepped out of the window. I could hear him muttering to himself, sounding angry, as I walked away.

"Hey!" he shouted as he leaned against the car.

I turned ever so lightly high out of my mind. "Do you know how to drive this thing? I'm used to being driven around—"

I smiled comically. "Yeah, I do."

He smiled, his teeth looking perfect. "Great!" he sighed in relief.

"Can you help me out?"

I took two steps forward. "I can, but for a price!"

He frowned. "I'm not paying you to drive me."

I chuckled. "Why not? You pay your driver?"

He contemplated for a second. "Is that your friend?" He gestured toward Tigress's direction.

I nodded and said, "Yeah."

He shook his head. "Unbelievable. Okay! You can drive me, but only you. Your friend can't come along, and how much are we talking?"

I stumbled back a bit. "Are you okay?" he asked, concerned.

"I'm fine—fine." I blinked twice and swallowed hard. "Um—fifty dollars to drive you."

"Fifty dollars?" He chuckled. "Why would I pay that?"

"You're lost, not me, like I said. I'm a young woman driving a man around on a night like this, so it's up to you." I shrugged.

He stood outside the car, contemplating his answer. I pulled out my minute phone and called Tigress. I explained what was happening and suggested she head back if I drove him home. Trust me, she wasn't fond of the idea, insisting on coming herself, but I told her no.

I hung up the phone and asked, "What will it be?"

He glared at me, frustrated, and I could see a flicker of irritation in his eyes as he tightened his jaw.

"Okay, deal, hurry up!"

I rolled my eyes. "Yes, sir!" I saluted, then signaled Tigress to go home as I headed for the car. I loved money, and when an opportunity arose, I seized it. I could have driven him home like a decent person, but I played the situation to gain a few bucks because of who he was. Besides, how do I know he wasn't a trick and backed out of asking for sex? He was a stranger, and sometimes that came at a cost. I wasn't working tonight, but I was about to drive a vehicle I'd never been in before. I made sure I would benefit in some way, especially with an asshole like him.

I took off my jacket, the leather making a soft swishing sound as I tossed it onto the backseat of the BMW. Sliding into the driver's seat, I felt his gaze lingering on me, causing sweat on my forehead. I had never driven a sports car before, but I reassured myself that it couldn't be much different from any other car. The pills I had taken were starting to take effect, clouding my mind and making my eyes water, but I was determined to hide it from him. As I gripped the steering wheel, I silently prayed that I wouldn't end up endangering us once I started the car.

He smoothed out his hair and locked the car doors.

"We are not in any danger out here, are we?"

I scowled, feeling sick to my stomach. "It depends on what you consider a danger," I said, starting the engine. I hadn't renewed my driver's license in seven years, but I hoped the police wouldn't be out tonight.

"I assume you're right." He leaned back in his seat. "Are we going to leave, or are we going to sit here all night?" he asked, raising his eyebrows.

I mumbled under my breath, mocking him and rolling my eyes. I took a deep breath and bit my bottom lip, pressing my foot on the gas, and the car revved loudly.

He fastened his seatbelt. "So, you know how to drive *this* car?"

I said in fear, "Yeah!" I smiled again, nervous. "Yeah."

"Let's get a move on," he demanded, waving his hand. "Do you know where The Grand Seasons Hotel is?"

I chuckled. "Who names a hotel that?" I said, gradually pressing my foot on the gas again.

"That's where I stay." I shifted the car into reverse, backed it up, and then straightened it out.

"Mm-hm," I replied, focused. I pressed the brakes, fastened my seat belt, and cracked my knuckles before gripping the steering wheel tightly. I took another deep breath, lifted my foot off the brake, and drove the car.

"I assume that means you know where the hotel is," he said, relaxing in his seat.

"Yeah." I smiled tightly, absorbed in my buzz.

The ride to his hotel was silent and awkward. He had closed his eyes, seeming to rest before we reached his destination. I could see him from the corner of my eye, and not to be dramatic, but he was beautiful for an asshole. His beauty was unlike any other man I had seen. It made me blush. His skin had a cool, golden, poreless smoothness. His eyelids were hooded, but his eyelashes were longer than mine, and his lips formed the perfect cupid's bow. I tried to focus on the road, but his proximity made my stomach flutter.

Traffic on the streets was light, and driving the BMW was easier than I had expected. I didn't think I would remember how to drive after seven years, but I proved myself wrong. The pill's effects made my eyesight slightly blurry, but I managed. It felt good to be on the road again without worrying about tricking or parking in dark alleyways. This time, I was in control and not treated like a sickness within society. It was the one thing that made me feel normal again—a miserable night transformed into an adventure. He didn't even have to pay me fifty dollars for the drive. I did it to mess with him, but I often had more dry humor than others, and only those who really knew me could tell the difference. However, I wouldn't say that to him because I needed the money, whether I wanted to admit it or not.

I questioned whether he was asleep or merely resting his gorgeous eyes. I cleared my throat to see if he would react, but he didn't move a muscle. In an attempt to disrupt the silence, I turned the radio on at a low volume and switched between channels until I found a country station. As I slowly increased the volume, he suddenly touched my wrist, startling me. His hands felt oddly icy and soft to the touch. I didn't move my hand for a moment, steering with the other until he opened his eyes.

He glared at me and said, "What do you think you're doing?"

I wanted to smile, but remained composed. "I just wanted to listen to some music."

He sighed heavily. "I'm paying you to drive, not enjoy the comforts of the car."

I turned off the radio and smirked. "Excuse me," I said, placing my hand on the wheel.

He closed his eyes again. "What's your name, anyway?" I asked, curious; the pills were making me more talkative than usual.

He didn't answer.

"What's your name?" I asked again, but he remained silent. I sighed and said, "Okay — you're either deaf or insulting."

He turned his head toward me and stared at me grimly. "You talk too much."

I giggled and smiled. "I think that's what the mouth is for. Don't you agree?"

"No."

"Well, I do, and since we're almost at your hotel, I should at least know your name."

He took a deep breath and said, "Sisto—my last name."

"What's your first name?"

He maintained a deadpan expression. "It's none of your business."

I bucked my dilated eyes. "Okay, Mr. Sisto." I pushed my hair behind my shoulders.

"Do you want to know my name?"

He looked out the car window. "I don't care to."

A sharp pain stung my chest. I knew I was blunt, but he was just an asshole—a giant, handsome pain in the ass. I didn't have to second-guess anything about him because I understood he wasn't a trick or curb crawler. He was genuinely lost, as anyone with his demeanor would likely scare away any working girl. His safest bet was to be seen as an undercover cop in our part of town. Besides, I honestly didn't care if he knew my name.

We finally reached the Upper East Side, where his hotel was located. I drove slowly, looking to my left and right to spot it. Truthfully, I had heard about it, but I didn't know what it looked like. The stories varied about the hotel. Some said it was hideous, plain, or industrial, while others claimed it was too breathtaking for the average eye. But I wanted to step inside someday, no matter how five-star it was. I've always wanted to know what the five-star treatment was like.

"Stop!" he shouted as I halted the car.

I was greeted by an imposing, towering building enhanced with striking red stripes, brightened by shimmering golden lights, and overwhelmed by many windows. The structure's apex was decorated in a vibrant green shade, reminiscent of Liberty's iconic stature. The building's aesthetic evoked strong associations with the American flag, with its bold red and gold hues, all while exuding an unmistakable industrial charm.

I practically bent my neck to look at the hotel. It seemed magnificent to me and the largest thing I had ever seen. I couldn't imagine what the inside was like, especially since I hadn't been inside a hotel before. The streets around us were bustling with fancy cars, businesses, restaurants, and people. It was different from what I was used to, but it was intriguing. I found myself on a different shore, and it made me excited.

I smiled as I glanced around. "Is this it?" He held his hand up in front of me, and I felt confused. "What?"

"Keys," he raised his eyebrows.

I took the keys out of the engine and carefully placed them in his hand. He mustered a smile and said, "Thank you." He reached into his pocket, gave me fifty dollars, and got out of the car.

I followed his lead, closed the car door behind me, and walked around to stand outside his hotel. I smiled as bright lights blinded me and inhaled the fresh air surrounding me. It felt as if an unknown sensation washed over me, cleansing me of everything I dared to know before. He walked ahead and spoke to the doorman, smiling and tipping him. His outfit consisted of an all-blue suit and a fitted shirt, topped with a blue trench coat. I could see, hear, and feel the taps of his dress shoes on the concrete. This made me smile even more, proving he was not just a figment of my imagination. His laughter felt like butterflies fluttering near my ears, and the glistening of his skin in the light made him seem like the prodigy of the sun. His hair resembled the finest silk, boasting a luxuriously smooth texture.

I adjusted my cheetah-print dress, zipped up my leather jacket, and slipped my hands into my pockets. The cold wind whipped my hair across my face as I noticed an empty bench by the bus stop. My feet felt reluctant to move, and my eyes were focused on Mr. Sisto.

I didn't want this experience to end, but it was getting late, and I was sure Tigress and Bambi were worried. I had one question that would force me to bid farewell to this night. I whistled and called, "Hey, Sisto!" I smiled, feeling my buzz simmer down.

He patted the doorman on the arm, then turned to me, his demeanor growing cold. He walked just a few paces, creating a noticeable gap between us. "What's the matter? Wasn't the fifty dollars enough?"

I rolled my eyes and smiled. "No, I just wanted to know if the bus stops here."

He sighed and ran his fingers through his hair. "Yes, it does. It should be one coming around 1:00 am."

"Forty-five minutes," I mumbled, my eyes appearing low.

"What?" he asked, annoyed. "Nothing," I shrugged. "Thanks again."

"Welcome." He tilted his head at me and began to walk away.

"Do you remember me?" I asked quickly as he was about to leave, moving toward the edge of the sidewalk. He halted, turning slightly with his hands in his coat pockets.

He seemed confused and said, "No. I don't. I've never seen you in my life."

I knew he wouldn't remember since he was occupied that day, breaking some poor woman's heart and not even looking me in the eye. Still, I needed to know even the slightest possibility.

"Okay—never mind."

He stared at me, lifeless once more. "Well—goodbye."

"Bye, handsome," I said, winking as I carefully crossed the street and hopped onto the bench, sitting on top of it. I tapped the heels of my black leather thigh-high boots against the bench seat.

Mr. Sisto entered the hotel, leaving me behind. He was the strangest man I had ever met. I was used to men with quirks and unusual habits, but he was different. It felt like he had a darkness within him, similar to mine, but he didn't hide it as I did. He presented himself honestly, not allowing anyone to truly understand him. It was as if he believed it was all or nothing. He resembled a robot devoid of emotion and distant. He was the most captivating embodiment of darkness I had ever encountered. I'm not saying he was a bad person, but something about him left a lingering emptiness. It made me curious about who he really was. I had only met him twice, seeing only the surface of him. I tried not to dwell on it, but it was imprinted in my mind. As I waited for the bus, recent events we shared replayed in my head.

I found myself wondering what his first name was. His last name was Sisto, so I figured his first name couldn't be something ordinary. It had to be something fancy, like an Oxford or Ivy League name. He seemed to exude pride and importance. It was as if he couldn't be bothered with the little people like he were untouchable. He acted like he ruled the world — a classic wealthy American man. It felt strange to be dismissed. I was used to it from my tricks, but it stung a bit coming from a man I barely knew. I wanted to mean something to him or at least catch his interest. I only caught a glimpse of what the lady at the restaurant experienced. I couldn't understand how she put up with him and fell in love with him because only love could make you endure someone like him. Still, even though he was indifferent towards me, it made me want to grab his attention even more.

I clasped my hands together, watching the cars pass by, feeling the wind on my face. Three names that would suit him best popped into my head: Richard, Christian, or Edward. At least, I thought they suited him. He was unpredictable. I didn't even know him, so how could I guess correctly? For all I knew, his name could be Stanley, a terrible name for a rich man. It would be horrifying if that were true. It would give me nightmares to think that such a handsome man like him could have a hideous name. It just wasn't right. I only knew four things about him: he was a heartbreaker, devoid of emotion, good-looking, and had money. What more could a girl want? Not that I liked him; it was just a passing thought.

I spotted the bus approaching and breathed a sigh of relief. I could finally escape the cold and get some rest. I've had an eventful night and wouldn't dare do it again. I was a night owl, but this prolonged experience was hell, especially in the fall. However, I was grateful to leave the apartment and embrace new experiences over the past two days. It was thrilling. I would carry it with me for a while, but not for the rest of my life. I had new memories, experiences, and people for that. I would estimate about ten years, and wouldn't remember this encounter or him. It was a sad reality to accept, but a truthful one, as he wouldn't remember me either, just like tonight. I felt insignificant in his eyes—a nonfactor.

Chapter 4

'Proposal'

I inserted a shiny quarter into the washing machine's coin slot and watched as the soapy water swirled around our dirty laundry. I was wearing a pair of inexpensive earphones while folding our meager amount of clothes. My music was playing at full blast to drown out the real world. One important thing to know about me was that I loved music, collected seashells, and ate frozen mangos. Those things defined who I was. I had been putting off doing my chores for a while, and I'd like to say it was because I was busy, but the truth was I was tired of the same routine, day after day.

It felt like places, people, and things were crumbling around me. Putting on a front, as I usually did in life, was hard. I was the strong, independent, and caring Rhiannon, but I didn't feel that way. It was taking a toll on me, and it started to show. I folded the last piece of clothing and placed it in the basket, then paced around, observing the peeling paint on the machines in the laundromat.

My eyes caught sight of a scuffle between two drivers outside who had crashed into each other. I watched as the police tried to break up the fight. It was not a fair battle; one driver sought to avoid conflict while the other driver persisted. However, I didn't understand the point of the fight when both their cars were in pristine condition, with barely any dents or scratches. It was common for me to witness such pent-up rage and anger because I had experienced it most of my life with my mother and her disposable relationships.

It was like clockwork. No one I've seen lately has been happy except for my friend Jenny and her brooding sister, Tigress. I hadn't seen Moe since early this morning when she was supposed to meet a "friend." It had been just me and my chores against the ticking clock of life. Everything seemed to be moving forward except for me and my obsessive thoughts. It wasn't the usual question on my mind about my survival, but rather about indifference.

The day before, he left me in a whirlwind. I couldn't clear my mind about what had happened. I had never experienced anything as shallow as this. I was used to being judgmental about situations like this. It wasn't me—at least, that's what I thought. I wasn't the emotional type to a certain extent. I could love and be kind from a family standpoint, but relationships were out of the question. Not that I stood a chance with someone like him, or if he even thought of me. The man didn't even remember me, but I remembered him.

It had to be the city affecting me because I was deceiving myself into thinking I could care for "men." Men were my income but not my life, especially not in my heart. Yet, I couldn't articulate what I was going through. He occupied my thoughts. It made me feel alive inside, like I was on the brink of something new. Back home, I didn't even glance at boys or men. They were inconsequential to me. I'd always been on my own, caring for myself, so trying to comprehend the matter beyond money and convenience was disappointing.

Mr. Sisto was a nuisance—a fantasy. It unnerved me that I was daydreaming about him. He disrupted my life, which I despised so much. I hated feeling mushy inside. I admit I felt an attraction to him because he was a handsome man. But not like this; maybe this is what people call a crush. It didn't go beyond that. I had no worries since I wouldn't see him again. We came from two different worlds— and unlike Jenny, I wasn't going to sit around and wait for someone to sweep me off my feet. That felt unrealistic to me. I was a prostitute, not a captive.

I stopped wandering around the laundromat and sat in one of the empty wooden chairs. The washing machine cycle seemed to move much slower than time. I sat there staring at the machine, wondering why I felt down on such a beautiful day—the one day it wasn't raining or foggy. I had miserable moments, but I was usually content and managed to smile and laugh. I couldn't understand it, yet today felt so different. I sang along to the music serenading my ears and didn't feel embarrassed because I was the only one there.

It was usually packed with kids, older people, and couples searching for a make-out spot. It felt so empty that if a coin dropped, you could hear it hit outside the mat. I crossed my legs, swayed my head to the beat, and tapped my finger on the basket beside me, reveling in the peace. But my thoughts kept circling back to him, no matter what I did. So, I closed my eyes tightly and took slow breaths. Flashes of his face and that night consumed my mind and body. I tried to sing louder and move with the music, but it didn't help, so I yanked the earphones out of my ears and placed them in the basket with my phone.

I pulled my hair back into a ponytail and leaned forward in the chair.

What made him so special to me? Besides his money and good looks, why was I attached to him? I couldn't care less about most people, yet I found myself thinking about a stranger here. I didn't know what to make of him. I had only met him twice, and those encounters were brief. It made no sense to desire him; he was out of reach for someone like me. His stunning brown eyes and thick, wavy hair made me smile, but I didn't mention how good he smelled. It made me feel mushy inside, and I wouldn't say I liked it.

Maybe it meant that I liked him. But why him?

My phone's ringtone jerked me back to reality as it filled the room. I rolled my eyes and glanced to see who was calling. It was Bambi. I answered the phone, and I could hear laughter.

"Hello?" I asked casually.

"Hey! It's me!" she shouted into the phone, the background noise overwhelming.

I frowned and asked, "Where are you? And why is it so loud?" I could hear her rush outside from wherever she was into the quiet.

"Oh, it's nothing; a friend invited me to his party."

"Mm-hmm—what do you want?"

She sighed. "I can't even call just to say hi."

I snickered. "No. Not when it comes to you. So, what is it?"

She exhaled. "Okay, well, I know you're going to the farmers market, and I wanted to ask if you could get me something."

I chuckled and replied, "And that's why you called me?"

"Yeah, why?"

I smiled into the phone. "What do you want?"

"A mango. I want to see how they taste frozen since you love them so much."

I stood up from my chair and opened the washing machine since it had stopped. "Okay—and since when did you want to step out of your comfort zone and try what I like?"

"I can't like the same things you do?"

I chuckled again. "No!"

"Bullshit. Besides, if I'm going to turn over a new leaf, I might as well do it completely, including eating more fruit." Someone on the phone called for her.

"Well, whatever, I'll get it for you. Is there anything else?"

She paused for a moment. "Mm—nope. I'll see you at home, okay?"

"Yeah. See you, bye."

"Bye!" she said playfully.

I tossed the phone back into the basket and transferred our wet clothes to the dryer. As I did, I noticed a stunning one-piece mixed in with our laundry. It wasn't mine or Bambi's; it looked too cheap for her and too revealing for my taste. I prefer my clothes to be simple and easy to wear. The piece was black and pink, held together by a circular metal piece, exposing the chest, back, and stomach areas. It looked cheap but was decent enough for work. I didn't have the energy to go shopping, so it would do for tonight. I tossed it in the dryer with the rest of the clothes and then sat back down.

I wondered if he knew I was a prostitute or at least suspected it. If I were a wealthy man, I would find it strange for two young women to walk the streets in that part of the city. Still, most modern women's outfits seem inspired by prostitutes, so who could distinguish the normal ones? I could have been heading to a party for all he knew. Not that his opinion mattered to me.

I probably looked like a mess that night. My hair was wild, and I wore the skimpiest outfit that looked like it was thrown together by chance. Did he find me pretty? On the job, it was men's instinct to call me beautiful because I offered them their one desire without emotional attachment. Based on the woman in the restaurant, he seemed to prefer dainty, stylish, and sophisticated women, easily attached and extremely beautiful. I was none of those. I had average beauty and style, and considered even the slightest emotion twisted. I could barely tolerate men, let alone those with money, even if their souls shone brightly in the room.

I didn't need a candle held up next to me to confirm I offered him very little. He seemed like a decent human being, but his actions were cruel. The image of that woman's heartbreak was still seared into my mind. He barely consoled her. He was as dark as they come—like tar at his core. Even my dull outlook on life wouldn't make me so bitter. He carried this anger that didn't require shouting or speaking for others to notice. It seeped from his every pore when you were near him. I might be making assumptions, but he wasn't a mystery; he was more like a disaster waiting to unfold. It gave me slight comfort knowing I would never see him again. I didn't need to be pulled into the abyss.

I slipped on my black leather thigh-high boots, paired with the one-piece dress I found earlier, and rushed to the vanity mirror to put on my pink wing. As I adjusted my hair underneath it, I noticed that the friendship bracelet Jenny had given me was missing. I instantly stopped what I was doing and rummaged through the drawers, the kitchen, and the bed. But I couldn't find it. I figured out two possibilities: that Bambi had sold it for some drugs or that I had lost it. I took a deep breath, calmed down before questioning her, and sat back down at the dresser.

"Moe!" I yelled suspiciously.

She was hogging the bathroom again, putting on her makeup even though it took her about three hours to get ready, and for what reason, I still don't know. "Yeah!" she replied.

"Have you seen the bracelet that Jenny gave us?" I asked, adjusting my wig for the last time.

I could hear her sigh. "No, I haven't. And no, I didn't take it."

"I didn't say you did." I turned on the stool, and she stood in the bathroom doorway. She studied me, and her mouth twisted into a vindictive smile. "But that was what you meant to imply."

I rolled my eyes and stood up. "Okay, let's say I was." I swallowed hard. "Did you take it?"

She chuckled and walked past me, sitting on the stool in front of the mirror. "No. I didn't. I still have mine, so you lost yours, obviously."

"I—"

She shook her head. "If I were going to take your shit and use it, I would have gotten a better deal with both bracelets." She shrugged. "Sorry to disappoint you."

I looked down and then back at her. "I'm sorry," I said, digging my heel into the floor. I sighed and dropped down onto the bed. "Well, Jenny is going to kill me for losing it." I giggled.

Bambi brushed her wig and said, "I doubt it. I bet he's treating her so well that even the smallest inconvenience won't matter now that she has money to replace it."

"It was sentimental!"

"So, she'll probably replace it," she laughed. "It's just jewelry at the end of the day, and it's nothing compared to your friendship."

I pouted. "Well, yeah." I traced the patterns on the bed sheets. "I just hate thinking about calling her and telling her I lost it."

Bambi admired herself in the mirror as she pressed her lips together, spreading her lipstick. "I guess—call her tomorrow or Tigress; she might handle it," she said, pushing up her breasts in her bold, dark red dress and turning to wink at me.

"I will."

She passed me a red lipstick, and I looked up at her. "I don't wear red."

"You should; it looks good on you," she said, extending her hand. "Here."

I rolled my eyes and took the lipstick from her. She guided me to the mirror and sat me down. I exhaled as I applied it to my lips, then pressed them together and formed a kiss to ensure it was applied correctly.

I shrugged. "What now?" I said, unimpressed.

She smiled and said, "Now you look stunning." Then she winked at me again. "Sometimes I wish I had your looks."

I looked at her through the mirror, feeling shocked. "Sure you do, Moe."

She nodded silently. "I do. Your youth hasn't faded."

I frowned and said, "Moe." She broke my heart, but she would always be beautiful in my eyes.

She dashed back into the bathroom to grab something before we headed outside. She came back with the mirror we had made years ago using seashells and rocks from the coast. I held my breath as she approached me with it, puzzled about why she had brought it.

She sat beside me on the stool and held the mirror up. "You are blessed and beautiful, even if you don't think so."

I lowered my eyes. "I never said I wasn't."

"That is far from the truth, little one." She pinched my cheek as if I were a child.

"How?" I asked defensively.

"You just don't. You notice these things with someone you have lived with for a long time."

I exhaled, annoyed. "I don't know what you want me to say," I shrugged, confused. "All this just because I said I didn't like wearing red lipstick."

She grasped my chin and turned my face to her. "Are you sure?"

I pulled my face away and said, "Yes!" I pushed the mirror out of my face. "Now, let's go."

She stared at me with a daring expression as if she were challenging me. Then I realized she wanted to toy with me using a false understanding of an assumed insecurity. I didn't mean to accuse her of stealing; it was just learned behavior based on her patterned behavior. I've been on her case lately, but it was because I wanted her to improve. However, I guess she didn't see it that way. I walked over to her and took the mirror, staring into it as if admiring myself. I kissed it longingly, then handed it back to her.

"Money awaits," I said cocky.

She dropped her smile, "Coming."

I picked up my jacket from the floor and headed out the door. "I'll wait for you on the steps."

"See you down there," she said shallowly.

I nodded as I slammed the door behind me, amused by the idea of someone trying to educate me about who I was or how I felt. I was blessed, all right, with the darkness of reality and the steady hand of understanding others before they understood me. If she wanted to tussle, I was ready to play. She might be able to win a battle, but I would ultimately win the war. In the end, it didn't matter, and I just wanted to get this night over with like any other. I loved Bambi, my friend and sister, but I felt she would ruin me if I let her. It was life, either way.

I marched my boots across the pavement to our signature spot, where we attracted tricks. Bambi followed behind me as I tried to avoid her. We had quarreled before, but for her to hit below the belt was surprising. She usually spoke her mind when upset. I wouldn't be shocked if she was as tired of me as I was of her. It came with the territory of living with someone for seven years. She hated that I kept her in check most of the time, but I hated it even more that I was the one doing it. All she had to do was clean up her life, and we wouldn't secretly harbor animosity towards each other. It implied what I already knew: we should have separated years ago.

I wanted it to be due to the nagging and not because of some hidden grudge against me related to Rio. He was dead, gone, and buried.

There was no point in dwelling on the past. He was a tyrant, and she was his victim. If anything, I saved her; it may sound heartless, but it's true. He exploited women, young girls, and boys. I did society a favor by getting rid of that scum. He meant nothing to me, but how could she not see that I loved her like family? And he hurt me, too, in unimaginable ways. He had to go, and I don't regret it. I told her the same thing, but it only showed that she was still naïve about the harsh realities of life.

A side effect of the constant drugs over the years—but we all couldn't be wise.

I saw Clarice standing in our spot and shouted, "Hey, Clarice!" I smiled with sarcasm.

She smiled in response. "Hey!"

My eyes burned with irritation. "It's nice to see you," I said tensely, rubbing her arm.

"I haven't seen you in a while."

I nodded. "Yeah, we've been busy, and I know you've been sick."

"Oh, I have, but I'm okay now."

I mockingly placed my hand over my heart.

"That's good. I wish you good health, but I wanted to tell you something."

She smiled as I gestured for her to come closer, and I whispered in her ear, "Do you see the fin on the wall behind you?"

She nodded and replied, "Yeah."

I frowned. "What does that mean?"

Her smile faded. "That it is your spot."

I nodded sharply and smiled. "Yes! So, it means get the hell off our spot."

She was speechless at first, but then became offended. "I—Fuck you!"

I rolled my eyes as she walked off. "No! Fuck you! You know this is our spot, bitch!"

She raised both middle fingers at me as she walked away.

"Yeah, yeah!"

Bambi shook her head as she popped some gum into her mouth. Who was she to judge? She did it all the time, and we had to as well. The others knew we had a spot on the block. They should have recognized it belonged to us every time they passed by that wall with the spray-painted fin. Whenever someone stood under that wall, it cost us time and money. Clarice understood that. Sickness couldn't possibly have given her amnesia.

"Harsh, don't you think?"

"I can say the same thing about you. You do it all the time."

"Yeah." She snapped her gum. "But you're not me."

"And I don't want to be!" I said with conviction. "It's our spot! Excuse me for following the rules that keep us fed and safe." A look of disgust crossed my face as she stared at me nonchalantly.

"Right," she said as she began to prowl the sidewalk, searching for tricks.

I sighed and rubbed my temple, preparing for the unbearable night. I slipped off my jacket and placed it on an old, abandoned street meter. I straightened my posture and held onto the streetlight pole, posing and waiting for passersby. I didn't believe I was wrong for defending our territory, and of course, Bambi sided with someone else just to spite me. She could be a real pain sometimes. I wondered if she realized she was the oldest among us because she didn't act like it. I wanted tonight to end quickly, then I could plan to leave this place and her for good. I tried to fight the urge, but felt restless and needed to be free. I felt trapped again, like with my mother, always taking care of someone else.

I wouldn't miss this neighborhood, nor would I miss that awful apartment. Everything around here was decayed, broken, and reeked. The people weren't too bad, but they settled for less. I couldn't do that. I had to be more than what meets the eye. I wanted to live somewhere cozy and find peace, a place near the ocean where the sun occasionally shone. I didn't believe in heaven or hell, but I liked to think this place was hell with a few fallen angels. I needed to improve my situation, or I'd be stuck with it for a very long time. I didn't want to be like Bambi, trapped here, eating myself out from the inside and nearing my thirties, no less. I felt pity for her; she saw me as the enemy, but I wanted to help.

I can't save everyone, but I can save myself. I had to prioritize myself or risk never leaving this life for good. I would never look back, no matter how much I loved her. It might not have shown on my face, but I was miserable. I tried not to take it out on others, but everyone, including Bambi, mirrored me—a reflection I despised. It knew me well. I couldn't escape or hide from it. It called out to me, but I didn't listen because what could I do to fix it? I felt that if I answered, my reality would be sealed, with no turning back.

I was determined to shape my own future. I refused to let anyone or anything hold me back. However, I understood that some people were making the best of their circumstances. It was challenging to remain open-minded about our situation, and it made me physically ill to consider the idea of being humble. I was compassionate at heart, but it shouldn't have been that way. I should have been able to pursue my own happiness without feeling burdened by others. All I wanted was to be happy and prioritize loving myself. I deserved at least one opportunity to lead me down that path.

I stopped posing and leaned against the streetlight as its brightness singled me out. I moved my heel back and forth on the grim pavement. Dirt was embedded in the cracks of the cement. I saw Bambi working her charm on a car full of what looked like college kids. My face twisted at the thought of hooking up with someone younger than me. All the money in the world couldn't make me do such a thing; I would rather starve for a week. She even pulled the girls out as she sweet-talked them. But seeing her back at work doing what she did best was nice, like most of us.

I gathered my thoughts as I mustered the energy to walk back and forth in our usual spot. I observed the passing cars, surrounded by the bustling nightlife. Tonight was unusually slow for me, and I was getting bored. Typically, I would have hooked up with two tricks and left by now. Out of sheer boredom, I began twirling and spinning to pass the time without caring how ridiculous I might look.

I mumbled the lyrics to Nirvana's song "Come as You Are," moving my shoulders to the beat. I smiled as I nodded along to the music in my head. I spun around on the edge of the concrete and fell backward onto a car. I screamed as I felt a sharp pain in my back. I fell forward onto the pavement, landing on my hands. Out of the corner of my eye, I could see Bambi running over from the car full of college kids to help me. I took some deep breaths to cope with the pain and put my hand out as Bambi stopped before me, saying, "I'm okay. I'm okay. I just fell," I said wearily.

She crouched down to examine me. "Are you sure?"

"I'm okay." I smiled to calm her down.

She exhaled, her lipstick smudged across her face. "You scared the shit out of me!" she said, lightly tapping my arm.

I laughed. "Sorry, but my back hurts like a bitch!"

We both laughed.

"What were you doing?" she asked with concern.

The kids in the car shouted, "We're not done yet!"

She rolled her eyes and said, "I know! Can I check on my friend first?" She mocked him as she turned back to me.

"Well, hurry up!" he said, frustrated. His friends were laughing in the car.

"I'm fine, really. I was dancing and not paying attention when I slipped," I said, rubbing my back. She adjusted my wig and kissed my forehead. "I'm okay. Go!" I urged playfully, pushing her lightly. "Please," I said with a slight smile.

"Be careful next time. I told you about being in your head so much."

I chuckled. "I know; it's a habit." I sat up, feeling sore and in pain.

Suddenly, the door of the car I had landed against swung open, and we both turned to look back. I was in too much pain to care, yet I still managed to say, "I'm sorry—about your car. I didn't mean to bother you."

"A limo," the croaky voice replied.

Bambi rolled her eyes. "Well, whether it's a limo or a car, she is sorry."

"Bambi!" I whispered, annoyed.

She shrugged. "What? You hurt yourself, and instead of asking if you're okay, he's telling you his 'car' is a limo."

I placed my hand on Bambi's arm for support, and she helped me stand up. The limo was extravagant and classic—stretched, pitch-black, with a shiny finish, resembling something from classic movies. The limo door remained open, but you couldn't see who was speaking.

"I'm sorry on behalf of my friend here; she didn't mean it."

Bambie cocked her head and scowled at me. "What?" I shrugged.

She crossed her arms, and I leaned in to whisper in her ear. "He might be a customer, so—" I said, widening my eyes.

"Are you okay?" he asked from the darkness of the limo.

I nodded and smiled through the pain, then stood with confidence. "I'm okay, baby," I said flirtatiously.

"That's good," the man replied as he leaned into the light. We still couldn't see his face, but his voice sounded familiar. I turned to Bambi and silently signaled her to leave, but she wouldn't.

"Can we talk for a moment?" he asked, speaking in a low, unclear voice.

I smiled and replied, "Just a second." I pulled Bambi aside. "I'm fine."

"I can see that," she chuckled.

"Then go!" I said through clenched teeth, frustrated.

She hesitated to leave. "Call me if something goes wrong."

"Oh, please! I can take care of myself." I rolled my eyes. "And fix your dress."

She looked down at her exposed nipple and gasped. "Shit! Sorry."

"Leave," I motioned for her to go.

She placed her hand on my face, and I kissed it. "Okay, okay," she said as she held my hand for a moment before turning back. I exhaled, faced him again, and walked with an alluring stride. I bit my lip as I leaned against the limo door in a seductive pose.

"Thank you for checking to see if I was okay," I smiled flirtatiously. The man leaned back into the limo seat, rubbing his knee with his hand. He remained quiet.

"What did you want to talk about, baby?" I said sweetly.

He chuckled. "Do you call all the men you meet, baby?"

"Depends—do you want me to call you something else?"

"No."

"Okay, then, baby," I smirked. "Don't leave me standing here all night."

He tapped his finger against his knee. "I won't," he said with a smile, displaying his perfect white teeth. "You're a working girl?"

"Working girl?" I giggled.

"You know what I mean."

"Am I a prostitute?"

He nodded. "Yes."

I smirked. "Yes, I am, but I can also be whatever you want me to be," I said, fluttering my eyelashes.

"Anything?"

"Anything for you, baby."

"Mm—come closer."

I grinned and moved closer. "You want to show me something, baby?"

He leaned forward and turned on the light in the limo. It wasn't who I expected. My heart stopped in my chest, and I stepped back quickly. I had to catch my breath as I dropped my smile and realized it was Mr. Sisto—the asshole who didn't remember me. I guessed he would now since he could see what I did for a living. Embarrassed, my cheeks flushed red, and I crossed my arms over my body as it felt exposed. I felt hot and nauseous as I stepped back even further, his eyes piercing my very existence.

He smirked and said, "It's nice to see you again, chauffeur."

I was flustered and didn't say anything. "What happened, cat got your tongue?"

I rolled my eyes. "What are you doing out here?" I asked, curious.

He reached into his jacket pocket and pulled out something. He extended his arm, and I could see that it was the bracelet Jenny had given me. I instantly smiled because I realized I had dropped it somewhere. Sorry, Bambi.

"I think this belongs to you. I've been trying to find you all evening to return it." I smiled tightly and nodded, taking the bracelet from his hand. I fiddled with it as I looked down. "Thanks," I said gratefully.

"You're welcome."

I sighed and looked up at him. "Is that all?" My heart raced in my chest, and my eyes could find no destination except his face.

"No," he exhaled, his breath forming clouds.

"Okay — what do you want?"

He smirked. "No more, baby?"

"What do you want, baby?" I asked flatly.

He sucked his teeth at my response. "If you don't want what I'm offering, then I'll let you go on your way." His expression turned icy. "I'm sure plenty of women in your position would want to hear me out."

I clasped the bracelet onto my wrist and tensed my jaw. "Okay — you have about three minutes to tell me what you're offering."

As he nodded and gestured gracefully, I hesitated for a moment before stepping into the luxurious limousine. The soft, buttery leather seats welcomed me as he closed the door behind me, shutting out the chilly night air. The warmth of the heated interior enveloped my shivering body, instantly providing a sense of comfort. He sat back and relaxed beside me, gently touching my pink wig and staring at me as if I were a familiar person transformed into a stranger.

Our eyes met when I turned slightly to look at him. He smirked, releasing the wig and moving to the seat across from me. He knocked on the window that separated us from the driver and said, "Drive!"

The driver replied, "Where are we headed, sir?"

"Just drive until I tell you to stop, but if you get tired, please pull over somewhere safe and secluded."

"Yes, Mr. Sisto."

He turned around and sat down in the seat, adjusting his coat. Then, the limo began to move, and my blood pressure spiked. I fidgeted with the bracelet on my wrist while silently waiting for him to speak. The anticipation was killing me. He was dressed the same as last time, but this time in all black, and his hair wasn't slicked back as much, yet still wavy.

I bit my lip and said, "You know this will cost you."

He stared at me blankly. "I know precisely that." He pulled out a roll of cash secured with a golden clip that said 'Playboy' on it. "How much for these few minutes?"

I settled back and crossed my legs, displaying my leather thigh-high boots. "A hundred dollars." If he was going to detain me, why not charge more than usual?

He appeared dumbfounded. "That's it?"

"Yes."

"How much do you charge an hour?"

"Fifty to a hundred dollars, depending on what I am asked to do."

"Mm-hmm — for someone who charges that much, why do you have tape holding your boot together?" I tap the tips of my fingers together. "I never said it made me rich." I smiled sarcastically. "If it did, I wouldn't be sitting here with you; I would have made millions by now."

"Mhm," he replied, pulling out two hundred dollars from the money clip and giving it to me.

"I asked for a hundred."

He shrugged. "I'm an overachiever, but I can always take the extra hundred back."

"No need." I placed the money between my breasts, upbeat.

He put the clip back in his coat and said, "I have a proposal for you." I nodded. "I originally came to see you to return your bracelet, but—"

"When they told you where I was and who I was, you wanted something more." I pressed my fingers tightly together. "And that is my assumption."

"Yes. You can say that."

"Okay—so where are we doing this, the limo or your place? I do use condoms, so don't even think about trying to convince me to do anything raw."

"Doing what?" he furrowed his brow in confusion.

"Sex! That is why you dragged me along, right?"

He rubbed his face in frustration. "No, not entirely."

I was confused. "Then why am I here, Mr. Sisto?"

He chuckled and closed his coat, bouncing his foot. "How about you let me talk first and then ask questions afterward?" he said anxiously. "I want to talk first."

"Okay, go ahead," I said impatiently.

"I remember you."

"What?"

"I remember you. You asked me yesterday if I remembered, and I do," he said, looking at me. I was going to bring the bracelet to you and then leave without saying anything, but I changed my mind."

I was still confused about what that had to do with my being in the limo, but I stayed silent to ensure he said everything he needed to. He remembered me, so was he expecting a prize? It was nice to know I existed in his reality to some extent, although I honestly didn't care whether I did or not. He was so serious about everything. But to pull me off the streets to tell me this felt strange. The limo didn't stop. It seemed we were on an endless drive, with much tension between us.

"They didn't tell me you were a—sex worker."

"They didn't!" I exclaimed mockingly.

"There's no need for that, and yes. They just said you were around this vicinity."

I straightened my wig with both hands and sighed. "Well, that's good to know. Are we done now? Because I have to work by the hour and make money." I turned to look out the window. "Since you have no use for me," I mumbled.

I could feel him staring at me. "I want you."

My eyes darted towards him. "You want me?"

He nodded, crossing his hands. "I originally intended to tell you this and leave you alone, but as I mentioned earlier, I have a proposal for you."

"And what is that?" I asked, intrigued with my stomach churning.

"You will be at my beck and call for about three weeks."

I laughed softly, clasping my hands tightly as my cheeks flushed. "I—you want me?" I pointed at myself. "For three weeks. Why?"

He remained stoic. "It's simple. You're beautiful, and you're in the profession of pleasing men without needing—"

"I know, an emotional connection," I said, breathing heavily.

He leaned back, resting his arm across the seat. "Yes, exactly that. Well, at least while I'm in the city." His gold watch ticked in the silence between us.

"Give me a minute to process this," I scoffed.

"Do you not want to take me up on my offer?"

I looked at him, confused. "I didn't say that. It's just that you're a rich man. You can have any woman you want. I can picture you meeting me here and there on occasion, but for three weeks straight?"

"I have needs, just like most men, but I don't want the burden of feelings getting in the way." He opened the fridge in the limo and grabbed a bottle of water. Taking a sip, he asked, "What do you think?"

I was at a loss for words. He barely knew me, and it made no sense. He didn't know me or my profession until about an hour ago, and now he needed my services. It was strange. He didn't seem like the kind of man to seek out this type of temptation. He appeared to lack temptation or urges altogether. He was so serious and off-putting most of the time, yet he was handsome. I didn't think I would see him again, not like this, anyway. I would be his for three weeks if I said yes.

"I don't know."

He rolled his eyes and sighed. "It's either yes or no."

"It's not that simple."

He scowled. "You are a prostitute. How hard could it be?" He swallowed hard. "I'm willing to pay you whatever you desire."

"What I want?" I lifted my chin.

"Yes." He smiled, looking frustrated.

"I want two thousand dollars."

"Two—for—three weeks?"

"We are talking mornings and nights."

"Okay."

I smiled. "Actually, make it four thousand."

"Four? No."

"Four!"

"Two!"

"Three!"

"Two!"

"Three!"

"Deal!" he chuckled. "No more negotiations. And I would have gone for four," he smirked.

He extended his hand for me to shake, and I quickly returned the gesture. We made a three-thousand-dollar deal, contingent on his follow-through. I tried to hide my smile but couldn't help it. I was one step closer to leaving that run-down apartment behind and starting my new life. Bambi would go crazy when I told her, but maybe I should wait until he reappears. I didn't want to let my hopes get too high about it all. I could only think about kissing his beautiful face, those lips, and his veiny hands in appreciation.

It was an opportunity I least expected, and he gave it to me. One thing I didn't understand was why me, besides him finding me attractive. There were girls on the streets and escorts who looked better than I did. Did he see me as heartless and dark like him? If he did, I wouldn't be surprised because I tended to be. I never know why people choose me for anything. For the first time, I felt closer to happiness than I ever had, and the night seemed more breathtaking than ever, with the city lights bouncing off the limo's reflection.

He instructed the driver to take us back to the previous destination. I couldn't help bouncing my foot as I tried not to stare at his captivating face. His nose was elegantly long, nothing like Pinocchio's. His beautifully arched eyebrows conveyed more emotion than his entire face as he focused on his phone. His finger tapped against his knee, and his sepia-colored eyes reflected off the phone screen. I decided to relax in the comfort of the limo by uncrossing my legs and placing them on the seat, sitting sideways. My head rested against the wall by the window as I stared into the traffic.

In the middle of texting, he asked, "What's your name?"

"They didn't tell you?" He shook his head, his eyes still on the phone.

"You can call me whatever you want," I said teasingly.

"I'd rather not," he replied without emotion.

"Does it matter?"

"If we're going to spend three weeks together, then yes." His finger kept swiping. I pressed my lips together, looking at his smooth, wavy hair, and said softly, "Rhiannon."

He stopped texting and glared up at me with a glint of kindness. He tried to suppress a smile and replied, "Rhiannon." He closed his phone and set it on the seat. "I like it. It's different." He smirked slightly.

"Thank you," I said, maintaining eye contact with him. "What's your name? Besides your last name, I mean."

He said with hesitation, "Lee. Leenardo Sisto is my full govern name."

"Lee. Lee. Leenardo."

"Don't wear it out."

I giggled. "I just wanted to hear myself say it. It's a nice name. It's different."

"Thank you."

He pointed toward my wig. "Take it off," he demanded.

"Why?"

"You don't need it."

"Well, I wear it for work."

He returned to the seat beside me, placed my legs over his, leaned forward, and said, "I paid for you; you have to do what I say."

I chuckled at the audacity. "You paid to talk to me, and I haven't seen the other money upfront yet, so technically — you haven't."

He tightened his jaw and handed me another two hundred dollars, asking, "How about now?"

I rolled my eyes and slowly took off my wig. As my curls fell, he tangled his fingers in them, his gaze fixed on me. "That's better," he said.

I smirked as I looked down at his lips.

"Also, I don't want you to pursue more clients tonight. I'll bring the money and the necessary paperwork to you."

"Okay." I smiled as I caught a whiff of his spicy cologne. "Wait? Paperwork?"

He smirked as the limo came to a stop. "I'll see you in the morning," he said, gently touching my back and opening the door. "Good night, Rhiannon."

As I exited the limo, I turned around and said, "Good night, Mr. Sisto."

"It's Lee."

I laughed softly. "Right—Goodnight, Lee."

Chapter 5

'Shiny New Toy'

The water droplets from my soaked hair trickled down my neck, leaving a cool sensation on my skin and eventually dampening my faded blue T-shirt. I rushed around the apartment, trying to pack my bags before he arrived. Luckily, the money I made last night gave me a small window of time to buy new products and clothes for three weeks. I stopped in the middle of the living room, wondering if I had forgotten anything, but I was sure I was all set.

I walked over to the stool in front of the vanity dresser and began putting on my jeans. My nerves were high, and I felt excited. This was the first time I had experienced something like this. The only thing that worried me was whether Bambi could keep up with the apartment while I was gone. She often forgot to take care of herself and the things around her. I flipped my hair out of my face, buttoned my jeans, then ran over to the wall and slipped my feet into a pair of white sneakers.

Unwinding from the day's excitement, I settled on the bed and dried my hair using a worn towel. As I finished, Bambi entered the room and placed her purse on the dresser. She headed to the kitchen, opened the fridge, grabbed a soda, and sat on the stool next to me. Her hair was tied up in a bun, and she wore a red tracksuit paired with black heels and heavy makeup. Sometimes, her style reminded me of a mafia wife from the movies. It felt like I had a poster child for Sopranos in the room with me.

I put the towel on the bed and noticed Bambi looking at me. I smiled and asked, "What?"

"Nothing," she replied, sipping her soda.

"Okay." I got off the bed, poured some curling cream into my hand, and worked it through my hair.

"Are you coming back?" she asked warily.

I flipped my hair back and smiled, confused. "Yeah. Why wouldn't I come back? It's just for three weeks."

"Why do you need to leave today? And why didn't he give you the money first?"

I walked back to the bed and dried my hands.

"I don't know, but he wants me for three weeks. He will give me the money when I'm with him, and we will look over some contract." I sighed. "You already know this. I told you last night."

She twisted the soda can in her hand. "I know! I just want to make sure you're safe and doing the right thing."

"Right thing?" I laughed. "You're acting like we don't face danger every day. We are prostitutes."

"Well, now that you mention it," she said, mocking me.

I rolled my eyes. "You can joke all you want, but I'll be fine."

"What if he doesn't show up and was just making things up?"

"A man I have seen twice now visited me last night and paid me four hundred dollars so that I wouldn't fuck any other men and claimed to want me for three weeks just so happened to lie about coming today." I shrugged. "Sure, he just lied for fun, or maybe I'm delusional," I said sarcastically.

She smirked. "I'm not trying to grill you. Look, I will miss you; that's all. The guy just gives me the creeps."

I chuckled as I tossed my jacket onto the bed and looked at her. "I'll miss you, and it's only three weeks." I sprayed some perfume onto my wrist, then placed it into one of my bags. "Of all the weird ass tricks you had, you find him creepy."

"You don't?"

"No. He seems fine to me. A little too serious, but still normal."

She sighed and turned to the window. "Are you coming back?"

I scowled, annoyed. "Yes! I'm coming back; why do you keep asking me that?"

Bambi placed the soda can on the dresser and gazed at me with glossy eyes. "Because I don't want you to leave me—me—for good."

I felt a lump in my throat when she became teary-eyed. "It's okay. I'm not leaving," I said, bending down to hug her. "I won't leave you." She sniveled as she turned to hug me back. "You promise not to leave?"

"I promise," I said, even though it was a promise I couldn't keep. "We will be inseparable, right?" Her voice trembled as she cried on my shoulder.

"Mm-hm," I spoke with sympathy, knowing I would leave for good, whether she liked it or not. I would like her to come along, but I understand we will eventually go our separate ways. Her hands gripped me as if she were desperate.

"Bambi, it'll be okay. We will be fine," I said as I pulled away from the hug, crying and sniffling.

We smiled wearily at each other as a knock sounded at the door. I hurried to the window, and Bambi quickly answered the door. I noticed his limo outside and turned to see his driver at the entrance, ready to collect me like a new possession at an auction. I could feel myself breathing shallowly and my heart racing. This was it: my ticket out of here, a fresh start to a new life.

"Mr. Sisto is waiting for you, ma'am."

I smiled as I grabbed my jacket and put it on. "Okay, I'm all set," I said, my eyes still red from crying.

"I was instructed to carry your bags." I nodded and pointed toward the luggage next to the door; he quickly walked in and picked it up. "I'll be waiting downstairs, ma'am."

"Okay." I smiled nervously as he closed the door behind him. Bambi stood beside the bed, and we exchanged a meaningful glance as if the world had just ended. I rolled my eyes and immediately hugged her again. "I want you to eat and get plenty of rest. Okay?"

"I will," she said, kissing me on the cheek.

We let each other go, and I said, "Well, I'll see you in three weeks, but I'll still call and check on you." I giggled, wiping away my tears.

"All right, little bird. Outside, the nest is waiting." She smirked. This was the first time we had truly been apart.

* * *

The driver opened the door for me to enter, and I noticed that Lee wasn't there. I placed my hand on the door and asked, "Where is Leenardo?" He looked at me with a deadpan expression and said, "Mr. Sisto had some business to take care of. He'll be joining us later in the evening." I nodded and got into the limo.

Once seated, I spotted cash on top of some documents placed on the seat. "What's this for?" I asked, looking up at the driver, his gray hair blocking the sunlight.

He smiled mechanically. "Mr. Sisto asked me to inform you that you should accept the cash as a down payment and read over the contract. We will make two stops, one at the clinic and another at a phone store, before heading to Mr. Sisto's residence."

Feeling confused, I smiled and said, "Okay—um, why are we going to the clinic?"

"As I mentioned, you need to read the contract to answer your questions."

I sighed. "Okay, and what should I call you?"

"Jenkins."

"Nice to see you again, Jenkins." I smiled as he closed the door.

I counted the money, decided on a thousand dollars, slipped it into my jacket, and opened the contract. Frustration washed over me as I read the terms. Even though I was a prostitute, I refused to allow myself to be trapped.

By all means, you must keep this binding deal a secret and will not not discuss it with anyone.

I've already broken a rule.

For the next three weeks, the willing participant will comply with both sexual and non-sexual demands. They are permitted to break the binding contract at any time but will forfeit any money not yet received. In the first two days, the participant will be tested for any diseases or illnesses, whether known or unknown. They must have an up-to-date phone and a contact number to be always reached. There will be no objections.

They must be in pristine health, meaning they must have no diseases or illnesses, eat healthily, and clean themselves daily. NO OBJECTIONS! The participant must only have sexual contact with the buyer unless the buyer states otherwise. The participant will remain in close proximity to their buyer.

Really? He calls himself a buyer.

There will be no objections; therefore, they will need permission from the buyer to go anywhere and whom they can invite over. There are rules to living with their buyer for three weeks.

Rule 1: No loud noises; always maintain silence unless they are alone in the apartment.

Rule 2: Condoms must be used at all times!

We can both agree on that.

Rule 3: No drugs allowed!

It's a good thing I left my stash at home.

Rule 4: The buyer and participants will sleep in separate rooms.

Rule 5: All sexual activity will take place in the participant's room.

Rule 6: Participants cannot enter the buyer's room and will never have permission to do so.

Rule 7: Always use coasters in the suite.

Rule 8: Do not exceed the agreed-upon amount with the buyer.

Rule 9: The buyer and participant will not be friends or engage in any relationship beyond the contractual one.

Rule 10: If the buyer enjoys the participant's services, they may be called upon again permanently.

After reviewing the rest of the contract, I discovered it was only five pages long. It mainly contained rules, sexual preferences, and highlighted sections for me to sign for consent. I closed the contract and placed it back on the seat. I didn't overthink the agreement; it was understandable — his money, his rules. It felt like I was a mistress, even though I wasn't because it was much more subtle than that.

The only thing I objected to was permission to leave or see anyone. He was a paying customer, not my pimp. It annoyed me to know that someone who apparently hadn't purchased a hooker before had the most ridiculous demands. But his money, his rules. I didn't want to be in a cage. I hate cages, and men tended to try to put me in one because of what I did, not who I was. I found that offensive because at least hold me hostage based on the fact that I am hot-headed, not because I slept with your best friend in the grimy dark alleyway. No one could control that.

It was clear he wanted a sex toy — something to play with and keep him company that didn't resemble an actual person. He didn't want to be seen with someone like me. He didn't want his reputation ruined, as if he cared. He didn't want a whore to behave like a whore. He felt different, I say, from all the tricks I have encountered. It seemed like he was hiding and preferred to remain in the shadows. He wanted an inanimate object.

I will admit I thought he would be here today. Considering how he tracked me down yesterday, you'd think he would be persistent. I wondered who he spoke to find out where I was. It wasn't Bambi since she was always glued to my side, and Jenny and Tigress were no longer around. It had to be the other girls on the street with whom I barely interacted. Some had big mouths, but we had a code to keep each other safe. Maybe he lied, remembered the place from the last time, and took a chance.

Whether he took a chance or not, I was grateful for the opportunity to improve my situation. I could see my goals closer than ever and had never been happier. I wanted to shout joyfully at the top of my lungs, but I settled for a nervous smile. I lowered the window and felt the breeze and sun on my face. It was a new beginning.

As we entered the apartment building, Jenkins trailed the luggage behind me.

"Wow!" I exclaimed, stopping in my tracks, captivated by the elegance of the lobby.

Jenkins smiled at me and remarked, "It's magical, isn't it?" He winked.

I nodded and gradually smiled as I took in my surroundings. "Yeah — A dream come true."

The building was nearly as tall as the Twin Towers and had a hotel-like appearance, but it was made of gray brick and pure glass. The lobby was cozy, dimly lit, and filled with exotic plants. It was empty except for the receptionist at the front desk. There were about ten 17th-century paintings in the space. However, that wasn't the best part; a giant fountain stood in the middle of the lobby. It featured a rose garden beneath the flowing water and a stone statue of a woman resembling a mermaid. I admired it as we walked to the front desk. Jenkins was discussing Leonardo's instructions with the receptionist, so I quietly slipped away.

I hurried toward the fountain and knelt beside it, admiring its structure and the roses. I leaned forward, inhaled the sweet scent of the roses, and then placed my hands in the water. It was ice-cold but felt magical on my fingers. It was the clearest and cleanest water I had ever encountered. The entire lobby smelled brand new.

Jenkins whistled at me, and I turned my head. "Coming!" I said as I followed him to the elevator.

I noticed that the elevator had a mirror beside us, but it was blurry. The music in the elevator was terrible—just commercial tunes. It would have been better if they had played classical music, as it would have made the ride to the top floor more relaxing.

"How long have you worked for Mr. Sisto?" I asked to break the awkward silence.

"Five years now—I believe," he replied with a smile.

"Not to pry, but is he normal?"

"Normal?"

"Yeah, he's not the type to be weird or off-putting?"

He chuckled. "If you're asking whether he's hostile or terrible, then no."

I nodded and mumbled, "Good to know."

"He's the funniest, kindest, and most generous man I've ever met, even when—"

I leaned against the elevator wall. "When what?"

He looked down sadly and said, "Nothing."

The elevator stopped, and the doors opened. "Here we are," he said as he hurried to the apartment door. I quietly followed behind, savoring the spaciousness of the all-white hallway adorned with dark-brown wooden apartment doors and red carpeting, softly lit by dense lighting. It was the first time I'd been in a place big enough to breathe and even run around like a child.

Jenkins paused in front of apartment 28 and slowly turned the key in the door. After opening it, he handed me the key and took my luggage inside. As I stepped into the room, I was overwhelmed with emotion. It was magnificent and cozy, with layers of white and black curtains. The decor blended early 90s and safari vibes, featuring white sofas adorned with floral pillows, wooden floors, cream-colored striped carpets, and framed sketches of people and objects. It even had a fireplace, and although I once thought I never wanted one, it made me wish for one in the future.

The kitchen was accessible through two large white doors, which created a striking contrast in style with the living room. The walls were tall and painted in a rich burgundy-red color with an ashy undertone. The cabinets and shelves were made from a sleek black and natural wood blend, seamlessly combining modern and Mediterranean elements. Three grape-shaped clear lamps elegantly hung from the ceiling, casting a soft, ambient glow throughout the space.

I strolled around the kitchen, running my hand along the walls and counters, admiring the spacious and beautiful design. It made me wonder whether he had interior designers or just good taste. I noticed the refrigerator and quickly walked over to it, peeking inside to see what was there. It was empty, containing only a lemon and an expired bottle of cheap wine. This disappointed me because I was starving. I felt warm and took off my jacket, throwing it onto the kitchen table.

Jenkins entered the kitchen and said, "I put your luggage in your room, but I will keep you company until Mr. Sisto arrives."

I nodded while I adjusted the gauze on my arm from giving blood at the clinic.

"Is it possible for us to get some food? I'm starving, and the fridge is empty."

Jenkins smiled warmly. "Yes, ma'am. It's been a long time since anyone has lived here."

"Really? He doesn't live here permanently?"

"No, ma'am, just for this business project venture; he'll stay here for three weeks."

"Ah, okay."

"I can step out and get something for you."

I nodded, then asked sincerely, "Can't I come along?"

"Uh, I was told to keep you here until he arrives. I can get you something, or we can place a delivery order."

I thought for a moment, irritated that I was already being held hostage like Rapunzel in a tower. I walked past Jenkins back into the living room and sat on one of the sofas. "Sure, that's fine. You can go ahead and place an order."

"Great," he said, his hands behind his back. He pulled out his phone. "Um— what are you in the mood for?"

"Fries and a milkshake," I replied as I bent down to take off my sneakers.

"Yes, ma'am."

I placed my shoes under the table and lay on the sofa, putting a pillow behind my head. It felt like I was resting on clouds as my body experienced the ultimate high of comfort. The couch was firm yet extra soft and had a fresh, clean scent.

"What time is he coming?" I asked, twirling my hair around my finger.

He remained focused on his phone. "He said he would be here around seven o'clock."

I rolled my eyes. "He'll be here in two hours; great."

"It'll fly by quickly." He placed his phone in his jacket pocket. "I'll be in the kitchen if you need me; please make yourself comfortable."

"Of course I will," I said condescendingly.

He walked into the kitchen, and the door shut behind him. I rolled over onto my hands and closed my eyes, hoping to rest before the food arrived. I felt nervous about Lee coming later. I was in unfamiliar territory, and there was no going back, not that I wanted to.

I woke up to see Lee perched on the table in front of me, alongside the food that Jenkins had ordered. Once I gathered my senses, I stretched a little. Lee softly brushed my hair from my face and remarked, "There she is."

He kept playing with my hair. "Come on. It's time to eat," he said, sliding my food to the table's edge.

I sat up on the sofa and rubbed my eyes. "What time is it?"

"Seven o'clock," he moved to the other sofa across from me.

I grabbed the milkshake and stirred it with the straw before sipping. I noticed that I also had a burger, not just fries. I swallowed carefully before asking, "Is the burger for me?"

He nodded.

I chuckled. "I just wanted fries."

"I know, but you need to eat. Fries and a milkshake aren't a full meal," he said, examining me with judgmental eyes. "No offense, but you are a bit malnourished."

"Thank you for that observation," I shrugged. "Some of us little people do not have the means to enjoy full-course meals every day," I said vigorously.

He smirked as he twisted his pinky ring around his finger. "Anything else, or will you sit here and watch me eat?"

"I might."

"You can't be serious."

"I might be," he sighed. "Did you read the contract?"

I took a bite of a fry. "Yeah."

He nodded. "What did you think?"

"I signed it and have no complaints other than needing permission to leave and see people."

"Okay—what's the problem?"

"The problem is I should be able to go wherever I want. I can't be stuck here."

He chuckled. "Well, it's non-negotiable, so you can always choose to break the contract."

I sighed deeply. "Right," I said, taking a bite of the other fry. "Is there any way we can work around this?"

"No," he said with a smile. "I never said you couldn't leave; I just mentioned that you needed my permission. So, talk to me beforehand or provide a schedule, and I'll try to approve it."

"Yes, sir," I said with a salute, feeling frustrated.

"I love for things to go smoothly, so please, please cooperate." He smiled again. "This will be the only time I ask," he said firmly.

A chill swept over me in the room, and I set the milkshake back on the table. "Okay, whatever."

It was only for three weeks; after that, I could collect my money and leave. It shouldn't be too bad. I just hated authority.

"Okay, now that we've got that out of the way, I want to say that we will not officiate our business until your results are back. Also, along with the money I promised you, you will get to shop and do other things for your comfort."

"Understood—Does that mean I'm getting an allowance?"

He cocked his head. "Something like that."

"Sweet," I smirked.

He nodded, tapped the cushion, and said, "I know Jenkins gave you a brief tour, so let me show you the rooms."

We walked down a medium-sized hallway, and I noticed about six doors lining the walls. One door led to his neatly organized office, while another opened into a peaceful meditation room. The remaining three doors revealed cozy bedrooms, each with an attached bathroom. The last door was at the end of the hall, but he didn't even mention it.

He paused in front of the second bedroom and said, "This will be your room."

As I walked in, I noticed my belongings next to the bed. The bedroom was absolutely stunning, the kind of space anyone in my position would dream of having. Its style mirrored that of the living room, featuring carpeted floors, tall white curtains, and comfortable furniture. It had a hotel room feel but with a cozy touch. Softly lit lamps around the room brightened a small closet and a single bathroom. I strolled around, taking in every detail, before finally sinking back onto the bed. I turned to face him and said, "It's so soft." I giggled as I caressed the bed. It was a standard-size canopy bed with all-white cotton sheets and white bed curtains.

He leaned against the doorway. "I'm glad you like it."

I knelt on the bed, pulled my bag onto it, and unzipped it.

"Well—I'll let you unpack and get settled."

I paused what I was doing and quickly asked, "What about the room down the hall?"

His back was to me, and he turned his head slightly, his hands in his pockets. "It's my room."

"Oh, okay."

"I won't show it to you, and you can't enter."

"What if it's an emergency?" He glanced at me. "That's what phones are for, and Jenkins." He exhaled deeply.

"Besides, Jenkins is just a door away if you need anything."

I smiled. "He lives here, too?"

"Occasionally. Now I'll leave you," he said, closing the bedroom door.

Without warning, I felt a sudden surge of energy. I bounced on the bed before collapsing back onto it, laughing with great comfort and joy. Then, I tossed my clothes onto the bed and went to the closet to put them away. As I did, I heard a knock at the door, so I paused what I was doing and opened it. It was Lee again.

"Yeah," I replied with curiosity. He handed me a bag containing a phone. "Thanks. I forgot about this."

"No problem. I set it up for you, and you can add anyone you want to your contacts."

"Okay. I'll make sure to save you as 'baby.'" I smirked.

He nodded and said, "Nice one," lingering by the door. "Well, see you later."

"See you later," I said as I shut the door, jumped onto the bed, and quickly called Bambi.

I was eager to tell her about how beautiful the place was. It exceeded my expectations. Judging by Lee's resigned demeanor, I had assumed he lived in a tall, large metal apartment building that felt cold, dark, and minimalistic.

He was the toughest trick to read; usually, most of them were perverts, abusive, divorced, widowed, or filled with pent-up rage, but with him, it was a blank slate. He didn't reveal anything unless he wanted to. It left me feeling torn between fear and intrigue. On the one hand, he was a puzzle I would be amused to solve; on the other, he made me question if I was safe with him. I mean, regardless of whether I could read him, it didn't guarantee my safety, but it did help me approach the situation in a certain way.

It was going to be three long weeks. I had hoped that Bambi would be okay without me, but I was surprised to learn she feared my leaving. I thought she would be the most supportive about it. She believed I would abandon her for good and choose him, but that wouldn't happen. He and I didn't need to be lovers, best friends, or even like each other, but we did need to find a certain level of understanding. I was a prostitute, so I didn't hold many expectations for a trick because they either viewed us as a fantasy or as a piece of meat to discard.

Time will tell how everything plays out. I wish everyone the best, even though I don't care much for most people in the world. I just wanted to come out alive and kicking, preferably with money in my pockets.

Chapter 6
'Turn Back Time'

A sliver of coldness lingered in the darkness, and I could hear it not far away. My body twisted and bent beneath its weight. I clutched my stomach in bed as it tightened from within. I felt the darkness coursing through my veins, inducing cold sweats. I tried to run, to escape, but it pinned me down, making it impossible to breathe.

I could hear it coming closer and closer. Though I couldn't see it, I could feel its presence. I kept drowning in it, falling without anyone to catch me. I tried to fight, but the darkness fought back, and I struggled to breathe. I screamed, but it couldn't be stopped. It consumed me, swallowing me whole as if I were nothing. It called out to me; it called my name. Then, I stopped trying to breathe or fight and let it take me. I was so weak, so broken, yet it carried me to a place unknown, even as I still felt heavy.

Then my eyes opened, and a beam of light shone on my face. I rolled over, only to realize it was just a dream. I sat up quickly, catching my breath and pushing the covers off me. I told myself it was just a dream, but my heart still pounded against the bones of my chest. "It was just a dream," I said, taking slow breaths. But aren't dreams supposed to be like shiny pearls from the sea, not nightmares shrouded in darkness?

I entered the kitchen to find an older woman cooking breakfast and Jenkins sitting at the table, eating oatmeal. I wasn't much of a breakfast person; it always made me feel nauseous, but occasionally, I could manage a breakfast sandwich or grits. I slowly approached the table and noticed a parfait. I quietly sat down and picked up a parfait in a plain white glass bowl.

Jenkins winked at me and said, "Morning."

I drizzled some honey on it and smirked. "Morning," I said as I eyed the woman cooking and asked, "Who is that?"

He dropped his spoon into his oatmeal and swallowed his last bite. "That's Ms. Amelia. She's one of the housekeepers and cooks who rotate in and out."

I nodded. "Okay," I said, eating some yogurt.

He placed both hands on the table, revealing the crookedness of his aged hands. "How was your sleep in your new, comfortable room?"

"What makes you think it was more comfortable than my last one?" I asked, taking another bite. He chuckled but then let his smile fade. "I didn't mean—I'm sure your last room was cozy. I was trying to say that—"

I laughed, smiled, and said, "I'm just messing with you. I had a good night's sleep."

He breathed a sigh of relief. "Oh, okay—good."

I scrunched my nose at him. "Is Jenkins your first name or your last name?"

"It's my last name."

"Mm—so your first is?"

"Kyle." He said, unimpressed.

I thought that having such a name was charming for an older man. "Not a bad name at all," I winked playfully.

He finished his oatmeal and asked, "What's your last name for future reference?"

I stirred my spoon in the bowl. "Hart," I said calmly, feeling a mix of spite and dread at the mention of that name after so long.

"Rhiannon Hart."

"Kyle Jenkins."

We both chuckled, and then Lee burst into the kitchen in his jogging attire, out of breath. His face was noticeably flustered as he grabbed a water bottle from the fridge. Sweat glistened on his lean, muscular body, leaving wet spots on the essential areas. I couldn't take my eyes off him as he gathered himself.

"Jenkins, I want you to take Rhiannon wherever she wants to go today," he said, licking the sweat from his lips.

"Yes, sir," Jenkins replied dutifully, standing up from the table, placing his dish in the sink, and then leaving the kitchen.

"I can go anywhere today," I said, sucking on my spoon.

"Yes, but only for today because I'll be busy. Then I'll check on the progress of your test results." He sipped some more water.

"The results are going to take a while." I stared at him flirtatiously, wanting to figure out what turned him on and off, even though it felt like reading a brick wall.

"I have ways to speed it up."

"Such as?" I asked, sucking on the spoon again.

"Money." He smirked as he ran his fingers through his hair.

I sensually licked the center of the spoon and asked, "What about the rules?"

He gripped the water bottle tightly. "We can break them for today," he said, maintaining eye contact with me as if fighting for control.

"Whatever you say, baby," I winked while biting my bottom lip.

"Don't stay out too late," he insisted.

"Okay—baby," I replied, smiling as I ate more of my parfait.

He sighed and emptied his water bottle, tossing it in the trash. "Before I leave, Amelia, let me introduce you to Rhiannon. Rhiannon, this is Amelia. She'll be staying with us for a little while." He smiled warmly at her.

She turned to glance at me without smiling, but offered a smile to Lee. "Welcome," she said tensely, glancing back at me. "Lee, your breakfast is almost ready."

He nodded and said, "Thanks, Amelia," before leaving the kitchen to the two of us. She had her hair slicked back into a bun and wore an all-black maid's uniform.

"It was nice meeting you, too," I said, trying to see if she would react.

She sighed visibly as if irritated. "You know he's married."

I dropped my spoon into the bowl and slid it back out the front of me. "No—I didn't know that."

He wasn't wearing a wedding ring. He didn't seem like the type to be married or engaged. It couldn't be because I would have never agreed if he were—not for three weeks, at least. If he wants a quick transaction in the back of a car or his limo, then whatever. It makes sense since he wants me to have permission to leave the apartment or go anywhere. He doesn't want his beloved wife to find out. I hate being lied to, even though I've lied more than anyone. Infidelity never ends well.

"Does she know?" I asked tensely.

She turned off the stovetop and faced me. "No, she doesn't, and I doubt she will." There was a formality about her as if the sight of me repulsed her. I was used to people quickly judging me based on my "profession." Their reactions were so exaggerated that they made the situation funny and annoying, as if the world had ended.

I shrugged off the prejudice, sat with one leg in the chair, and smiled teasingly at Amelia. "Why do you say that?" I asked, playfully feigning ignorance.

She scoffed, "No need for you to know. We were dragged out here for whatever this is." She pointed at me. "Mrs. Sisto would be ashamed." Turning her nose up at me, she plated Lee's food.

I smirked. "I promise to keep it a secret if you can," I said, placing a finger over my lips before leaving the table. "So, how about we do our jobs as best we can, okay?"

It wasn't my fault that he was an unfaithful man. We are all unfaithful to something in life, but mostly to ourselves.

"Women like you have no respect for the home anymore."

I turned quickly and asked, "And what kind of woman is that?"

"A—Jezebel!" she exclaimed, her eyes wide with irrationality.

I laughed uncontrollably, struggling to catch my breath. "I'm sorry," I gasped, then composed myself, saying, "Close enough for me." I winked as I left the kitchen.

We drove past countless shopping centers that looked like miniature palaces. The city appeared as gloomy as ever, but I admired how certain places could shine like stars in the sky. I wondered if everyone was drawn to shiny things the way I was, but not compulsively—more in an "I deserve this one thing" way. I didn't want to admit it, but it felt wonderful to be treated with an ounce of importance, like a princess.

"Stop here, Jenkins!" I shouted as I spotted the Coach store. The limo came to a stop, and Jenkins replied, "Are you sure, ma'am?"

"Yes, if there's one thing I want in life, it's to see a coach and get the most expensive piece." I grinned.

Jenkins hurried to open the door for me, and we entered the store together. We were startled to see a giant fabric dinosaur statue reminiscent of their purses. There were also cute light-pink stands displaying their merchandise and other items. I wandered around the store while Jenkins waited by the door. It felt like I was being watched. I didn't need a bodyguard; it's not that he felt like one, but it made me ponder. Did he know Mrs. Sisto as well as his boss? I usually don't feel uneasy about these kinds of things. Still, it began to dawn on me that some poor woman was waiting at home for her husband while he was out here buying whores and breaking the hearts of sophisticated women just because he could and didn't love her enough to stop.

It reminded me of my mother, who tended to depend on the most terrible men. She was addicted to them. She married three times: one was a cheater, another was a junkie, and the last one was a heavy hitter if you catch my drift. She had poor luck with men. I remember the times she would cry, fight, and lose her mind over her first husband. He wasn't a good liar, so he didn't bother to let her know he had stepped out on her. The girls were always younger and prettier, which drove her even madder. It gave her major anxiety, leading to the pills she would take with two glasses of white wine.

As a child, I couldn't understand much of what was happening. But I did recognize when she took it out on me, calling me a whore, ugly, and worthless. We were so close once upon a time, but when I turned thirteen, she saw me as the villain in her story. It was always that I made her husband look at me willingly, or that I wore that short skirt on purpose to distract them, or simply the fact that I was born into this world. Everything was my fault when things didn't go her way; she had the world as a whole to blame, but she chose me.

And how did it feel to be the chosen one? It felt like I had fallen into a deep, pitiless hole set aside for me since the beginning of time. It took me to places I couldn't imagine. I developed a minor addiction to pills, but other than that, I turned out great—the number one prostitute for hire. It's just that I hoped I wasn't the reason his wife developed a pill habit or any ill will towards her life. If anything, I wished she was clueless because knowing is power, but more often, it was heartbreaking.

I selected two purses and a few clothing items to buy. As I approached the checkout, I noticed a jewelry counter across from me displaying a beautiful teal pearl ring. I set down my items and quickly looked, fascinated by how exquisite it was. I adored seashells, pearls, and anything else crafted from the ocean. It made me think of the girls and how I missed them. It had only been three days since I last saw them, but it made my heart tremble. I missed them, yet I would see it as practice for when I decide never to look back at the Lower East Side.

I gently lifted the ring from its display holder, feeling the weightlessness of its intricate design in my palm. As I slipped it onto my finger, the cool metal contrasted beautifully with my warm skin tone, creating an elegant look. It made me long for the sea and sand as I used my finger to caress the shiny pearl. I checked to ensure no one was watching me before closing my eyes and saying, "Thank you for blessing me, high seas."

"Do you see anything you like?" he asked as I felt him hover beside me. I opened my eyes to find Lee standing behind me. He leaned against the counter, his face close to mine, his reddish-brown eyes looking down at me. The rush of blood hit my heart, making it beat faster, and my cheeks flush. I stood there, frozen and curious about why he was there. He had business to attend to. I looked around him and noticed that Jenkins was gone, leaving us alone.

"Yes, I did," I turned to meet his eyes.

His hooded eyes studied my face. "Is this all you're getting?"

"Mm-hm," I said, nodding with my nerves frayed. "You surprised me. I assumed you had business to handle."

He shrugged casually and said, "It's all been taken care of. Does it really matter?"

My mouth curved into a smile immediately. "No, I guess not," I glanced down at the pearl ring.

He brushed my hair away from my face once more. "It looks great on you."

"It does, doesn't it?" I asked, raising my hand and admiring the ring.

He sighed and stood back, then said, "There's one more place I want us to visit before we head back."

I scowled. "One more stop. I just left and haven't even shopped like I wanted to."

"I know, but we have things to take care of."

"Like what?"

He stared blankly and replied, "You'll see."

"Okay," I said, feeling disappointed.

"Also, your results came back negative."

I was confused. "I donated blood just a day ago. That's impossible."

"As I mentioned, I have methods to further things," he said with a smirk. "Tired of me already?" he asked mockingly.

I smiled mischievously and stepped in front of him. Then I swiftly wrapped my arms around his waist and stood on my tiptoes to look him in the eye. I said, "I could never tire of you, baby," using my finger to trace his beautiful, curved chin.

His pupils flared as he pulled my hands away from his tiny, muscled waist. He gripped my arm firmly but not aggressively, whispering, "Hurry up, and don't do that again." His tone was impassive as if I had repulsed him. "Got it?" he asked harshly.

I winced as I placed my hand over his and said, "Yeah. Now let me the fuck go!" He released my arm, straightened his sleeves, and forced a smile at the cashier and me then left the store.

Amelia was worried about me ruining a home when she had the mastermind at her doorstep. Maybe it wasn't that I couldn't read him; perhaps it was just that he was a heartless bastard who couldn't flirt or take a compliment, or so it seemed. If he was married, then I felt sorry for his wife. He confused me so much. One moment, he was calm and treated me like a human being, and then, in another moment, he acted as if my touch would taint him—as if he was above me. But, as I said, I rarely expected tricks, too—especially those with money.

I dropped the shopping bags onto the floor as we entered the apartment. He whistled at me as I tried to head for my room. I turned slowly, and he said, "You and I, office, now," he demanded.

I glared at him, annoyed, as he walked ahead while I followed him to his office. He sat at his desk and gestured for me to sit. "Please," he said anxiously.

"What's going on now?"

"We need to review the contract again or establish some boundaries."

I rolled my eyes. "You hired me to fuck you, then scold me for trying to do so."

"Why do you have to be so vulgar?" he asked, clearly annoyed. "Look, I did hire you to—please me, but I have rules and boundaries that help me feel comfortable doing that. It seems, however, that you show no regard for them." He rested his hands under his chin, his elbows resting on the desk.

I sighed, "Okay. What are your boundaries, sir?"

"You will not touch me like that unless I give you permission. You will not kiss or touch me affectionately until I say so. You will call me Lee or Mr. Sisto. No more 'baby.' It was cute for a while, but now it's annoying." He began to write on a piece of paper.

I was caught off guard. None of the things he mentioned were included in the contract. This didn't make my job any easier either because I had to satisfy someone without being able to engage physically, and I began to doubt the deal. It felt like it was changing whenever he wanted it too, and I didn't like it.

I chuckled. "You didn't mention any of this in the contract. How am I supposed to know what you like if you don't let me do what I need to?"

"Just ask me, and I will tell you."

"You're so confusing; it makes my head hurt."

"I'm happy to help," he said with a tight-lipped smile.

I crossed my legs and sat back in the chair. "Does your wife know you have a prostitute for hire?" I asked directly, staring vindictively.

An eye for an eye.

He abruptly stopped writing and looked up, astonished. "What did you say?" A crease formed between his eyebrows.

"You heard me. Your wife? Does she know you're paying for hookers?" I smiled sarcastically.

He dropped his pen on the desk and leaned back in his office chair. His eyes turned red, and his demeanor changed drastically. He radiated heat as if he wanted to blow a hole through the wall. I could sense him trying his hardest not to explode. The room was silent for a moment.

I wondered what he would say. Probably the usual, like most tricks. She isn't sexy anymore, I have urges, or she nags too much. He made me angry, so I would do the same to him. He humiliated me because he decided to change the rules. It made me content to know he was imploding on the inside, and I had a hand in that—either way, his wife deserved better than a cheating, cold piece of shit anyways.

He was tense. "Who—who told you about her?"

"Ms. Amelia," I replied mockingly, adding a hint of sweetness to my voice. "She said you were married, and Mrs. Sisto would be very ashamed of what you're doing," I said tauntingly.

He licked his teeth, and his eyes looked sad. "I am—I was married."

"Oh, well, divorce is the trend these days," I mocked harshly.

He chuckled softly and said, "We didn't get divorced." He glanced down, shut his eyes, and took a deep breath. "She passed away in a car accident two years ago."

I lowered my smile as my heart dropped to my stomach. It couldn't be. I had every right to shame him. It couldn't be. I couldn't even speak. I just couldn't.

"I will speak to Amelia about the misinformation. But now you know, and for the record, if my wife were alive, I would never, ever do such a thing to her." He reopened his eyes as his hand slammed lightly on the desk. The tension in the room heightened, and the looks on our faces were riddled with confoundment. "I love—I loved her too much for that."

I uncrossed my legs, took a deep breath, and said, "I'm sorry." My eyes pleaded for forgiveness for my ignorance. He looked away again. "I'm truly sorry; I was unaware. My condolences."

"It's not your fault. You didn't know. Thank you." I nodded as I shifted to the edge of the chair. "I will respect any boundaries you have from now on. Once again, I'm sorry."

He sniffed and said, "That will be all." He turned away so I couldn't see his defenselessness.

She did it on purpose. She had to because who would act as if the deceased were still alive unless they were unhinged? She wanted me to slip up, and I fell for it. I knew better, and here I am, feeling terrible for antagonizing a man over his dead wife.

I stood in the doorway and turned to him. "Leenardo," I called out.

"Yes." He turned immediately to look in my direction.

"I am. You know, really — sorry," I said genuinely.

"It's okay," he said, slowly processing everything.

"Okay," I replied, trying not to sound insensitive or come off as any more reckless than I already was.

✳

I sat on the floor in my room, listening to "Rhiannon," my mother's favorite song by Stevie Nicks. She loved it so much that she named me after it. She would play it morning and night, and I would join her. I liked to think it described me perfectly. I firmly believe that the name you are given at birth is one you grow into, and sometimes, the naming of a child truly matters.

I tapped my foot on the floor, letting the music flow through me as I tried to avoid thinking about what had happened earlier. I could tell that both sides felt humiliated. It wasn't like me to take information and run with it; I should have double-checked with Jenkins. Amelia would be a problem in the long run, so I needed to steer clear of her. She must have had strong feelings against the late Mrs. Sisto because it seemed that only hatred could motivate someone to do something so heinous. I was a prostitute, not a disease, but in her eyes, they might as well have been the same.

I played the disc again. I had already listened to it about three times, and that was when I realized how terrible I felt about the incident. I hummed along, holding my headphones closer to my ears, belting out the best part of the song that repeated my name. I closed my eyes as a wave of emotions washed over me, becoming fully aware of what I felt.

It brought up old feelings and memories and didn't feel good. A dead wife? It made me wonder why he hadn't said anything. Although it wasn't my business, I found myself burdened with this new piece of information. I never wanted to know about a trick's life, but they often shared their stories willingly. We listened and pretended to care, even if we didn't.

I wanted to avoid the feelings that troubled me, but my mind kept bringing me back. They flashed in my head repeatedly, making me want to curl up in embarrassment. I paused the music, took off the headphones, and placed the recorder in the closet. I rubbed my temples as I turned around and saw Lee standing in the doorway with a large white box. As he entered the room, he set the box on the bed while I stood by the closet door. He pulled down the bed curtains and pushed the front curtains back. I closed the closet and turned my back to it.

He looked over at me and asked, "Are you clean?"

"Clean? Like, did I shower?"

"Yes."

I nodded. "Yeah, I am," I said with a suspicious chuckle.

He pointed to the box. "Put this dress on; I'll be back soon."

I leaned forward, reaching out my hand to stop him from leaving. "I—um."

"Yes?" he asked calmly.

I could see and feel the intensity radiating from his eyes.

"Never mind. I'll wear the dress," I said, wanting to ask a question I already knew the answer to.

He smiled at me sincerely, then vanished.

I walked over to the bed and sat beside the box. I noticed it had the name "Alana" written on it. I lifted the top off and pushed back the papers inside. There was a dress—it was sheer white, with pearls dangling from the back. I took it out of the box and held it up. It was beautiful yet daring, flowing

237

down to the floor. I gently placed it on the bed and removed my clothes. I could see myself in the mirror not far from the bed. I slipped into the dress, and its smooth texture felt soft against my skin. Walking to the mirror, I admired my reflection, smiling at how lovely I looked in such an elegant dress. It reminded me that I could shine among the glamorous things. I picked up the sides of the dress and spun around, full of delight. Being near something so lovely and perfect for a woman born of the ocean was breathtaking.

I quickly ran to the bathroom and sprayed myself with perfume to make the moment more provocative. It smelled of cherries and desire. I smirked and crawled onto the bed, sitting upright on my knees with my hands in my lap, waiting for Lee to return. My heartbeat was fast as my mind ran through a million ways this transaction could go. I read the contract, but seeing him in action was different. He didn't seem like the confident type but more rigid. He was already strict with everything else in his life. I tilted my head back and took a deep breath, letting my hair fall off my shoulders. All I could see was the pale cream ceiling over the bed, and it felt like time was racing, and this moment felt odd. I was more confident about tricks and didn't usually care, but I felt — on edge with him.

The door creaked, and I instantly looked ahead of me. It was him. He stood tall, his hair damp and mostly bare, with a towel wrapped around his waist and wearing a necklace with two gold bands hanging from it. I smiled faintly, keeping my eyes fixed on him as the uneasiness crept in even more. He looked away as he reached into the box and retrieved another piece of sheer clothing — something I hadn't noticed when I opened it.

What was he doing? I asked myself.

His jaw tightened. "Come here," he ordered.

I stood up from my knees and moved to the end of the bed. I sat still as he gently placed the fabric on my head, resembling a veil, indicating that this was a wedding dress. I tried to touch it, but he caught my hand and said, "Don't disturb it. Leave it as I placed it," he insisted firmly.

I nodded, queasy. "Okay, Lee." My tone was sweet and hesitant.

He was semi-tall, and slender with a narrow waist. When wet, his hair appeared dark brown. He paced back and forth in the room, searching for something. I sat on the bed, still as a statue, my legs crossed, and observed his cold, distant behavior.

"Where is it?" he said softly.

"Where is what?" I asked restlessly.

He appeared all over the place and said, "The camera. I had a camera in here, but I can't find it."

"If you're talking about the small teal one, it's under the sink in the bathroom."

"Why is it there?"

I shrugged and chuckled. "I don't know."

He walked into the bathroom and quickly came out with the camera. He stood in front of me, adjusting the settings. Then, he asked me to return to the center of the bed, and I complied. I sat as I had before. I was becoming restless as if I were paid to exist around him. He snapped a picture of me, then gestured for me to pose another way that concealed my face, and I obeyed. He took another photo. He wanted me to pose this time to showcase my hair, but I was to be tangled in the bed curtains, so I did. He paused to examine the photos but showed no emotion toward them. He looked back at me and suggested I lie flat on the bed, and I did.

He gently lifted my chin with his finger. He adjusted the dress, lightly brushing over my nipples. He took another photo, making me turn my head in opposite directions, then a close-up of my breast. "Stay still. Don't move." I lay still on the bed, feeling bored yet flattered to be admired. I heard him set the camera on the dresser, and then he loomed over me. We were face-to-face, inhaling each other's breath and feeling the heat of our bodies. He caressed my cheek with his thumb, gazing into my eyes as he pulled the fabric tight around my face before kissing me. His other hand stroked the side of my thigh.

The kiss felt like a gentle, longing peck on the lips. His beard was soft against my face, and then he kissed me tenderly on the forehead. He moved lower, kissing my nipples, stomach, then my inner thighs. My breathing grew shallow as I became wet. He held onto my legs as he pressed kisses against my vagina, making me hot. I bit my lip as I gently grasped his shoulders. I felt his warm breath against my folds, his tongue entering me. I moaned as he did wonders inside me, making me crazy. I let go of his shoulders and clenched onto the bed as his tongue curled around me and over me.

I cracked the skin on my bottom lip as I bit down again, this time harder, to avoid screaming. I felt the heat rise from my stomach to my chest as I moaned Leenardo's name.

"Say my name again." He demanded, and I complied.

"Say it again!" He demanded, and I submitted as he gripped harder onto my legs.

I could feel my body shake as a small rupture went off inside me, and then I relaxed. I caught my breath while remaining still on the bed. He slowly released me and then placed one last kiss on my lips, noticing the tiny drop of blood on the veil.

He licked his lips and said, "Remove the dress."

I nodded and stood up, taking off the dress. "Please!" he shouted. "Be careful with it."

Confused, I looked at him and replied, "Okay." I removed the dress and veil carefully. I was naked once more. I crawled onto the bed and sat down.

He gently folded the dress and veil and placed them back in the box. Turning away from me, he removed his necklace, which had two gold bands attached. He kissed the necklace, then leaned over to kiss the box before setting it on top. He whispered, "I love you, Alana." But I pretended not to hear it. It was a cold day for a broken soul. He stood still, lifted his head, exhaled, and looked back at me with darkness in his eyes. He dropped his towel and rushed over, pushing me face down on the bed.

His hand tangled in my hair, forcing me to spread my legs. I winced as he pushed inside me harshly. I closed my eyes tightly as confusion washed over my body, and pain as he thrust roughly. It felt as if I was going to break. He pressed my face into the bed harder. I could barely breathe as he treated me like a rag doll with no worth. He pulled my hair like he wanted to rip it out of my scalp as he fucked me. I felt the coldness around me as I tried to imagine something happy.

My hand turned red as I gripped the bedcovers, stifling my screams. He wasn't as gentle as before, but it seemed he was doing it only for her — Alana, and not me. He let go of my hair, causing my head to fall back onto the bed while his hands gripped tightly at my waist. The loud sound of our bodies slapping together stung my ears. I tried to hold back my tears as I felt an emptiness inside. I sensed him slow down as he released inside me, then collapsed onto the bed. I opened my eyes, feeling as if there were a hole in my chest. I lay on the bed, lifeless, just as I had felt for most of my life.

He sat back up and went into the bathroom, tossing the condom in the trash. I curled into a ball, closed my legs, and pulled the covers over me. He returned and put his towel back on, walking past me without acknowledgment as he picked up the box. "I'll deduct the stain you left on the veil from your pay. Goodnight." His voice was rough and flat as he slammed the door behind him and left the room.

I grabbed the pillow above me and rested my head on it to ease the pain in my neck. It was a cold night, and even though my body felt sore, I felt even more like a broken toy.

Chapter 7

'Siren'

If given the chance to journey to any place, I would set my course for the ocean. Its vast expanse, frigid depths, and enigmatic darkness held a profound allure for me. In spite of my fear about its unknown origins, I was captivated by its perilous nature and its genuine ability to cleanse. The touch of the ocean against my skin evoked a sense of completeness within me. I was enamored by its enduring presence in the world's history and its promise to persist into the future. The call of the sea was a siren's true home and served as a guiding light for lost souls. If I were to choose anew, I would undoubtedly return to the ocean, where the sharp, towering, and corrosive rocks starkly contrast with its boundless expanse, creating a sensation of belonging and familiarity.

The myth varied across different countries, altering the meaning of a 'Siren' over time. Most viewed them as giant birds with a woman's head disguised in a beautiful illusion, while others depicted them as dark and mysterious mermaids who were both deadly and enchanting. This presented a stark contrast but led to the same fate in the end.

I was born on a beach in a small town called Blue Creek to my mother, Lulu Hart. She was forty years old and single. It was normal for her to soak her feet in the sand and inhale the salty scent of the ocean. This, she said, calmed her mind. It took only eight minutes for her to start having contractions, which she dismissed because I wasn't due for a few days. When her water broke, she was in immense pain and all alone. She gave birth to me single-handedly, with the waves washing away the blood beneath her. After only two pushes, I came into the world, crying and screaming.

She didn't even know what to name me, but she liked to say that before she pushed me out. I stood up in her womb, trying to crawl to the surface, ready for this world, as she held me in her arms amid the blood and fluid. She looked at me with so much love and said, "The high seas have blessed us."

Eventually, she named me after her favorite song, "Rhiannon" by Stevie Nicks. She believed she could connect with the music better than anyone else. She said, "I felt like a free spirit wrongly accused by the world. I often felt as if I didn't deserve to exist. My life was tough, but I cherished my freedom and the pursuit of the life I wanted. People called me crazy for wanting to better myself and honor that small spark within me. In the end, I found myself alone and without dreams, forever chasing that elusive white horse leading me out to sea."

Like the rest of the world, she was once a child and now a woman. She used to be an artist and sang beautifully. She had the potential to be anything she desired, but for some reason, she gave up on life and never looked back. I tried to console her many times, but she found my affection repugnant. It felt like a sign of weakness to her, but in reality, her refusal to confront her brokenness was what truly made her weak.

My mother and I didn't have a good relationship; I was her child, which was the extent of our connection. She tried her best to guide me, but I felt I didn't know her. She remained a mystery, as she rarely spoke about her life before my father came along. She occasionally shared one or two details about him when she was in a good mood, but he felt like a ghost in my life. She only had one faded old picture of him, and he was strikingly handsome. But that was all I had: a beautiful man trapped in an image.

She was a troubled woman. If you met her, you might believe she was insane because her moods shifted so rapidly. I struggled to like or befriend her, yet I still loved her. It felt profoundly human to me, but that was simply how it was. She may have had a mental illness, but she refused to let doctors evaluate her health unless she was on the verge of death. She was estranged from her family, though her sister and brother would check in on her occasionally. I'm unsure how often they had fallen out in the past.

Her parents were as overprotective and abusive as she was toward me. They treated her the same way she treated me—making me feel insignificant while also making me feel like everything. I had to grow up quickly because of her. Imagine being a parent to a parent, fighting every day to prove your worth and remind yourself that you matter.

She loved folklore, myths, and the sea. She was addicted to them and felt they made her life worth something. Night and day, she obsessed over that. I began to believe in it myself and still did. Anytime she was down on her luck and received a blessing, she thanked the ocean. She thought it had spirits that watched over the earth and gave the land its prosperity, so she prayed to them, thinking they would bless her in many ways—especially with me, though she didn't want me.

She often said, "May you be blessed by the high seas," a phrase that has stayed with me even now. I didn't think she was completely crazy, as I believed in those spirits, too. We would go down to the beach every day, and I watched her pray to them. It might sound unbelievable, but they would gift her pearls and seashells.

It felt so real. I believed they were real. She doesn't know this, but one night, while she was passed out from her pills, I walked down to the beach. The sky was dark, brightened by luminous stars. I could feel the cold wind from the shore as I jumped over the white fence and buried my feet in the sand. I approached the sea, knelt down, and closed my eyes. I repeated the exact words she used to pray with, and all I could hear was the ocean, the movement of my legs on the sand, and the wind. Then, when I opened my eyes, I saw a tail sparkling against the darkness of the sea, swimming away. Before me lay three magnificent blue pearls. I grabbed the pearls and ran back home, believing I was blessed.

Ever since that day, blue has been my favorite color, and I have been captivated by the lore of sirens. My room's walls were covered with drawings, posters, and movies featuring them. In my mind, they felt real; however, I knew deep down that they served as an escape from my unhappy life. In a way, I didn't care about the truth. It was the closest thing to feeling alive and understood. You didn't have to be a prostitute to relate to a siren; you just had to be a woman.

I learned to swim so I could swim at night, hoping to encounter one, but I never did. I would gaze at the moon, pretending to be stranded in the distant sea, searching for a home. I thought maybe my mother didn't give me life, but the sea did, and I washed ashore while she claimed me. I didn't belong in her world, and she didn't belong in mine. I would cry, looking up at the moon and shouting at the sea to take me home. I wanted to go home, but I was— home.

It was the evening when I finally decided to run away, and my mother and I fought. We weren't speaking to each other. Our usual arguments centered around her belief that I was an ungrateful and spoiled child, while she viewed herself as a loving mother who always got the short end of the stick. I was supposed to start community college the next day, but I felt desperate to escape that town and her overwhelming presence. I quietly crept into the hallway and left a note, taking one last look at her before crawling out of my bedroom window and catching the next bus out of town.

I met Bambi, Jenny, and Tigress, who quickly became my best friends. They showed me the ins and outs of being a working girl. We grew so close that I decided to share the special ritual my mother and I used to perform. Since they had never been to the beach, I felt inspired to look for one near the city. By chance, I found a perfect spot. When we visited, we took the time to pray to the spirits of the ocean, usually at night or just before sunrise. We danced around a bonfire like a group of witches worshipping the night.

We were given pearls and seashells, just as I had been before. However, one night, we received an old, worn-down hand mirror. We cleaned it up and adorned the back with our treasures. We would gaze into the mirror as if it whispered secrets from the sea. If you looked closely enough, you could see the ripples of waves shifting within the mirror's surface. I cherished them, and they loved me, but not enough to honestly share my beliefs. They sometimes pretended to agree with me to boost my spirits. It was understandable, as my thoughts did seem absurd to the average person.

It had been a long time since I last saw the ocean and felt the grainy texture of the sand. It wasn't that I didn't want to go anymore; my life had become consumed by sadness and responsibilities related to Bambi. I just never had the time. I felt the sea understood me just as much as I understood it. I hoped it hadn't forgotten me.

Sometimes, I imagined myself sitting on the treacherous ocean rocks, my blue, scaly tail swishing back and forth. My translucent skin, veined and shrouded with pitch-black hair, remained still. With my reptilian eyes, I waited for prayers to echo through the waves from desperate women and little girls searching for meaning in their lives. I could feel the cold breeze on my sensitive skin as I began to sing for the ocean and the moon, my long, thick, bone-like nails reaching out to the two things that accepted me the most.

I didn't need a sailor to wash ashore or pass by in a boat for me to survive. All I needed was myself and my destination: home. But I wondered how my mother felt about my leaving. Did she read the note? Did she put up missing posters? Did she rejoice, or was she devastated by losing a part of herself? I didn't know. I sometimes missed her and her crankiness. I loved it when she would call out to me, excited about our day at the beach. I cherished the way she sang me to sleep and how she tried to understand my teenage mood swings. Most of all, I dearly missed our late-night conversations over frozen mangoes.

If I closed my eyes and concentrated hard enough, I could vividly recall what she looked like before I left. Her hair was brunette, longer than mine, but fine in texture.

Her curls were tighter than mine, especially in their natural state. She had bronzed skin with a yellow undertone. Her dark brown eyes sparkled, and charming freckles. Her eyebrows were faintly bushy, and her high cheekbones became more prominent when she smiled. Although her teeth were a bit crooked, her smile was lovely.

She was beautiful even when she couldn't see it. I missed her, but I longed for a better and healthier future even more. It took a toll on me to do what I did. I did not run or hide from it, but it left behind a darkness. The same darkness she carried before me. Sitting on that same rock, I could feel a heaviness in the air, waiting to consume me and make me even more miserable than I already felt. The sea and the moon held it at bay for a time, but I knew it wouldn't be long before it would destroy me.

It surrounded me like an entity trying to break free. I couldn't let that happen, even though my outlook on life was bleak. It felt like whatever she had passed down to me lingered in the air. Still, there was one thing she passed on that I didn't mind: singing. I rarely sang in front of others, but when I did, it felt serene, as if I were calling out to the sea and its waves. It was the one thing that deepened my love for music. It was poetry woven with sound, prayer accompanied by a rhythm, and words infused with genuine emotion. It became a habit I could call my own, free from negativity. Like the sea and the moon, it felt like home.

Chapter 8
'Rotten heart'

"I am not yours, not lost in you. Not lost, although I long to be. Lost as a candle lit at noon,"

– Sara Teasdale

Tiny air bubbles floated to the surface of the bathwater as I held my head under, my pitch-black curls adrift like sea urchins in the ocean. I felt weightless while immersed in the water. It was peaceful and relieved my mind. I wiggled my toes playfully, dreading the moment I had to get out. I didn't want to face the world again just yet.

I wondered if this was what sirens felt underwater — this freedom of existence and lightness of form. It was nice, quiet, and the most peaceful I had felt in a long time. It felt as if the world didn't belong to me, and I didn't belong to it, but I was here. Soon, very soon, I would be home.

Suddenly, a shadowy figure emerged, grabbing me by the

shoulders and pulling me out of the water, causing me to choke at the abruptness of no longer holding my breath. It was Jenkins, clinging to me and panicking.

Coughing as I struggled to catch my breath, I said, "I'm fine—I'm fine!"

He leaned against the tub, worry etched in his eyes. "Are you okay, ma'am?"

I nodded while battling to regain my breath. "Yeah—I was just relaxing underwater." I chuckled and smiled.

He scowled. "It didn't look like it."

I giggled. "Well, it's true. And it's not the best way to drown unless you want to die painfully," I said with a smile, reassuringly.

He stood up and composed himself, smirking. "You scared me."

I leaned against the side of the tub. "Sorry," I said sweetly.

"Mm-hmm. Do you need anything while I'm here?"

"Yes. Can you bring me a bag of ice? My neck feels sore," I said, lying and stroking it to make it convincing.

He winked at me and said, "Of course."

As he left the bathroom, I climbed out of the tub, soaking wet. I wrapped a towel tightly around myself and cautiously approached the bed. I gently sat down, dried off, and then put on my robe. I used the towel to dry my hair while contemplating how to spend my day. I had already called everyone and discussed nothing important, and I didn't feel like napping. I ran my hands through my hair and stretched out my legs, feeling the soreness in my body. It hurt, and he was the reason for it.

I found it creepy and sad that he made me wear his wife's wedding dress, excuse me, deceased wife's wedding dress, and had sex with me as if I were her while in it. He was damned beyond imagining. 'Alana' was her name, and it was beautiful. He had to be a different person when she was alive. I didn't even know what she looked like, whether she was a good person, or if he was. But his first impressions didn't suggest that he was. I didn't want to be a vessel for the dead in any shape, form, or meaning. I was hardly living already.

A knock came at the door. "Are you decent?" he asked kindly.

"Yeah! Come in."

He opened the door, smiled at me, set the bag of ice beside me on the bed, and handed me his phone.

I scowled in confusion. "Who is it?"

He whispered, "Mr. Sisto."

"Why?" I asked, annoyed.

"I called him to let him know what happened."

I rolled my eyes. "I was relaxing, Jenkins!" I whispered, bothered.

"Rhiannon!" Lee shouted sternly on the phone. "Rhiannon!"

I held the phone to my ear and took a deep breath. "Yeah—yeah, I'm here."

"Why am I getting calls at the office about you trying to drown yourself?"

I laughed, then covered my mouth. "I wasn't trying to drown myself." I put my hand over the phone. "You've got to be kidding me, Jenkins!"

Jenkins shrugged. "Unbelievable," I said, shaking my head.

I uncovered the phone. "I was relaxing underwater, and he just assumed I was hurting myself, a point I made to him."

He sighed. "I hope not."

"Well, I wasn't so—"

"Is this about last night?"

I rolled my eyes again, wanting the conversation to be over. "No! I couldn't care less about that. It was a misunderstanding, okay? I'm fine."

"All right," he said calmly. "I'm glad that you're okay."

"Thanks," I said, understanding.

"But I do need one thing before we close this conversation."

"Like what?"

"I am attending a friend's event tonight, and I'm taking you with me. Amelia and Jenkins will be off. It's a small fair with an elegant theme. I'm unsure what to expect, but I want you to come."

I sighed heavily. "I can stay here by myself. I don't need a babysitter. It's not like you need me there."

"As nice as that sounds, no, you will come with me. Reason or not."

"You're an asshole!"

"Sue me! I'll see you at eight. Wear something nice. Now give the phone back."

"Whatever!" I yelled back into the phone before handing it to Jenkins, who was hovering in the doorway. "I hate you," I mouthed to Jenkins as he walked away with the phone, talking with Leenardo.

I quickly closed the door behind him and lay down on the bed. I picked up the bag of ice and set it between my legs, soothing my sore, aching vagina. It was going to be a long day for me.

I hurried out of the apartment and put on my coat while Leenardo waited downstairs in the lobby. As I rode the elevator, I slightly opened my jacket to make sure my outfit looked presentable. When the doors to the front lobby opened, I stepped out and was confronted by a stranger. I was in complete shock. I smiled as I walked up to him, unable to believe my eyes. He had shaved his beard, revealing his bare face and heart-shaped features.

I wanted to touch his face but remembered the rules, so I kept my hands to myself. His skin looked smooth and baby-like; he appeared slightly younger. "You shaved your face," I said, fascinated.

"Yeah, I did," he exhaled. "I wanted to try something new."

I leaned in a little and studied his face closely. "Mm — it looks nice," I smiled.

"Thank you," he said warmly, likely trying to lighten the mood. "And—you look lovely yourself. You'll fit right in," he said, flicking the ribbon in my hair.

I opened my coat and twirled my pitch-black mini-dress in front of him. "Well, thank you, sir." I giggled.

He chuckled and smirked. "All right, we need to align our story if anyone asks how we met and how we know each other."

I nodded. "Just tell them it's none of their business."

He scowled in response, which I assumed was because the people were his friends. "I'm not going to do that," he said.

"Why not?"

"Because—because—because I can," he whispered, frustrated. "I want you to say we're friends and met while I was on business."

"Okay, what if they ask about the business, the day, and how long we've been friends?"

"The Doberman expansion project, August 9th, and for two and a half months," he said as he counted on his fingers to think. "Repeat that back to me," he said, wiping his lips with his thumb.

"We're friends. We met on August 9th when you were working on the Doberman expansion project, and we've known each other for about two and a half months."

He nodded and smiled. "Good. Good, now let's go before we're late." I tapped his shoulder, and he turned from holding the door. "Yes?"

I hesitantly adjusted his turtleneck and said, "It was crooked."

He looked down to touch his collar. "Thanks."

"Welcome," I said cheerfully as he opened the door for me.

"You're more excited than I am!" he exclaimed lightly, taking in his surroundings.

"And you're not?"

"I've known them long enough not to be," he shrugged.

We stood on the sidewalk while he whistled for a taxi. I buttoned my coat as the wind began to howl and chill me. Meanwhile, Lee seemed unaffected by the cold, acting as if he were a furnace.

"I never took you for a taxi, man," I joked.

"I'm rich, not snobby." His eyebrows furrowed as he waved his hand to hail a taxi. "Duly noted," I said, crossing my arms and freezing.

A taxi pulled up in front of us, and Lee opened the door for me to get in first, then he followed.

"You couldn't find any other drivers tonight?"

"No. Jenkins is the only person I trust to drive the limo."

"Picky much."

He laughed, not with coldness but with genuine warmth. "Rhiannon, I'm just being cautious. You should understand."

I smiled and replied, "Oh, I do." I snapped at the driver to catch their attention. "Can you please turn up the heat?" I whined.

"Yes, ma'am."

"Thank you."

Lee turned and glared at me. "What?"

"Nothing," he replied, closing his coat.

I shrugged with delight and said, "Whatever."

I tried not to show it, but for all my protests about going, I was actually excited about attending his friend's event. It's been a long time since I went to a fair, and I was glad not to be stuck in the apartment, bored, watching basic cable and waiting for him to fuck me. Also, it would be interesting to see the kinds of people he hangs around, not that I couldn't guess from the top of my head.

"What's the event for?"

He looked up from his phone. "It's for charity and to celebrate their anniversary."

"Wait. Are those the same friends who were too drunk to help you get home?"

He chuckled. "Yeah."

I smiled and said, "Hmm, so they enjoy parties."

"Very much."

He put his phone away and looked at me. "What about you?"

"What about me?" I smiled, feeling nervous.

"Do you like attending parties or events because of your profession?"

I looked down and giggled, then met his gaze again. "Somewhat." I sighed. "I'm more of a homebody."

"That's not so terrible."

"I think it's the country in me," I joked, laughing. "How about you?"

"Hmm," he replied playfully. "It depends on the occasion, but I'm like you. I enjoy going into hibernation."

"Okay," I said, nervously biting my nails.

"Are you from the South?"

I nodded.

"What part?"

"Um, Blue Creek, Maryland," I said, a smile spreading across my face. "It's a charming little town that feels like it's nestled within another small town, almost as if it has its own distinct charm."

"It sounds—"

"Livable." We both laughed. "I recommend it if you want to escape from everyone and enjoy the countryside."

"Mm," he said, his eyes smiling.

"How about you? Were you born and raised here?"

"I was born here, then raised here and in my parents' home country."

"Which is?"

"Sicily, Taormina." My eyes brightened. I should have guessed he was Italian or Sicilian because he was much more tanned than the average person. I suppose the dirty blonde hair threw me off.

"What's it like living there?" I asked, curiosity coursing through me.

"It's—" he bit his bottom lip. "It's a beautiful place full of culture. I haven't visited in two years, but I hope to take some time off to return. The sea is a stunning blue, the food is exquisite, and the people are lively. It's hard to put into words, but you really must experience it for yourself."

"You had me with the stunning blue sea."

"I'm happy to welcome new tourists into my home." He winked at me in a friendly way and then used his finger to wipe my chin. "You had a little—lip gloss," he pointed out.

"Thank you, what a gentleman."

"I'll take that as a compliment rather than a joke."

"Do with it as you wish," I teased, moving to the cab window. I watched the city lights fade behind the taxi as it drove down the highway. "Do you miss it?" I asked a hint of sadness in my voice.

"What do you mean? Sicily?"

"Yeah."

"Sometimes I do, but not as much since my wife passed away."

"I'm sorry."

"It's not your fault; it's just life."

"I sometimes miss home, too."

He pinched my leg, and I looked at him, startled. "You are your home; remember that," he said as he rested his head against the seat, turning away from me.

I nodded and murmured, "One can only imagine." I turned to look back out the window.

The cab stopped in front of a colossal mansion gate. Leenardo asked the driver to lower the window. He peered outside to talk to the guard. After three seconds, the guard buzzed us in, and we were let out in front of the mansion. It was a typical mansion—large, made of brick, with a garage full of cars and an unusual landscape—nothing impressive.

He paid the driver and grabbed me by the waist as he led us to the back of the venue. My kitten heels dragged across the pavement, struggling to keep up, but the property was massive. Since it was dark, only faint lights and low-cut grass were visible.

I could hear the sounds of people, making my heart skip a beat. My heels began to sink into the grass, and as I could no longer keep up, I stopped. He turned to face me, and I removed his hand and attempted to pull my heel out of the dirt.

"My heel is stuck," I said, frustrated and cold.

He released a resigned sigh and gently crouched down, placing his warm, soft hands on my leg. He adjusted my foot and lifted it from the muddy, wet, and cold grass. He looked up at me with his burnt sienna eyes sparkling against the night's darkness and asked, "I didn't hurt you, did I?"

"Mm—no," I mumbled, nervous.

"Okay," he said as he rose back up, then quickly picked me up into his arms. It happened so fast that I was too stunned to speak. He kept pace, nearly reaching the backyard gate. A million things raced in my mind as he carried me over the threshold like a bride. It was a tingling that erupted inside my stomach. I didn't know what to make of it, but it made my face feel scorching hot.

He used one arm to open the gate and gently set me down. The back of the mansion was enormous, buzzing with activity. There was a Ferris wheel, a carousel, game booths, and various food options. The theme resembled a fair but had an Alice in Wonderland twist, with elegant decor and workers dressed as the Red Queen, the March Hare, the Mad Hatter, and the Tweddles. I even wondered if I might spot the Red Queen's sister.

"Hey! Lee!" his friend called out to him. He grabbed my hand and walked to meet them. A man not much older than Lee stood next to a woman. They must have been the friends he was talking about who were partygoers.

"Hey! My macho man!" Leenardo exclaimed with more joy than I had ever seen him show. He hugged his friend while I stood in the shadows, trying not to be noticed.

"How've you been?" his friend asked, holding his face affectionately, love shining in his eyes.

Lee grasped his hands and replied, "I've been good." He looked at his friend with longing.

"Okay," his friend whispered, then embraced him tightly, and the hug lasted longer than it should have.

I peered beside me, fascinated by the lights and joy in the atmosphere. It filled me with contentment to at least enjoy the night. A woman's hand reached out to me. "Hi! I'm Isabella," she said cheerily.

"Oh—um, hi." I shook her hand.

"You came with Lee, right?"

"Yeah, I did." I smiled nervously and tugged at his coat,

breaking up his hug with his friend. Everyone exchanged glances. He stuffed his hands into his pockets, and I moved closer to him, hovering a bit.

"Please excuse my rudeness. Isabella and Edward, this is Rhiannon. Rhiannon, meet Isabella and Edward."

"Hi."

"Hey."

"Hello."

Edward was about the same height as Leonardo and had a similar complexion. He had short brown hair, a crooked nose, and an overbite, but he also had striking cheekbones and a well-defined chin. Then there was Isabella, a real knockout. She was slim and had a pear-shaped figure. Her hair was the same color as Edward's but was shoulder-length and bone-straight, and she had a pinkish-reddish complexion.

"Edward is my best friend, and Isabella is my cousin," he said, smiling. "Rhiannon is a friend I met recently."

"Friend?" she said, skeptical.

"Yeah. A friend."

"Mm—Lee, since when have you ever gone out and made friends?"

He shrugged. "I still have people skills. I'm in the business of it."

"Sure, Lee," Isabella winked. "Well, it's nice of you both to make it. I really appreciate it," she said, glowing and holding onto her husband's arm.

Lee moved away and kissed his cousin on the cheek. "I wouldn't miss it for the world." She held onto his waist and smiled enduringly.

"I know you wouldn't because if you did, I would kill you," she joked, and everyone laughed. I noticed a bit of dirt on my red stockings, so I brushed it off. Leenardo looked back at me and asked, "Are you okay?"

I glanced back up at him. "Yep. I just noticed a little dirt." I straightened up and crossed my ankles.

"Rhiannon?" Isabella called, her chocolate-brown eyes fixed on me, full of curiosity.

"Yeah," I said, light and sweet. Lee stood next to me, holding my waist.

"You look lovely." Leenardo rolled his eyes and scoffed. "No, seriously. I love what she did with the red and black outfit. It fits the theme perfectly." Her smile remained unwavering as she turned to look at both of us, studying whether one of us would fumble under pressure.

"Thank you." I smiled nervously as I blushed. People rarely complimented me, and it only made things more complex than before. It emphasized how little I thought of myself, as I couldn't recall a day when I genuinely complimented myself, no matter how small or significant. I was so excited to come that I tried to dress up at least.

He chuckled and tightened his grip around my waist. "I knew you were happy to come."

I nudged his stomach with my elbow, and he flinched. "No violence, please," he laughed.

"You will live." I smiled widely and sarcastically.

Edward wrapped his arm around his wife. "Well—it's great to see you, Lee. We have plenty of entertainment and food, so please enjoy yourselves." He gave his arm a gentle pat.

"Lee, we'll talk later, okay?" Isabella said, her white dress flowing charmingly.

Leenardo nodded in agreement as we watched them greet more guests. He let go of my waist and put his hands back in his pockets. "That went smoothly. Don't you think?"

"I think it went well," I said with a tight-lipped smile. I could feel my stomach growl as we stood still in the cold. "I'm hungry."

"Okay, then go eat." He waved his hand.

"Aren't you coming?"

"No. I might—"

"Yes! You are coming along with me to eat and do some rides, or I will tell everyone I am a prostitute, and you paid me to come."

He stood there, confused and speechless. "How do you know they will believe you?"

"They don't have to. It's the rumor that counts and plants a seed of doubt in their minds about your character, whether they believe me or not."

He licked his chapped lips and smirked with intrigue. "You could have just asked me to tag along."

"Sorry, that's not my forte."

He rolled his eyes and pulled me along as we headed for the food stands. "I want pizza, and you're paying." I smiled as he held onto my wrist, firm yet gentle.

"Whatever you want—Rhiannon," he said as I could hear the tension in his voice.

I bit my lip. "I love it when you say my name," I teased, smitten.

He shook his head. "You're going to be the stress of me."

I wanted to do more than that. Trust me.

*

We came across a game booth called the Red Queen's Painted Roses. It showcased a cardboard castle and artificial rose bushes, complete with hoops for tossing balls and stuffed animal prizes dangling high above. The carny was dressed entirely in white, with splashes of red throughout their outfit.

"Wanna play?"

He took a sip of his lemonade and said, "I'll watch."

I rolled my eyes at how reserved he could be. "Come on!" I whined. "It'll be more fun than just standing around." He seemed as if all the fun had been drained out of him. Despite being wealthy, he looked incredibly miserable. If I were rich, I would seize every opportunity to enjoy life.

"Please!"

He glared at me, irritated. "Okay—but what do I get in return?"

He straightened his posture and tensed his jaw.

"What do you want?" I asked flirtatiously, hoping it would come across as confident.

I watched him contemplate his desires, a smirk spreading as he sipped more lemonade. "We'll do whatever you want, and I'll determine the cost later."

I didn't like the sound of that.

"Um—I don't know. It sounds like I will be indebted if I do so."

"Not in debt." He frowned playfully. "Consider it an extra treat after all the fun, especially for me."

I shrugged in curiosity. "Okay," I said quickly, complying; it wasn't as if I needed much convincing with his confidence and mystery.

He gave the carny some money for about three rounds of the game. I aimed to win the stuffed Cheshire cat with its diabolical smile. It was always my favorite character in the movie, and it made me feel represented. I kept my legs close together and bent my knees, trying to handle the ball in my hand carefully.

Lee stood behind me, then whispered in my ear softly. "Take the shot."

I remained focused and said, "I will once your hot breath stops burning my ear." I winked in a taunting manner.

He stepped back a bit, smiling with his hands clasped behind his back. "I'll give you that one."

I turned to look at him. "Okay," I said, tossing the ball into the hoop without glancing. The carny praised me and allowed me to choose a stuffed animal: the Cheshire cat.

I gestured toward the booth and said, "Your turn." As I savored the victory, I showcased my skills. Besides his brooding and dark demeanor, I was intrigued about what lay beneath the cold exterior of someone I called Leenardo. There had to be more to him. Though it was rare, he did seem to smile and laugh now and then.

He sucked his teeth, picked up a ball, and stared at me before tossing it into the hoop. "Your turn," he said, cocky and competitive. He declined a prize because he didn't want one.

I handed him my Cheshire cat and tossed another ball into the hole. It was as if an alarm had sounded, leading us to four more rounds of throwing balls until I had about five stuffed animals in my arms.

"Okay!" I shouted, standing down. "No more. I have too many prizes to count."

He placed his hands on his hips playfully and said, "Let's see, one, two, three—"

I laughed and said, "Okay, okay." We smiled at each other, our spirits high, his eyes brighter than ever, and my mood cheerier than before. He took some of them from my arms into his as we walked away from the booth.

"What are you going to do with all of these?"

"I don't know. Some girls back home have kids, so I'll see if they want them."

"Mm."

"But I'm keeping my cat," I said, nuzzling my face into it. He looked at me, both perplexed and amused, his laughter echoing beautifully with the sincerity behind it. "You're different," he said with a smile, the cold air hitting his teeth.

"Is that a good thing?" I asked, shifting my eyes out of curiosity.

"Yes, it is," he said as our eyes met the unknown allure between them.

I hurried to a table, placed the stuffed animals on it, and took the rest from his arms. He sat down and asked, "So, what else do you want to do?"

I grinned widely and pointed at the carousel. "I've been dying to ride it."

"Isn't that for kids?" he said with a mocking tone.

I rolled my eyes. "No!" I replied, my face perplexed by such outdated thinking. "Anyone can get on it." I crossed my arms. "I've wanted to do this since I was a little girl."

"You've never ridden one?"

"Sadly," I replied, trying not to dwell on the past.

"Why?"

I exhaled. "Because I just haven't." I made a pouty, sad face. "See how it's calling our name?"

"No. I can't." He crossed his legs.

"You're sad, you know that— You're no fun at all."

"Sorry."

"Well, I don't need you. I'll ride by myself!"

"Good idea." He nodded.

As I walked toward the carousel, I turned and shouted, "You're missing out!"

He just sat there with the same dull expression on his face, but I didn't mind. It was good to have fun. In a way, it healed my inner child. I was experiencing things I had never had the chance to do before. He didn't know it, but I had never been to a fair. I lied about it. My mother believed it was a waste of time and insisted that I spend my time with her or focus on school. We rarely left the house except for necessary errands or to pray by the sea.

The carousel stood majestically in the heart of the bustling fair, its vibrant paint gleaming under the glow of fairy lights. Each horse had unique colors and expressions, evoking a sense of nostalgia for childhood — illustrations depicting charming cities and boats gliding across the sea, precisely painted to tell a story. As the gentle whir of the carousel turned, the soft sounds of laughter and music filled the air, creating a magical atmosphere.

I felt the corners of my mouth tighten as I smiled, watching the horses ride in the wind. I clasped the bars surrounding the carousel, waiting for my turn. I followed the motion of the blur created by the lights and horses in the wind. My eyes spun in circles, and my body surged with a rush of excitement. Then, it slowly came to a stop. I rushed up the stairs, passing the people leaving as I walked around, trying to find the horse I liked the most to ride. I used my hand to caress the horses' marble skin and the metal poles, sending shockwaves through me. By chance, I spotted one that was white with a pink saddle and a melted smile. I felt the abrupt coldness of the surface as I hopped on. I considered naming it since I would ride it, even if it were just once. "I'll call you Candi," I whispered. I liked to name things as it calmed my fear of the unknown, as if I understood it.

It wasn't like it was some magical force or spirit of the ocean. It was a simple wooden horse—an object, but one that would give me life for just a few minutes. Only two more people were on the ride as it started up again. It felt like I was riding the wind as it moved slowly and then sped up. I grasped the pole tightly, looking up at the blaring lights overhead and around me, embracing bodily freedom. The cold slapped against my legs, and the wind ruffled my hair. The other horses concealed me within the ride as I moved like a flash of an image stuck in a zoetrope. Escape. Freedom. Two words I like to think mean the same thing. It had been this big dream for me. It meant that one day, just one day, I would transform like a caterpillar in a cocoon. I would be able to break free and spread my wings. I would fly so high that I could see the world below me, even while looking through a darker lens. I would happily create my own life without worries—just peace and beautiful scenery.

It might mean revisiting the ocean, diving into the sea, and embodying the spirit I was meant to be. It would be painful, but in my way, beautiful. I would possess these dark attributes, yet such an enticing tail that it could shine brightly at night among the ocean rocks, sea, and moon. I could swim for miles, consuming the blessed water in my newfound lungs. It would bring me tranquility.

For so long, like love, I felt I didn't deserve it, but unlike love, I wanted freedom and nothing else. There was so much you could do with love for others besides yourself. It tended to drain you, leaving you hopeless and unwilling to pursue the higher form of yourself. The only person who could save and understand me was me. I was my white knight on my white horse.

I wondered whether closing my eyes and letting my arms roam free in the wind would transport me to that part of my life where everything was resolved—a ripe age when the darkness faded to the point that light could penetrate through. Knowing I had a long way to go was overwhelming, but perseverance was my virtue. I didn't need anyone like they needed me. I could either sink or swim, and the first choice wasn't an option.

Candi rode up and down, and I felt caught in a tornado, the carousel battling against the chilly wind while the twinkling lights blinded me. As I gazed into the mirror, a familiar shadow appeared behind me on the horse, far off in the distance. I turned to look, and it was him. It was Lee, watching me as if he wanted me to sense his presence.

I smiled and said, "You came!"

He nodded gently and replied, "I did!"

I laughed, feeling a sense of camaraderie between us.

"I'm glad you did!"

The ride started to pick up speed, and I held tighter to the pole while glancing back at him. He remained still, hardly moving on the horse. I extended my hand to him as a symbolic gesture of our shared experience, even though he clearly had done this before. He didn't hesitate and reached back, despite the distance, rolling his eyes and laughing, yet showing a hint of understanding while finding my behavior strange.

"Having fun?" he asked, fascinated by my joy.

"A lot!" I responded as I leaned back, gripping the pole, and closed my eyes, feeling the ride's motion, the wind, and the adrenaline coursing through my body.

I didn't want it to end. It was the most fun I had. Sometimes, I found it weird how I enjoyed having fun through the simplest things instead of partying or drugs. Fun was a high all its own, something humans had to experience and couldn't fabricate. It was a feeling you genuinely wanted to feel. No pill, drug, or alcohol could recreate that. If it could, that would mean you wouldn't have to confront your unhappiness, trauma, or the fact that you agreed to a voluntary death.

And I wasn't ready for death. My life had barely begun, although I had faced misfortunes that didn't make me wise or mature—just damaged. I wanted to hold onto a slight resemblance of it or take it for myself because no one had ever fought for me to have a good life. It hurt to know that I had to fight every step of the way, even for the broken things. I didn't want the white picket fence or a big family; I cherished the quietness of the ocean and the serenity of feeling high, thinking that I would be okay. I loved everyone I knew and cared for them, but would they feel the same if I were to leave forever?

I opened my eyes to see the carousel stop as I sat back up. Lee approached me at a slow pace and leaned against the mirror. His nose was bright red, and his eyes were glossy from the cold. I just sat there and smiled while giggling with my hand covering my mouth.

He shook his head at me and said, "I see you can be—"

"A child?" I asked, swooning at the moment.

"No, not childish." He licked his bright red lips. "Adventurous is what you are."

I dropped my hand and stood on the opposite side of Candi. "Why would you say that?"

He put his hands in his pockets and sniffed in the cold. "You're the only person I know who would give directions to a stranger you met once in a restaurant and then drive them to their hotel the day after without worrying that they might be dangerous or even accepting a proposition from them. That's quite an experience, especially considering your profession."

I burst into giggles again and said, "Well, I don't know what to tell you." I stared him down, unwavering. "I'm just me." I shrugged casually, using my finger to caress the vibrant paint colors and carvings on the horses as I walked swiftly toward the carousel's rusted metal staircase.

"Whatever that means," he said, following behind me. "So, where are we going next?"

"Really?" I asked, puzzled.

He smirked and said, "Yes."

"Okay—um, I'm thinking about the teacups," I said excitedly as I walked backward.

"You certainly have a knack for moving around, I see." He raised an eyebrow.

"Maybe." I bit my bottom lip and hurried over to the teacup ride.

He chuckled softly and called out, "Wait up!" as he ran after me. I was having fun, he was having fun, and we were enjoying ourselves. It had been a while since I had experienced such a thing.

Chapter 9

'Beauty & The Beast'

"Lost as a snowflake in the sea."

-   Sara Teasdale

The bones in my knees cracked on the dry carpet as his hot creaminess drizzled down my chin. I made intense, uneasy eye contact with his ash-burn eyes as he gripped my hair tightly, thrusting himself into my mouth roughly. I curled my tongue around him as he potently moved within me. I held onto his thighs with a deadly grip.

My face was overstimulated from the smell of sex and secretion. I could feel my eyes roll back into my head as I nearly gasped for air, his dark-blonde hairy legs scraping against the palms of my hands. It felt like pins against raw skin, particularly his hair, which was plastered against my face.

My lips were rubbed raw as he thrust two more times before squirting his pale, thin-creamy emission deep in my throat as his muscles and hand gripping my hair relaxed. His face flushed with pleasure as he fell back onto the bed. The depth of his eyes was dark and devoid of reality.

I breathed through my nose as I weakly rose from the floor and rushed to the bathroom, spitting into the toilet with immense disgust. My bare body rested against the cold, elegant toilet as I pulled the handle to flush it. I gently massaged my head, as it felt sore.

I heard him shuffling around in the bedroom while I longed for quiet. I grasped the toilet as I managed to pull my dead weight off the floor. I put on my robe and turned on the sink's hot water, filling my mouth with scalding water, swishing it around, and then spitting it back into the sink.

I plunged my hands into the water and splashed my face to wake myself up. It was around eight in the morning, and I had been woken up for Leenardo's enjoyment. I grabbed a face towel from the bathroom closet and patted my face dry as I stepped back into the bedroom.

He finished buckling his pants and dug around in his pockets, pulling out a couple of hundred dollars and tossing them onto the bed. He didn't even say good morning and reeked of strong alcohol. He nodded and drunkenly stumbled out of the room, avoiding my gaze and slamming the door behind him.

I glanced at the money lying on the bed, took a deep breath, and returned to the bathroom to brush my teeth. It was another dreadful morning, and I needed a shower to wash away the lingering smell. I scrubbed my teeth with my toothbrush, fuming at the tenderness of my head and the minty toothpaste running down the side of my hand. I was used to being treated like meat or an object to discard, but that didn't mean I had to accept it.

The way he tossed the money onto the bed made me furious. He might as well have thrown it on the floor for me to pick up. And why did we always have to have sex in my room? Why not anywhere else in the apartment? A girl like me would think that catering to a wealthy man meant passion and adventure, but it was just gray mornings and endless nights filled with emptiness.

He was both ominous and predictable. Or is that merely the side he revealed to me?

I knocked on my apartment's chipped and rotting door, waiting for Bambi to answer. I heard a slight movement behind the door, but it didn't open, so I knocked again. "Bambi!" I shouted at the door, knuckles itching from the rough, dry, white wood.

"Bambi!" I called again, and this time, a voice responded.

"Yeah, yeah! Hold on!" she shouted back, unlocking the door.

As she opened the door, she stood naked while a man got dressed in the room. He was older, balding with gray hair, and had a body covered in hair like a werewolf. His protruding belly was so large that it appeared he was pregnant. I noticed a wedding ring on his finger, and he wore a cheap suit so poorly made that visible stitches were holding it together. I rolled my eyes as she smiled nervously while he walked out the door. The sound of his rough dress shoes echoed across the old, checkered floor of the apartment building.

"Hello," he said, offering me a polite but slightly embarrassed nod. I turned to the side to let him out without saying anything, and I entered as she closed the door behind me. I didn't care that she was fucking a client. It was what we did, but in the apartment, it crossed the line. The number one rule was that what we did stayed on the streets and never came back home. I was gone for about a week, and she was already acting disruptive and reckless.

I wrinkled my nose at the pungent smell in the room and the dirty dishes scattered around the kitchen and on the table. I knew she could be lazy sometimes, but did I have to keep up the apartment all on my own? I sat on the stool before the vanity mirror and placed my bags on the floor beside me. Bambi threw on some underwear and pulled out a cigarette, taking a drag.

She sniffed while exhaling smoke and said, "So, what brings the newfound Queen back here among us—peasants?" She teased, noticing my newly purchased clothes.

I chuckled. "You're not peasants, and I'm far from a Queen."

"Mm-hm," she said with a hint of sarcasm.

"You couldn't be bothered to clean?"

"Nope. But I'll get to it."

"I bet—and why would you even think about bringing a trick in here?"

She choked on her smoke. "You know the rules."

"Well, the rules don't apply when you're gone!"

I scowled in repulsion. "Bullshit! Of course, they do, especially when I come back and have rando's knocking at the door for what you're selling."

"Did you come back just to scold me?" she asked, rolling her eyes.

"No! I came back to check on you, not just by calling, but I will if I have to. It kept you safe all this fucking time."

"I don't even know what to say to that."

"Whatever!" I said, tired of her shenanigans. "Don't do it again."

"Fine!" she snapped back at me, her small breasts bouncing disturbingly.

I looked around the room, its lifelessness more profound than ever. Because of the thinness of the decrepit walls, the sounds of our neighbors were louder than usual. It made me feel hollow, as if nothing worthy of life could even sprout in such a place.

"I brought presents," I said, handing her a stuffed animal. "I wanted to see if you'd like to hang out and catch up."

She dropped down onto the bed. "Let's see, I'm still in poverty, doing things for money, and most of the people I was close to have left." She said with bitterness in her voice.

I exhaled and leaned on my knees. "I didn't leave you. I'm coming back, but until then, we can shop and do whatever else you want." I said, raising my eyebrows playfully with a smile.

Bambi blew out more smoke. "You're already tired of the castle."

"It's far from a castle," I said, looking down. "Trust me."

"I doubt that. Look at your fancy clothes and brand-new manicure — French tip, no less!"

I laughed in her face and sat back up. "It's just surface-level stuff, Bambi. Dressing a whore in fancy clothes doesn't change what she is. It just creates the illusion of being more than what she is."

She nodded and held the stuffed animal tightly. "Whatever you say, philosopher." She tugged on its ears and glanced at me, deep in thought. "You brought me a bear."

"All the other girls took the good ones," I replied with a shrug. "Let it make you think of me."

She rolled her eyes and smiled. "Yeah, right!" She threw the bear at me, and I jumped up to hug her.

"Okay!" she shouted as I bounced on top of her. "I'll go with you!"

I rolled over laughing and lay beside her. "I missed this," I said, nostalgic.

"You only have two weeks, right?"

I sighed. "Yeah."

"Well, there you go. You'll be back home in no time."

"Hopefully, with all the money I'm saving, it means a new life."

"With three thousand dollars, I doubt it."

"He gave me that, but sometimes he gives me more when he feels like it."

Bambi turned to face me. "Is he a good fuck?"

I giggled. "Um—he knows how to eat, if you know what I mean." She slapped my arm, covering her mouth.

"Is he big or—" she asked teasingly.

"I'm not telling you that!"

She seemed disappointed. "Is he at least handsome?" she asked, with curiosity and excitement, wiggling her feet.

"He is gorgeous."

"Mm-hm."

"It's as if the sun kissed his skin and hair. He reminds me of a golden retriever but without the friendly and loving part." I sighed anxiously. "He treats me well enough." I turned onto my back and rested my hands on my stomach, and Bambi remained silent.

I smiled at her, and she looked back at me with sympathy. "Does he hurt you? Because if he does, you don't have to stay, especially for money."

"He fucks rough, but no, he doesn't hurt me." I winked and sat up. "He couldn't if he tried." I stared at Bambi over my shoulder. "Come on, get dressed. We are going out." I said, slapping her ass.

She got out of bed and turned on the shower in the bathroom, then peeked her head out.

"I love you," she said with fear in her eyes.

I felt a lump in my throat before I could speak. "I love you too," I said, aware that when I got home, it wouldn't be long before I had to leave, and she wouldn't be coming with me. That's why moments like this mattered and why I was helping her. It would give us both a chance at a new life. We didn't have to cut each other out of our lives; we just needed to go our separate ways.

I pulled down my sweater sleeves and looked out the window. I used to do this as a daily ritual to brighten my mood, regardless of who or what was on the street. It reminded me that I was human and that the situation wouldn't define or hold me back. My emotions sometimes got in the way, but not this time. I couldn't let my past or present prevent me from a better future because of my comfort. It had kept me safe for a while, but it was time to move on, no matter how much it pained me to do so.

We took a detour after shopping and eating out because Bambi was eager to see the apartment. He allowed no guests, but I pleaded with Jenkins to make an exception just this once, as long as he wasn't home.

The limo stopped in front of the apartment building, and I clasped her hand.

"Look."

She popped her gum and asked flamboyantly, "What?"

"As a precaution, don't touch anything, take anything, or even breathe too loudly. I don't want Leenardo on my case, nor Amelia, because she would love to get me into a lot of trouble, okay?"

She shrugged nonchalantly, but I tightened my grip. "Okay?" I shouted.

"Okay—jeez, if I had known coming here would heighten your fears, I wouldn't have asked."

We stepped out of the limo, and Jenkins looked at us with concern as we entered the building. I would expect him to have some confidence in what we were doing; besides, Lee wouldn't be back until around seven o'clock.

I opened the door, and she dashed into the apartment.

"Shout if you need anything, ma'am."

"Ma'am? She's far from that!" she laughed mockingly.

"Thanks, Jenkins," I said, feeling polite yet tense. He went into the kitchen, and I dropped my purse onto the table by the front door. Bambi wandered around, exploring the other rooms and gasping in disbelief at how different this place was from our apartment.

I snapped my fingers and said, "Don't be too loud!" I glanced around me. "Amelia will hear you and tell Lee all about it, so keep it as quiet as possible."

"Sorry," she whispered. "Your room is charming. Who knew you were living like a true queen?" she squealed, overflowing with excitement.

I giggled and said, "Shh!"

"Oh, right." She chuckled happily, then flopped onto the couch, propping her feet on the coffee table. I sat down next to her and nudged her feet off.

"No feet on the table. It's Murano, and it's expensive and rare."

She looked at me, perplexed. "Rich people's worries."

"No. Those are Leenardo's rules and boundaries."

"Oh. He has boundaries. Wow." She giggled. "New-age men, I guess."

I sighed and leaned back on the couch. "I respect it. But he's going to kill me when he finds out you've been here," I said nervously, rubbing the sofa.

"He won't, and besides, this place is—"

"Everything someone like us would and could ever want for a lifetime."

"Yeah—if only he felt generous enough to give."

I chuckled sarcastically and replied, "I doubt it, but it's not his responsibility either."

Bambi rested her head on my shoulder, and I rested mine on top of hers. We sat in silence, staring at the fancy coffee table.

It felt like a still moment, trapped in the flow of time and space. Having her by my side, talking to me without a phone pressed to my ear, was lovely. Still, somewhat, it also felt like I was going insane with loneliness in such a beautiful place. The shiny things and muted colors couldn't sustain my happiness forever. I needed more. That's why I didn't require anyone else to improve my life but myself. I could be the only one to pursue what I wanted and find my happiness. I had small moments this past week, but longed for them permanently. Bambi couldn't cure my darkness for long, and no one could.

I liked to think of us as sisters or sometimes as mother and daughter. She was broken, and I wanted to be her fixer, even though I couldn't fix anything. As much as I loved her, she carried as much darkness within her as I did. However, it didn't have to define her. She just needed to want to evolve and improve her life, just like I was trying to do. We were two people with distinct beliefs, morals, and souls. Although I often hesitated to hope for much in life, I found myself wishing for her. She had immense potential, and I wanted her to recognize it, regardless of the challenges and setbacks she might face. I wanted her to live forever.

I wanted her to be a part of my life forever. I wished for her to believe in life endlessly. It felt like it was all or nothing, but she was giving nothing. I wanted her to fight alongside me so we could ride off into the sunset together, but there wasn't much I could do. I was merely Rhiannon. Changing my own life was already difficult. I would miss her, and I could sense the future animosity radiating from her skin. I wanted it to be that way, but it wouldn't be — and that was okay.

The front door slammed shut, startling us and causing us to jump off the couch. My nerves were at an all-time high as I saw Leenardo standing in front of us. I needed the money, and this couldn't jeopardize my plans — not this one little break of his rule.

He placed his trench coat on the coat rack beside the front door and slid his hands into his pockets. It felt like he would scold me like a father who had caught his daughter breaking house rules.

He tilted his head and asked, "Who is this?"

"This is Bambi, my roommate from back home." I grabbed her wrist and pulled her next to me. She obnoxiously popped her gum in my ear and smiled, displaying all her teeth and gums. "Nice to meet you, handsome."

I rolled my eyes.

"I don't know if you remember me from the night you knocked her over onto the sidewalk while I was standing next to her, making sure she was okay. But that was me." She giggled. "You're younger than I expected." She squinted her eyes at him.

He smirked and said, "I take that as a compliment."

"How old are you?" she asked nosily. I nudged her.

"Bambi!" I said through clenched teeth. "I'm sorry she doesn't have manners and asks many questions."

"You mean like you?" he joked sourly.

"I—" I said, chuckling with a slight smile.

"He's got a point there," she said. I looked at her in frustration.

"I know I'm not supposed to have guests over, but—"

"But?" he interjected roughly, sighing. "No guests, so she has to go. I'll deduct it from your pay—first and only warning." He nodded politely at Bambi.

"Why?"

I nudged her again.

"What! Why can't she have guests over? This place is practically fucking empty."

His eyes turned icy, and his jaw clenched. "I get it. You're the fun, no-nonsense friend, but this is my place and rules. If you and Rhiannon don't like it, you can help her pack her bags." He winked mockingly.

"Damn! That is so cold, man. So cold!"

"Shut up!" I gestured for her to sit down. "I'll have Jenkins take her home."

"Thank you," he said, leaving the living room.

"Why can't you ever shut the hell up?" I asked Bambi, bewildered.

She scoffed. "Why were you acting like a scared little puppy?"

"I'm not afraid of him, but he pays me, so I have to cater to his needs if I want to get paid. You know that, and I know that, just like any trick, we play into their fantasy."

She sat on the sofa with one leg folded beneath her. "I know, but he's too handsome to be so—"

"I know he can be strict at times."

"Strict? Shit! He's more like a damn sergeant," she laughed, popping her gum again.

"Stop!" I hit her arm. "Stop popping that fucking gum and put on your coat."

"Jenkins!" I shouted, my anxiety rising. He peered through the kitchen door.

"Ma'am?"

"Leenardo has come back, so can you please take Bambi back home?"

He nodded with a piece of fruit in his mouth. "Yes," he mumbled.

Bambi walked over to the rack, removed her coat, and put it on. We exchanged smiles, leading into a hug, just as Jenkins suddenly appeared behind us, keys in hand.

"I'll call you tomorrow."

"Okay," she said, pinching my cheeks.

Lee walked back into the living room, grabbed his coat, and put it on.

"Leaving so soon?" he asked mischievously.

Bambi smirked. "Early morning, baby." She winked. "And I see you are too."

"Yeah, why are you leaving? You just got back," I said, crossing my arms. "Wait, why did you come back so early?"

He dismissed my questions with a laugh. "It's none of your business. Nice seeing you again, Bambi." He walked between us and left, with Jenkins following behind him.

"You know it's impolite not to escort me out," she said.

"You are right about that," I said, curious about Lee's destination.

We followed them into the elevator and eventually arrived at the lobby. Jenkins was waiting by the limo with the door open for Bambi, but Lee was nowhere to be found. Bambi decided to stall Jenkins so she could find out what I had discovered. I scanned the street for Lee until I finally spotted him nearby, getting ready to ride a motorcycle.

It was sleek, black, and sharper than anything I had ever seen.

I quickly approached him and stood in front of the motorcycle. I extended my arms as if that would stop him from driving and asked, "Where are you going?"

He simply stared at me, blank and silent. I could feel the rage bubbling up inside me. He returned to the apartment to issue demands and make my guest leave, abandoning me to my vices and boredom. I kicked his bike and called out, "Where are you going?" He shot me a piercing look while fiddling with his bike helmet.

"It's none of your business! And don't ever kick my property again."

"So many demands, Mr. Sisto," I mocked him.

"Watch it," he said, annoyed.

"What? You want me to make my guest leave while you go out and have fun, leaving me to rot in that gorgeous apartment, bored out of my mind?"

"It sounds like a problem for you."

I crossed my arms. "Oh, really?"

"Yes, it is. She can be your guest, just not at my place, and you can go out."

"We already hung out!"

"It's not my problem!" he said, revving his bike. "I don't know what you're trying to do, but please stop before it leads to something you won't like."

I sighed, stepped away from the front of his bike, and stood on the sidewalk. "I don't want to cause trouble. I want to know where you're going?" He stayed silent again.

"I deserve to know."

He paused, looking at me with confusion. "You do?"

"Yes! You woke me up this morning out of your mind—My mouth and body are still sore." I choked. "I may be a prostitute, but I'm still human and deserve to know more about my client than just his damn rules."

He smirked, confused. "I don't owe you anything." I placed my hand on the bike and looked back at Bambi, signaling her to go. She nodded and got into the limo, with Jenkins appearing relieved to drive off. "I'm not saying we have to be best friends, but if the contract states it could lead to long-term employment with you, we should have some common ground."

"I doubt I have anything in common with you," he said, looking me up and down with a glare.

I slowly removed my hand and replied, "I'm used to tricks treating me like shit, but for a man who loved his dear wife, he sure knows how to treat women. I—"

He set his helmet on the bike and hopped off, standing directly in front of me at the mention of Alana. "Did I touch a nerve?" I said confidently. "It seems you're human, after all."

He chuckled and looked around, bewildered. "Why do I have to tell you anything or for you to know anything about me?" he shouted hoarsely.

"I don't know!" I shouted back. "Maybe it's because I want to learn more about you beyond just you fucking me and being strict." I was out of breath, pacing back and forth. "I'm not saying I'm in love with you or even that I like you, but we need a common understanding and to respect rules, boundaries, and each other." I laughed cynically. "A mutual business partnership."

He nodded and put his hands on his hips. "A mutual business partnership."

"Yeah," I said, defeated. "I would like not to wake up and think you are a crazed man, ready to murder me in my sleep." I made intense eye contact. "All offense!"

"It wouldn't change anything if you did because hypothetically, I still could."

"Well, that's not your call, and yes, you are correct, but it wouldn't hurt."

"So, what are you asking?"

"I'm asking you to hang out with me sometimes, even attempt to — consider commonality between us as business partners. It would calm my worries a lot."

"You don't seem like the type to worry."

"You are wrong about that."

He chuckled and paced back and forth, pondering what I had said to him. He shook his head as if what he was about to do was forbidden. It seemed as though I was uprooting his life or stealing his belongings. I only wanted to dig a little deeper and understand that he was human, even though he treated me like anything but. He was hot and cold; one moment, he was a decent man, and the next, he was cruel, stepping on me as if I were nothing — a bug beneath his shoe.

It felt like going brick by brick with him. It was strange because I didn't care to know the tricks entirely; I just wanted to understand why they did what they did. It was interesting to realize that everyone was accustomed to their own darkness. Most of us were slaves or victims of something beyond our control.

He sat on the bike and loosened his helmet. "I was—I am going to a museum," he said sincerely, though he still seemed a bit distant. "It's one I usually visit around this time."

I smirked. "Okay."

He handed me his helmet.

"Safety first."

My eyes widened as I asked, "You want me to come?" I knew breaking the ice would take some time, but not this fast. Nevertheless, it was a start.

"No, I just want you to hold it." He seemed irritated. "Hurry up!" I put on the helmet, making sure my hair was tucked in, and tightened it. Carefully, I got onto the bike and wrapped my arms around his waist. I felt his body jerk, but he didn't say anything.

"Hold on tight," he insisted.

"Okay," I murmured, secretly thrilled.

My thighs were pressed against the bike's leather seat as I clasped his waist; I felt his muscles and the road bumps beneath us. My head rested on his back as the wind caught my eye, blurring everything around us.

Through the bike helmet, everything seemed to zip by faster than lightning. I experienced his perspective each time he rode. I was used to my world spinning slowly; perhaps his felt like it was moving at a rapid pace. It was stimulating to feel that rush while weaving through traffic. The combination of fear and excitement was intoxicating, almost like a drug.

It sounded ridiculous, but I could have sworn I heard my heart beating in sync with the bike's speed and the wind. Did his beat the same as mine, connected to the rhythms of nature? It had no other reason to beat that way.

I closed my eyes, feeling the heat radiating from his body. I didn't want to let him go, as it felt so good to fight against the cold. I was so caught up in the moment that I forgot to bring my coat while running after him. It must have been the adrenaline from the debate that kept my body well-lit.

I didn't care if someone liked or respected me, but I did care about commonality. I needed to understand him to get along with him. It felt strange to know only two things about him and nothing more. It was irrational for him not to want to know me or allow me to learn more about him. I could be a scammer, murderer, or lunatic. I thought I was more trusting, but he seemed to beat me to the punch.

However, it wasn't trust he felt, but rather cockiness — vanity. He didn't trust me, but had such confidence in himself that he believed he couldn't misjudge the next person. In his own eyes, he was always right. This realization made me think that it was likely the reason he was so demanding and strict about things. He always needed to be correct, but disguised this need as setting boundaries.

Our bodies jolted with the bike's sudden stop, and the tires screeched. When I opened my eyes, we were parked in front of a gray art museum building shaped like junkyard metal. We both got off the bike, and I took off my helmet, revealing messy hair. I walked to the museum door and adjusted my hair as Leenardo entered the building ahead of me.

It seemed things were off to a good start, and I meant that in the most patronizing way.

I slowly strolled into the space, noticing a front desk and a tall, thick wall with a noticeable maze behind it, which I assumed was where the paintings were. I spotted Lee leaning against the wall, waiting for me, and I hurried over so as not to delay any longer. I stood beside him and smiled.

"It's about time," he said, annoyed.

I nodded. "I could say the same," I replied with a wink as I walked ahead, taking in the antique paintings from various eras on the wall. I felt him watching me from behind, trying not to show his preference for a specific painting on the far east side of the museum.

He stood proudly before a giant painting, his eyes fixed on it and his body stiff. The painting was enormous as it hung on the wall. The frame was golden and worn. The description at the bottom read: The Kiss of the Sphinx by Franz von Stuck, 1895.

"Is this what you were in such a rush for?" I asked sincerely.

His face tightened, and he stayed quiet. "Well?" I pressed again.

He quickly turned his head. "Yes. If that means you'll stay quiet, then yes!" he whispered before sitting on the bench in front of the painting.

I remained in my place and asked, "Why?" while I stared at his back.

He sighed. "It has sentimental value."

I nodded and moved closer, standing at the end of the bench. "Does it belong to you?"

"You sure have a lot of questions," he said, side-eyeing me with his shoulders slouched. I giggled a little and glanced at the painting. "Yeah—I do."

"Well, stop. You're giving me a headache. Just observe the art and be quiet," he demanded, keeping his gaze fixed on the painting.

"Okay," I said softly, sitting on the edge of the bench.

The painting seemed just out of reach. However, that didn't prevent me from understanding it. At first glance, I recognized its marvel. The background was a deep red, reminiscent of the blood that flows from human veins. The shadows were so dark that you had to squint to see clearly. A gigantic rock stood prominently, on which a sphinx-like woman lay, kissing a kneeling man. They were both naked, but only he was visible while her face remained concealed.

I gazed at the historic brushstrokes of the painting. I loved how devoted they were to one another as lovers. It was as if she took his last breath, and he loved her despite her monstrosity. He was her prey, and she was his temptation, much like many mythical creatures or women.

Others looking at the painting might assume there was no choice being made and that a monster was swallowing him. They would see him as her meal, while I viewed her as the ultimate goddess being gifted what many creatures like her couldn't have—love, devotion, and passion.

I saw myself in the painting as if a past life had returned to haunt me. We were practically the same if you replaced the wings with a scaly tail. I sat on a rock by the ocean, facing a mere man who offered me nothing but, in a desperate way, sought them out under the guise of temptation, even though they were essentially alike. I just wasn't the woman he desired and never would be.

I shifted on the bench a bit more, which caught his attention. He looked at me for a moment before turning his gaze back to the painting. Relaxing, he said, "You asked why this painting is significant to me." He slid his hand inside his coat and gently touched his chest. "It's sentimental. I never cared much for it until I met her. It was her favorite painting, and around this time of year, she would want to come here and admire it." He fiddled with something hidden in his coat. "She used to say it reminded her of the kiss of death."

"Why?"

He chuckled and placed his hand back on his lap. "Because she saw love and death as one, two sides of the same coin."

"That's beautiful."

"Not really, especially since she's gone. But for her, I keep traditions alive. It's the best thing I have left of her."

I didn't care much for the world, but my heart always ached for the widows. The men and women left with a love they would never hold again. They were the ones who felt forgotten. It was a sad truth: love, often viewed as the savior and healer of humanity, couldn't shield us from the pain of loss.

"What do you see when you look at the painting?" he asked me.

I shrugged lightly. "I see temptation and love." My eyes scanned the painting again. "I see a man and woman in the burning fever of twisted fate."

I turned to face him, and he was smiling. "I like that. Twisted fate." He leaned on his knees and looked at me. "Do you want to know what I see?"

"Sure."

He smirked and said, "I see beast and man. Yes, there could be love there, but I think it's more of an obsession than true love. He's not prey, and she's not a predator, yet in an opposing manner, they harm each other. As you mentioned, they are stuck in a twisted game of fate driven by lust."

"Morbid," I said as we kept eye contact.

"Yeah, it is, but that's how it looks to me." He looked down and took a small breath before leaving the bench and continuing to walk around.

"All these paintings on the wall are various forms of a game of love, lust, and loss that society has faced for centuries, though we are experiencing it now," he said, his hands behind his back as he looked my way.

"She's not a beast!" I whispered fiercely, my voice bouncing off the museum walls.

He frowned and asked, "What?" I sighed and walked to the other side of the museum.

"I said she's not a beast. She's a woman and just as human as everyone else."

"And why is that?"

"Sphinx or not, they have emotions and desires like anyone else. They may appear beastly, but that is because men often view women as a fetish or temptation, something so terrible that it seems wild and unmanageable. This perspective reveals a reluctance to admit that they, too, see themselves in a similarly horrid and lustful light."

He scoffed, and I smiled.

"Just like you. Rough and wild."

He nodded and tucked his hands into his pockets, then stopped walking. "You might be right."

"I am right."

"I never took you for a philosopher," he said, his tone low and condescending.

"You underestimate me in many ways," I said as I continued scaling the walls of paintings, absorbing the worldly art I had only seen in books as a kid. "But then again, I did think you were a judgmental piece of shit," I smirked, avoiding his stare.

"Did I offend you?"

I looked over at him. "No, but I thought I would help your interpretation a bit."

We both sensed each other's annoyance. Even with our differences, I was beginning to understand what shaped him into who he was. It felt like heat radiating from our eyes as we silently stared at each other. Then he suddenly clapped his hands, jolting me out of the trance between us.

"It's time to hit the road." I nodded and walked toward the door. "Did you learn enough about me?" he asked as he followed behind me.

"Not enough, but I will soon."

He chuckled. "Does that mean I have to listen to you ramble about your little life?"

I stopped in front of the door and turned around. "No. I couldn't care less."

"If only you felt the same about me." He winked.

"That's different, and you know it," I said, pushing the door open with my foot as I walked out.

"If you say so," he replied, unfazed, as he took off his coat and handed it to me. "Next time, bring a jacket."

He hopped onto the bike while I put on the coat. "Do you have any other demands?" I asked sarcastically.

"No."

I put the helmet back on and braced myself for the ride back. He started the engine again, but before he pulled away, he placed his foot on the sidewalk and wrapped my arms around his waist.

He turned his head slightly and said, "I'm not crazy or an axe murderer."

"Okay," I said sincerely.

"I wanted you to know that, so you have no reason to be afraid of me."

I smiled, feeling guilty. "I'm not afraid of you." I leaned in closer, resting my chin on his back. "I just want to learn more about you. I'm not asking you to tell me your favorite color or what keeps you up at night, but just enough to properly judge your character. Okay?"

"Mm," he said tentatively as he revved the motorcycle.

I rolled my eyes, seeing my breath inside the helmet. "Deal?" I asked, my voice muffled.

"Deal." He sniffed in the cold, then rode the bike into traffic.

Chapter 10

'HeartBeat'

"You love me, and I find you still. A spirit beautiful and bright."

- *Sara Teasdale*

I flipped through the television channels, but nothing seemed interesting, and there weren't many DVDs in sight. Once again, I found myself alone in the apartment. Lee had some business to finish, Amelia had the day off, and Jenkins was visiting family.

Since the girls had already made plans, I had no one to call or hang out with. It was Halloween, and I felt bored and hungry on the couch. I turned on the Western channel and headed to the kitchen to find something to eat.

I pushed open the heavy white doors. Swinging open the fridge door, I saw nothing but leftover breakfast and healthy snacks. I frowned in hunger, then opened the freezer, which contained only frozen vegetables and one pack of ground beef.

Amelia cooked most of the meals every day, and they were good, so there was no need to order takeout or cook for myself. I had two choices: order out or cook. I would rather do neither since I had become accustomed to someone else doing it. I slammed the fridge door closed and tossed the ground beef and frozen vegetables onto the kitchen counter.

I planned to combine the two, but I didn't know what yet. I stopped the sink and ran lukewarm water into it, placing the frozen ground beef in the water. Then, I dragged my feet back out into the living room, and to my surprise, Leenardo came through the door with groceries.

He closed the door with his foot and said, "Are you just going to stand there, or are you going to help me?"

I snickered and playfully shrugged. "I don't know. I love it when a man struggles."

He looked frustrated and tired. "Rhiannon," he warned.

"The key word is 'please'," or you might end up holding them forever." I crossed my arms.

"I'm serious."

"Me too! There's a poor guy still holding them till this day."

He smiled tensely and asked, "Can you—please help me?"

"I love it when a man begs." I bit my lip and giggled.

"Rhiannon!" he shouted dramatically.

"Fine!" I rolled my eyes, unfolded my arms, grabbed the groceries, and headed back to the kitchen. He had brown paper bags, which were not very useful because they broke easily and snagged on silk gowns. I stood at the kitchen counter, rummaging through the bags, when he followed me in. He set the rest of the groceries on the table, took off his coat, and draped it carefully over the chair.

As he removed his gloves, I noticed his hands looked cold, red, and veiny.

I slid onto the stool at the kitchen counter and opened a bag of chips. "I never took you for a shopper," I chuckled jokingly.

He sighed and began to put away the groceries. "I haven't done this in so long."

"Mm—what made today different?" I took a bite of a chip.

He shrugged and said softly, "I don't know. I just felt like it today."

I nodded. "If I had money like you, I probably wouldn't shop either." I chuckled again.

He opened the fridge, placed some food inside, and then turned to me. "I assume you're the one who put the ground beef in the sink?"

"Yep," I said cheerfully with a smile.

"Do you know how to cook?"

I waved my hand and said, "Somewhat, but if you count cooking pasta as a talent, then yes, I am."

"It'll have to do." He shut the fridge and headed to the cabinets.

"Why?"

"Well, since we're the only ones here on Halloween night, I thought it would be a good time to get to know each other. What better way to do that than over food? You'll be lending me a hand during dinner."

"Eh—I don't know," I said, unsure of my cooking skills since the only two things I had cooked were pasta and fries.

"Don't worry. I'll be your teacher, so you'll be fine." He shut the cabinet door and set a large skillet and two pots on the counter.

"Okay." I set the bag of chips on the counter and clasped my hands. "What are we making, chef?" I asked as I crossed my legs, my long silk nightgown draping gracefully.

He tried not to smile. "Definitely not ground beef. We had enough of that last week." He laid out all the ingredients on the counter and started bringing out bowls and utensils of different sizes. "We will be having garlic butter steak bites and mashed potatoes." He slid the raw potatoes toward me along with the peeler, then walked over and grabbed a pink box from a bag. He opened the box, and I spotted an Oreo cheesecake.

I smiled and leaned against the counter. "For dessert?" I asked, raising my eyebrows in delight.

He smirked. "Of course," he said in a croaky, hushed voice. "No place is better than—"

"Patsies," we both said. He closed the box, smiling and looking intrigued. "Do you know the place?"

"Who doesn't?" I said, rolling up my robe sleeves and starting to peel potatoes in a bowl. "When the girls and I had money, we would find the time to order from there on special occasions." I smiled.

"We might have more in common than I thought." He gave a slight smirk as he unplugged the sink.

*

The sizzle of garlic and oil in the skillet filled the kitchen as Leenardo moved his head to the music playing on his phone. He wore a purple apron that didn't quite match his outfit but made him seem more approachable. I chopped the last of the potatoes, slowly approached the oven beside him, and dropped them into a pot of scalding hot water sprinkled with a bit of salt.

I stood next to the counter and watched as he flipped and turned the steak in the skillet, bobbing his head and singing along to the music. It felt like observing a rare breed in its habitat. He was either brooding or just plain angry most days, but today, he seemed normal. I wasn't sure whether to be skeptical or happy about it.

I observed him quietly as he cooked, pondering the questions I would ask him. I knew I had said I wanted to know more about him, but what would I even ask?

He turned slightly and asked, "Hey—um, could you bring me the Marsala?"

"Mm-hmm, where is it?"

"The second cabinet to the left over there," he said, pointing to the cabinets by the fridge.

I opened the cabinet, grabbed the Marsala, and quickly handed it to him. "Thank you."

"I'm going to watch TV. It seems you've got the cooking covered from here." I walked over to the door, and he turned down the burner on the stove and set the spatula aside. "Wait," he insisted.

"Do you need something else?"

He nodded, reopening the bag of chips and taking one. "Let's talk."

I looked around, confused. "Talk?'

"You said you wanted to get to know each other, so talk." I felt nervous, and I had no questions prepared. I was in a tough spot. I spoke without thinking, and now I didn't know what to say to him. At least I knew one thing: he looked good in that apron. I wondered if he wanted to follow my terms or was curious about me, too.

I approached the counter slowly and sat down, opening my hands for him to share the chips. "Um—I don't know. What do you want to share with me?" I said anxiously. He poured some chips into my hands and then laughed. "You're funny. You know that."

I smiled and looked down while eating some chips. "I try to be," I said, winking. He dusted the chips off his hands, placed them in the cabinet, and leaned on the counter with his arms crossed. "Tell me," he contemplated. "How did you get to be where you are?"

I couldn't help but chuckle because no one had ever asked me that question before. It took me by surprise since it was so complicated. My whole life felt like a Rubik's Cube. I took my time answering him. I slowly bit my bottom lip and said, "I didn't have a great home life, so I ran away at the age of nineteen and never looked back." I sighed and then avoided eye contact. "I—um, money was tight, so I did what was best for my livelihood."

He kept his eyes on me, staying focused. "Mm—how long?" "Seven years." I forced a smile. "A cruel testament."

He grasped the wine bottle and popped it open. "Want some?"

"Yeah, sure." He nodded, grabbed two wine glasses, set them in front of us, and filled them to the brim. I pulled the wine glass closer, caressing it with my finger.

"Now, you tell me. What brings you back here?" I asked, taking a sip of wine, and he followed suit. "I was called and asked to join a project we have with the city." He sipped more wine, savoring its flavor on his tongue. "I lived here for about three years before."

"Amelia mentioned that you brought her and Jenkins here with you."

He nodded and held the glass firmly. "Yeah—um, I live just outside the city. I think we're all adjusting."

I played with the glass rim and asked, "What was your wife's name, if you don't mind my asking?" I knew her name but wanted to hear it roll off his tongue. "Or not."

He looked me in the eye and exhaled slowly. "Her name was Alana Giordano-Sisto," he said, his mouth curving into a beautiful smile. It was as if he were in a daze. "She had vibrant auburn hair that went past her waist and a beauty mark on the right side of her chin." He closed his eyes and savored the scent of the wine. "She was my everything; she still is." He chuckled and reopened his eyes.

I smiled with sympathy. "What was she like?"

He set down his wine glass and checked on the steak in the skillet. "She was like a ray of sunshine. She had a big heart and was so open-minded." He added onions to the skillet and then checked on the potatoes. "She seemed sweet," I said to gauge his reaction and inquire for more information.

He burst into laughter and turned to face me. "I loved my wife very much, but she was anything but sweet. She hated people just as much as I did. She was a true New Yorker." He rubbed his lips together. "I loved that about her. She was kind but never tolerated anyone's nonsense."

I nodded, sipped my wine, and raised my eyebrows in agreement.

"Why did you agree to my proposition?" He stood tall and confident.

I shrugged. "Your charm." I joked, but his gaze lingered on me. "Okay." I sighed. "I thought you were good-looking and remembered you, so I figured, why not? More money for me."

He appeared serious again and chugged the last of his wine. He looked over his shoulder and said, "The potatoes are ready and need to be drained." He tapped the counter to command me.

I rolled my eyes, grabbed the drainer, and walked over to the stove. He was behind me, hovering to make sure I did everything correctly. "I don't know about you, but I'm starving."

He sighed, leaning past me to turn off the stove. "I'm starving, too."

"You look like it." I gasped, punching his arm while mashing the potatoes in a bowl.

"I'm not that malnourished," I laughed.

"I'm not so sure about that," he joked, leaning against the counter. "Here, you need to mash harder," he said quickly, standing behind me and lightly touching my hand to forcefully guide it in mashing the potatoes.

"I got it," I said, appreciative. His hand still held mine while he used his other hand to pour melted butter and then milk into the bowl with the potatoes.

"Watch as I stir gently, allowing everything to mix harmoniously." I nodded, knowing he didn't need to hold my hand to guide me, but I didn't mind for some reason. I wanted him to linger a little longer. Our faces were close together, our cheeks sharing warmth. It was strange how I could feel the strength of his veiny hands holding mine firmly while he kept his eyes on me as I tried to focus on the bowl.

It sounded like a swooshing noise as we stirred and stirred. I could feel his neck pulse as he leaned on me, continuing to talk about the mashed potatoes, even though they seemed ready. Eventually, he released my hand and handed me the parsley to sprinkle over the potatoes in the bowl. My hand felt burning hot and sweaty as if I had plunged it into hot water.

"See? Cooking isn't so bad," he smirked.

"And you're not a bad teacher." I lied since he hardly taught me anything, and anyone could make mashed potatoes. At least he did most of the cooking.

"Mm—a compliment." He smirked again and took the bowl from me. He placed the potatoes onto our plates, followed by the bites. Then, he drizzled gravy from the skillet over the food and sprinkled some additional parsley on top. Using a napkin, he wiped the plates clean like a chef and carefully set the forks beside them.

He wiped his hands on his apron and refilled our glasses. "Alright," he sighed. "Dinner is served."

"About time." I smiled and returned to the living room, plopping down on the sofa and deciding what to watch on TV. Channel after channel, I finally found a horror-comedy movie I liked, and then Lee stumbled out of the kitchen and sat down next to me. The film was a low-budget horror flick from the 80s called Elvira: Mistress of the Dark. I had seen it a few times, and it was one of the classics. It never failed to make me laugh.

I sat cross-legged on the couch as I took a bite of steak. I wished it were well done, but it wasn't. The movie had just started, and I could feel his eyes on me. I looked at him and asked, "What's wrong?"

He toyed with his food. "Nothing. It's just—are these the kinds of movies you watch?"

"You haven't even given it a chance. It just came on." I giggled. He shook his head and ate some potatoes. "What movies do you watch?" I asked, leaning back on the couch.

"Not much," he chuckled. "I grew up watching old films. My parents were obsessed with them because that was how they learned English."

"Mm. My mom loved old westerns." I dropped my fork onto my plate. "And now I'm obsessed with watching The Good, the Bad and the Ugly." I giggled again. "Well, at least the one with Leonardo DiCaprio," I smirked.

"Wear my name out, why don't you?" He joked.

I smiled and said, "No, but seriously, what movies?"

"Um—Roman Holiday or Breakfast at Tiffany's."

I laughed and said, "No, seriously." He had to be joking because he seemed to be one of those people who watched documentaries or legal dramas.

"I am."

"Oh! — Well."

"My parents really liked Audrey Hepburn." He winked and chuckled. "But to be fair, I have a guilty pleasure for rom-com movies from any era." He exhaled and set his plate on the coffee table. "It reminds me that life isn't so bad."

"That is optimistic." I finished my potatoes.

"You're not going to eat your steak?"

I looked at him queasily. "No."

"Why?"

"Fully cooked meat is more my style. Sorry," I shrugged, grabbing one of the pillows from the couch. "No offense taken," he said, trying to watch the movie.

A few minutes passed as I laughed persistently at the movie, but Lee remained unamused. Still, he stayed to watch it with me. I felt hurt that he didn't like my movie choice, but not everyone has to enjoy the same things to get along. By this time, I was lying on the floor in front of the television on a pile of pillows. My mouth ached from all the laughing, and my eyes were wet from crying.

It was pleasant to experience peace amid my thoughts and the world around me for a moment. It felt like tasting the freedom I so desperately craved, if only for once in my life — well, twice. I just hoped that no matter where I ended up in life, it would be somewhere I could be happy and see the ocean.

I glanced over my shoulder at Leenardo while I laughed. I had thought he was asleep, but he was actually watching me. I stopped laughing and returned his gaze. His arm rested across the top of the sofa, and his body was relaxed, with his legs sprawled out. He seemed anxious and bored, so I turned around and sat up.

"You don't have to watch it with me anymore."

He nodded. "Maybe I want to."

"It's clear that you don't like the movie, so—"

He rested his head on the couch and sighed, "You don't know that."

"So, tell me, then, so we can get this over with, and I can get back to enjoying the movie."

He quickly lifted his head and scowled. "I'm not going to say that; I never said I didn't like the movie," he grunted in frustration.

"Yes, you do!"

"No! I don't!" he said firmly. "Now, stop bothering me and watch the movie."

"Liar," I said, tossing a pillow at him. He flinched in shock, and for a moment, I thought he would get angry and shout, but he didn't. Instead, he threw a pillow back at me, sparking a pillow fight between us.

One after another, we aimed at each other's faces and bodies. I wished for a storm of feathers to rain down on us. But the pillows weren't cheap, nor would they break from the blows we exchanged with each other. They were so soft that they could slip out of our hands, resulting in a potential exchange of fists. We were in a delicate situation, and I didn't plan on losing, especially not to a blonde, red-eyed beauty like Lee.

We chased each other all around the apartment. It wasn't on my list of things to do on Halloween, but it was fun. He was enjoyable, and I appreciated that. I liked it when he emerged from his horrid shell and resembled a human. If only he had done it more, these weeks would have gone more smoothly. I wondered if he realized what he was doing. Did he know he was having a good time? Did he understand that he chose to let me in halfway?

It felt like he took long strides as we played. He was so lanky that he resembled a creature I couldn't quite picture. His broad shoulders and long limbs were like a frog springing from one place to another. I felt like prey running from him, dizzy from the room spinning because of it.

We both tripped and landed on the floor beside each other. I lay on my back, my belly full of laughter, and my body aching from the friction against the floor. He lay facing me, his head propped up on his hand, smiling as we laughed.

"I think we missed the movie."

"I don't care," he said, laughing.

"Me neither." My hand tried to stop my mouth from laughing more. "I had a great time tonight."

He moved closer to me, almost towering over me, and looked at me in an unfamiliar way. "It was nice. I enjoyed it, too."

His eyes searched mine as we smiled at each other. At that moment, it felt like the room had turned blue — not a dim blue, but bright as a sapphire radiating charisma. If we stayed quiet long enough, we could hear the thumping of our heartbeats against our chests and our shallow breathing. He inched closer, his mouth almost touching mine.

There was a forcefield between us, pulsing to be set free and ignite the room with fire. I felt my stomach drop and my chest cave in as I realized what was about to happen. My face burned red, and my throat dried up. As he began to lean in, I contemplated breaking the number one rule. I knew I shouldn't, but everything in me wanted to. It hurt to consider it, but no matter how much I yearned to fulfill my desires, it wouldn't lead to my freedom.

I quickly turned my head and sat up. "Cool," I said, blushing.

He paused for a moment, closed his eyes, and then lay back beside me, a hint of disappointment on his face as he turned pale. "Yeah, cool," he echoed after me.

The television showed reruns of the same movie, its scenes flickering in the dim light of the darkness as I woke up to Leenardo's absence. The soft sound of a piano playing a lively tune echoed down the hallway, filling the room with stillness. I stretched my arms wide, feeling a slight stiffness in my muscles as I sat up, yawning deeply to shake off the remnants of sleep. With a click, I turned off the television, plunging the room into quiet, and gradually peeled the blanket away from my body, feeling the cool air against my skin.

I slipped my feet into my slippers and headed to the kitchen for a glass of water. As I filled the glass, the music grew louder and more erratic. I took two sips of the water, then placed the glass on the counter and followed it down the hallway. It was the most beautiful sound I had ever heard, but it began to annoy me. I listened more closely, trying to trace its origin. I let my ears lead me as I stopped at the end of the hallway. It was the room next to Lee's, and the door stood wide open.

He said I couldn't enter his room, not the one next to it, so I braced myself and peeked through the door, spotting Leenardo at the piano. It was the only object in the room besides the bench he sat on and a chair in the far corner by the window. It was orange and resembled a seashell; it sat alone and was dusty. He didn't notice me, so I tiptoed in, leaving my slippers by the door.

He was so absorbed in playing that I managed to dust off and sit in that same orange chair. A marble glass of alcohol rested on top of the piano, with the bottle right behind it. He seemed drunk again and out of his mind as he played until his fingers bled. He drank glass after glass while I watched him descend into a breakdown.

Everyone had their vice. Me and my pills. He and his bottle. It wasn't anything I hadn't seen before, but I felt pain for him. He could be so much happier one minute and then the saddest person in the room the next. It must have been exhausting. I wanted to comfort him, but he wasn't mine, and I doubted he would feel the same for me.

He was sweaty, drunk, and red-faced. He seemed as if he could burst from how much he had to drink. I was about to leave when he picked at the keys again for a dramatic finish to his piano playing. It sounded like ocean waves crashing against each other—brutal yet angelic. Afterward, he rested his head on the piano and fell silent.

I clapped as loudly as I could to get his attention. He quickly sat up and grabbed his glass, startled by the sound, as if about to throw it at the ghost in the room—that was me.

"Hey, hey. It's just me," I said softly. He laughed and then fumbled back onto the bench, and I rushed over lightly on my feet to catch him. I took the glass from his hand and placed it on the piano. Lee was out of it. I could snap my fingers, and he wouldn't understand a thing. He sat down again to regain his bearings while I leaned on the piano.

"What—what are you doing in my room?" he asked, slurring words.

"This isn't your room. It's a piano room."

"No—no difference." His eyes drooped as he swallowed the last of the whiskey. "I told you not to come in here." He slammed the glass down onto the piano.

"I wouldn't have come in here if you hadn't played so loud and woken me up from my sleep," I said, frustrated. "And be more specific next time about the rooms. Say, do not enter my room and the room next to it!" I screeched. He twitched in irritation.

"I'll make sure of that next time," he said with a smug and arrogant look. He was even more insufferable when drunk than when sober. I wanted to wring his neck, but this wasn't my problem, and neither was this situation.

"Well, keep it down, okay. I'm going to bed." I stood up and looked at him with pity, then turned to leave. As I walked away, I could hear him sniffling, so I looked back and saw him crying. I paused, then turned to face him. "Lee," I called out to him.

"What?" he shouted, pouring more whiskey into his glass.

"Is something wrong?"

"What do you think?" he asked rudely. "I thought you were going to sleep," he said, mocking me.

"I am. I—I want to make sure you're okay."

He stared at me and said, "Do me a favor. Don't play shrink, and don't make this an opportunity for bonding because it isn't." He glared at me, sadness in his eyes and destruction in his hands.

I slowly moved closer. "Okay, I won't."

"Thank you." He lifted his glass toward me.

"What can I do? Huh?" I chuckled. "Because, unlike you, I want to be able to sleep peacefully tonight."

He sighed and gulped down the alcohol from his glass.

"I want to forget," he began to cry. "I want to forget," he repeated, and I nodded.

"Okay," I whispered.

"Can you do that?" he asked, his voice sincere and broken. He reached out his hand to me, and I hesitantly clasped it. "I can do that, Lee."

He set his glass down and held onto my waist, resting his tear-streaked face on my stomach. He wrapped his large hands around me as I caressed his hair. He silently cried about whatever was weighing on his conscience. I continued to comfort him until he stopped crying and looked at me with his fiery, swollen eyes. I smiled at him with sympathy and said, "It'll be okay, Lee." He used his thumbs to stroke my stomach slowly, then lifted me onto the piano, closing it with his hand to create more space.

Was this what he liked? Did he want to be pampered and comforted like a bird with a broken wing? He could be rough in bed, but in the end, he craved gentleness and understanding. This was something Alana, his wife, must have been familiar with. I didn't see him as that kind of trick, but I should have known better. Most widowers, in some way, wanted to be comforted and experience a hint of a woman's embrace, as they did before their wives died.

It was eerie how his emotions flowed inconsistently, but I suppose death or love could do that regardless of how long it had been. Unlike others, these factors didn't make me indifferent to love. I found it sweet and caring to love someone so deeply that you could feel like bursting into a million pieces. I didn't know what to think about it. For a long time, I felt I didn't deserve it, and I still don't.

He gently kissed my cheek, removed my silk robe, and placed it on the piano beside me. He laid me down and hiked up my nightgown. Then, he took my robe into his hands and folded it, laying it over my face. I felt him pull down my panties, and I could sense the coldness of the room against my bare skin. He unbuckled his belt, and his pants dropped to the floor.

He pulled me closer and kissed me from my ankle up to my inner thigh. The softness of his damp, plump lips made me tingle. He hovered over my vagina, and I could feel the warmness of his breath. His tongue teased my clitoris as he flicked at it, making me jolt. Then, he clasped onto my legs tightly, licking and sucking any and everything in between, making me lose my mind.

He held onto my legs so tightly that I thought they might break in his grasp. I arched my back as he curled his tongue inside me, hitting the right spot. I could feel my body tremble and shake as it washed over me, filling me with exhilarating pleasure.

He let go of me and let me rest for about five minutes before swiftly and gently pushing inside. It caught me off guard as I grabbed his shirt, tearing it open and revealing his abs. I couldn't see anything because he covered my face, plunging the room into darkness. I wasn't scared, but I definitely didn't want a repeat of last time.

"Lee," I called out, but he remained silent. "Lee!" I yelled.

"I'm here." I took a breath as he filled me up. The thickness of his curved penis absorbed every inch of me.

"Don't leave me sore this time," I said, taking deep breaths. "You can do whatever you want, but please, not so rough this time." I felt him lean over me and kiss my cheek again, then whisper in my ear, "Only if you scream loud enough."

I giggled with worry. He clasped both my legs, spreading them wide and far. He pushed deeper into me, and I gasped at the pressure because I still felt slightly tender.

My hands reached for the piano as he moved slowly within me. It felt like torture as he relished in my wetness while he picked up the pace, and our moans bounced off the walls of the apartment. The piano felt like a slippery surface, so I instantly held on to Lee's waist as he thrusted inside me. His kisses touched my forehead and cheeks, but never my lips.

My nails dug into the skin on his back, ripping and tearing at the immense pleasure I felt between my legs. He didn't care, as it appeared to motivate him. He was still rough but not harsh to the point that it felt like my cervix was breaking. I almost swallowed my tongue as I tried not to scream.

"Call me baby," he demanded. I moaned even louder. The sensation I felt made it hard to even speak. I couldn't form a word or a sentence as he moved faster. "Lee!" I called out.

He leaned over me again and said, "I know.' He kissed my mouth briefly. "Call me baby," he demanded again.

I bit my lip as I grew wetter, parting my legs wider for him to enter me more deeply.

"Baby," I whined, catching a glimpse of his smile through the fabric of my robe. "Say it again."

"Baby," I said, whimpering. He let go of my legs and clasped my hands, bringing them over my head and holding them down as he roughly and swiftly thrust harder. "Baby!" I whined again.

"Good girl," he said, breathing heavily between his moans.

I began to clench onto him as I felt a burning sensation between my legs and stomach. He hissed and flinched in pleasure as he kissed me once more, thrusting quickly while I screamed "baby" as loud as I could. In just two seconds, we both reached the end together as he fell on top of me.

Then, he stood up and touched the piano as he caught his breath. I closed my legs and removed the robe from my face. I widened my eyes as they adjusted to the bright lights in the room. I sat up, and he stepped back. I pulled my legs onto the piano, placed my hands between them, and regained my senses.

His face was puffy yet beautiful. He glared at me and said, "Don't ever come in here again." He tugged at his pants, closing them.

I stayed silent. "Do you understand?"

"Yeah," I mumbled, still out of it. "You understand!" he yelled, approaching me and grabbing the sides of the piano. It surprised me. "Okay—okay!" I said, unafraid but confused.

His face was twisted as if he were holding his breath, and his hands were piped red. "Good," he said, his voice croaky. "And never sit in my wife's chair again." He peered up at me, looking cross.

"Yes, Mr. Sisto," I said firmly. Leenardo was back and even more out of control.

"Never forget it!" he hissed at me before leaving the room angrily.

"Trust me, I won't!" I shouted back, jumping off the piano.

I couldn't wrap my head around his existence. At times, it felt like what I had experienced was a dream, and I might wake up at any moment. He was like Jekyll and Hyde. He wasn't a bad person, but he could be an asshole. His twisted nature had a way of revealing his darkness. A huge shadow loomed over me and this place. It didn't scare me, but it made me suspicious of what state he was truly in. Everyone had demons, but none like this. I was accustomed to Bambi and her drug-induced outbursts or her running through the streets naked, but what if this led to real harm?

He seemed like a blank slate from the moment he caught my eye. It made me think about how all this could be dangerous. Something inside me urged me to run, but I didn't want to. I needed the money. I needed a chance for a future, and relying on tricks wasn't helping, nor was Bambi. I needed his money for my escape. All I had to do was endure another week.

Until then, I would steer clear of him unless he requested my presence. He made it impossible to satisfy him. He was so fickle that it made me want to punch a hole in the wall or run him over with a car. He didn't care for me, and I didn't care for him. I desired only the money. I didn't know what he wanted, but it must be something dark and disturbing because who in their right mind would hire a prostitute like this other than a lunatic?

I must have a talent for attracting the shattered and broken.

Chapter 11

'A Flip Of The Tail'

"Yet I am I, who long to be. Lost as a light is lost in light."

\- *Sara Teasdale*

The sand and rocks crawled between my toes as I gazed at the ocean. Its formidable waves and salty water looked as if they were lathered in soap. I kept my eyes closed while I listened to the sea, wind, and air around me. It felt incredible to be close to home, to smell the ocean, and to feel a familiar wetness in the air touching me.

Who would have known that I would be standing here waiting for the inevitable to happen seven years ago? I longed for freedom—something I couldn't have just yet. One more week, and I would be home free—just one more week.

I walked forward into the ocean, wetting the lower half of my body as the water brushed against me. I spread my arms, leveling my hands over the rising water, hoping to find clarity as I inhaled the saltiness from the ocean onto my tongue, which scratched against my throat.

I wanted to swim away. I wanted the waves swirling around my rigid scales and flapping tail to carry me. I could feel my claws emerge as my mind flashed with the events of the past two and a half weeks. I wanted someone or something to sink them into for my pent-up frustration. I had always endured for others for far too long.

I suddenly felt the urge to dive into the water and swim away, leaving all my troubles behind. It called out to my spirit, vigor, and very being, yearning to break free and live unrestrained. It felt like an addiction.

But I couldn't leave just yet; I had unfinished business to take care of. I didn't know what that was, but as much as the sea beckoned me, my darkness did, too. It wanted to collect what it was owed, and I planned to serve it its final dish before I departed.

I clasped my hands, floating in the icy water, praying to my home and fellow sisters. I prayed and prayed — this time, not for a gift or blessing, but to be brought home.

"Rhiannon!" Jenkins called out, trying to get my attention.

I opened one eye and glanced back. "What?" I shouted, annoyed by the interruption.

"Mr. Sisto wants to talk to you!"

I rolled my eyes. "Why?"

"He just does! Come out of the water, now!" he said, holding the phone close to his heart and smiling with all the care in the world reflected in his eyes. I sighed, intending to release all the tension in my body. I forced a smile to avoid offending Jenkins. I walked back toward the shore, approaching Jenkins and grabbing his phone while soaking wet in a light blue, filmy dress.

"Yeah," I said with a tentative ear, hoping the phone call would be quick.

"Listen—uh," he paused for a moment. "Yeah!"

"I need you to do me a favor again."

I clenched my jaw. I had done him enough favors as far as I was concerned. I needed this arrangement to be over. I smiled at Jenkins, making it appear as if everything was fine, and then turned to look back at the ocean. "What favor?"

"I had a date for a friend's party, but she bailed at the last minute, so I'd like you to come with me."

"Do I have a choice?"

He chuckled. "If I gave you one, would it make you feel better?"

"I'll take that as a no."

"I asked, didn't I?"

"If that helps you sleep at night. Listen—do you really need a date? I mean, I'm sure your friends know you're single, so what does it matter if you're there alone? I'd prefer not to show up on your arm."

"I understand." He paused once more. "But I need you, so you'll be going."

"Why?" I asked softly, curious about why I was even needed. I was just a prostitute hired for sex, not for public appearances.

"Do you need a reason?" I nodded and glanced down at the rawness of my cold, red toes on the gritty sand. "Yeah, I do. This time, I honestly do."

"I pay you, right? Huh? If you need a few extra dollars to be by my side, I'd be happy to help with that."

"I mean, there's so much money can do," I said, the flashes of last night replaying in my mind. My heart raced.

"How much?"

"Lee."

"How much!"

I stared off into the distance past the ocean, wanting to explode. I wanted to be free, and I would be. "I'll accept whatever you want to pay me."

"Is this about last night?"

"No," I said, aware it was about last night and every night I had been close to him and his insanity, not to mention the bruises that had formed on my thighs.

"It doesn't seem that way."

"That's too bad, Lee, because it's not about last night."

"Okay, then, tell me your price." "Really, I don't want anything."

He scoffed. "Give me a number. Everyone has a price, even you, Rhiannon. What can I offer you to be by my side willingly?" He clicked his teeth. "Mm?"

"Another three thousand dollars," I said, displeased with myself.

"Done! I'll send it to you, and I expect you to be ready in about two hours."

"Okay," I said, hearing his smile over the phone.

"Good, see you in two hours, and wear something nice."

I chuckled. "Of course. I wouldn't want to let you or your friends down."

"I would hope so."

I sucked on frozen mangoes while we sat idle in the limo. Leenardo was conversing on the phone about business as usual. It was almost time for him to leave since the project he was working on was nearly finished. I looked through the window, observing people coming and going at the party.

The estate was quite large and well-maintained. The first level was made of white wood, while the lower level featured cream and gray brick. Numerous windows allowed a dim, yellowish light to shine through — one balcony was visible from my vantage point. The property was surrounded by lush green land, including trees, shrubs, and nearby houses, giving it the classic charm of a white picket fence estate.

I took a bite of a mango, my fingers gripping the bag tightly and wrinkling it. It was hard to ignore the smacking sound my mouth made when it came in contact with the fruit, but it highlighted how silent it was between us.

He hung up the phone and put it in his coat pocket.

"Did you really have to bring those?"

"I'm hungry," I replied, chewing. "Why?"

He glared at me and said, "Mm—I'm not sure. Maybe it's the constant sound of your chewing that's annoying." His mouth mimicked mine.

"There wouldn't be any chewing if you hadn't shown up an hour early and rushed me. I hardly ate today."

He smirked. "And that's my fault?"

"Yes," I replied, nodding as I took another bite of mango.

He closed his eyes, clasped his hands, and took a breath. "Okay," he said as he opened his hands and moved to the edge of his seat. "Leave the tension for later. The party will have food, and I want you to be on your best behavior." He forced a smile. "I would appreciate it."

"Mm," I said, zipping up my bag of frozen mango slices and putting it in my purse. "When you mention tension, how much are we talking about? Big, medium, or small?" I said to tease him.

"What— what are you talking about?" he looked confused.

"What you said earlier: "Leave the tension for later." I didn't know we had any," I chuckled.

"Who cares?" he said with wide eyes. "If you don't start with me, I won't start with you."

"I thought we were on the best possible terms, Mr. Sisto."

"I don't understand why we're debating this."

"Debate?" I said sarcastically.

"Rhiannon!"

"What?" I shouted, annoyed. "What is it?"

"You've had an attitude since I've seen you. I don't know what it's about, but drop it and save it for later. This is one of my closest friend's engagement party, and I don't want you ruining it for whatever reason." He demonstrated with his fingers. "I'm this close to losing my temper, and trust me, you haven't seen me angry."

"I doubt I'll want to," I giggled. "I'm not afraid of you, and you could have just asked me to behave politely instead of demanding it." I rolled my eyes and crossed my arms. "Besides, stop lecturing me about your friends and their behavior. Have I embarrassed you at all until now?"

He stared at me.

"Exactly, so stop with this illusion that I'm "embarrassing" you. I'm a professional." He leaned back into the seat and rubbed his temples. "Whatever," he mumbled. "Let's just get this night over with."

"I couldn't agree more." I tapped my red heels on the carpeted floor, the faint sound echoing in the silence as the limousine door swung open. The vibrant color of my shoes contrasted sharply with the rich, pitch-black carpet, forming a striking visual that mirrored the complex emotions building in my chest.

As I looked up, he stepped out of the limo and gestured for me to take his hand. Once we exited, I felt the refreshing air that cleared and cooled me from the stuffy limo. We walked arm in arm through the doorway, entering an estate filled with a mix of people laughing as everyone stood still, focused on whoever was speaking.

We moved closer to the center of the crowd, brushing against strangers and feeling invisible. I attempted to peer into each person's space but couldn't discern who they were. I only noticed a dinner jacket and a man's hand resting on a woman's waist. Her stunning, flowing cheetah-print dress showcased her arms and back.

Lee stood next to me, clearly impatient. I whispered, "I didn't take you for someone with more than one best friend."

He glanced at me from the corner of his eye. "Of course, you wouldn't," he shrugged. "I do have a life beyond what I show you."

I agreed with him. I knew nothing about him except what he had told or shown me, and I didn't care anymore. I wanted the money and to run off into the sunset, with or without Bambi.

"We can both agree on that."

He sighed as if he were already over the conversation. "Wouldn't it be nice if we could do it all the time?"

The crowd at the estate began to clap and then dispersed, so he took my hand and pulled me to the front with him. I stayed close behind as he approached his best friend. "His name is John Devo," he whispered quickly to me.

Two people stood in front of us, talking to John and his fiancée. John was the most ordinary man I'd ever seen. He had light brown hair, blue eyes, Eurocentric features, and a stout build. Even though he was a plus-sized man, his skin was pale with a yellow undertone.

"Is there anything else I need to know before we speak to him?"

He stretched his fingers while holding my hand and said, "He's from England." He chuckled and added, "We met during our university years."

I tilted my head and rolled my tongue around in my mouth, pondering how coincidental it was that his name was John and he was from England. He sounded just like Jenny's John—unless! The couple walked away, and to my delight, I spotted Jenny standing beside Leonardo's best friend. We made direct eye contact.

We squealed in unison and left our dates, rushing to hug each other and jumping around like kids. She looked as beautiful and elegant as ever. We embraced tightly, feeling like our limbs might break from the tension.

Tears filled my eyes as I tried to take in everything around me.

"You were supposed to be gone," I said through my tears.

"I understand." We let go of each other. "But John wanted to wait and have the party here with his friends." We laughed, our hearts brimming with love.

"I'm so glad then because I get to see you," I said, giggling and holding hands with Jenny. "What are you doing here?" she asked, swallowing her tears.

I turned to look at Lee. "Remember I told you about Leenardo? He brought me here."

She nodded. "Ah! Yeah, I've heard so much about you from Rhiannon and John." She smiled. "You're more handsome than they both described."

"Thank you, Jenny." Leenardo nodded politely, and I smiled again, excited to see someone familiar.

"Not more handsome than me, my love," John smiled with his lower teeth.

"No one's more handsome than you, pumpkin," she winked at John, blowing him a kiss. He returned the gesture and said, "Come here, lad." Leenardo smirked and hugged him tightly, patting his back. "It's great to see you."

"Yeah, it's been a while."

"How have you been?"

"Oh, you know, just home and work. The usual."

"Mm-hmm."

Leenardo fondly patted his arm. "Congratulations to both of you on your engagement," he said with a smile.

"Thank you," Jenny said, her red curls bouncing in the light as her figure peeked through the translucent cheetah-print dress. "And Rhiannon, we have so much to catch up on! I need to tell you all about the wedding plans and so much more!" she squealed excitedly.

"Lay it on me!"

"Oh, right! I forgot," she laughed. "John, this is Rhiannon, my best friend in the whole world." She hugged me from the side.

"Hello," I waved.

"And apparently, Leenardo's date." He winked at him.

"Yeah, she is." Lee looked down at his shoes and then back up. "I'm grateful for that because my original date bailed on me, but as a good friend, Rhiannon came with me."

"I love helping." Everyone exchanged smiles. "Alright, we'll let you boys catch up, okay?"

"Okay, love." Jenny kissed John on the cheek, and I glanced at Leenardo. He shoved his hands in his pockets.

"See you later."

"Okay," I said softly, almost as if I were seeking permission.

Jenny grasped my wrist and dragged me through the various rooms until we finally found ourselves in a photo booth situated in what appeared to be an empty dining room. She drew the curtain behind us and arranged me against the booth wall with her facing me.

"Alone at last," she giggled.

"You could have at least let me take off my coat," I said playfully, gently pushing her shoulder.

"I'm sorry," she replied, catching her breath. "I just wanted to get out of there."

"I can relate," I chuckled. "It's a relief to see someone I know besides Leenardo, but I thought you liked John."

She rolled her eyes. "He's great! Being around wealthy people every day, discussing ski trips, business stocks, and future vacations has exhausted me, especially when questioning our relationship." She caressed her engagement ring. "I'm sorry we haven't talked in so long, but I've been preoccupied, as you can see."

I smiled and held her hand. "Just breathe. You can do this."

"I don't know. Maybe I'm in over my head thinking I can fool myself into being a housewife or a mother. I'm terrified," she said, her eyes soft and full of emotion.

"It's okay. I'm sure you'll adjust after the wedding. If there's one person who deserves this more than anyone, it's you." I pinched her cheek. "Maybe even have lots of orgasms." I joked to cheer her up.

"Ew!" She slapped my arm and laughed.

"He doesn't give you any?" I chuckled along with her.

She bit her lower lip and said, "Occasionally. He is surprisingly a good lover and gentle, too."

"I knew you were leaving for a reason." We laughed again. "There are always three reasons a woman marries a man: he's either funny, rich, or good in bed."

"Or all of the above," Jenny smirked, and I nodded in agreement. She leaned back against the curtain. "What about your prince charming? How's it going?"

I shrugged my shoulders. "It's going." I pulled my hand back and fiddled with my coat. "Do you think they know?"

"Know what?"

"Know about each other hooking up with prostitutes."

Jenny pondered. "Probably so." We laughed. "Who cares? I'm marrying John, and you're—"

"I'm in a business partnership, but it feels like a prison sentence."

"Why? Is he a weirdo or hurting you?"

"Well, he's not a weirdo."

"Okay. Does he hurt you then?"

"Define hurt?" I joked, but she looked serious. "No! Not on purpose, at least. I think."

I took off my coat and placed it on my lap in the cramped photo booth. Jenny looked worried. "What?" I asked, knowing she'd lecture me about safety again.

"I sensed something was wrong between you two." Her eyes were filled with worry. "Just leave him."

"And go where? I'd be breaking the contract, and I have only one week left with him, so everything's fine."

She shook her head. "You just said he hurts you," she whispered cautiously.

"I never said that." I rolled my eyes. "It's not like I have a black eye or broken bones. He can have sex a little rough, that's all." I nudged her arm. "Don't worry about me. I'm fine."

"You made enough money from him, right? You can go anywhere now."

"So, you say, so stop! I'm not leaving. Look at me; I'm alive, healthy, and unharmed." Jenny shook her head again. "You know how this goes. I'm okay."

"Alright, but if something happens, call me, and I'll come get you."

"Mm-hmm."

"I'm serious. You can live with us until you get on your feet."

"Mm-hmm."

"Promise." I sighed, trying to ignore the humidity in the photo booth. "I can take care of myself, but I promise. So, does this work?"

"Yeah." She stepped outside the booth and plugged it in. "There." The booth lit up with lights, and the screen loaded. "This was leftover from his last party, and we forgot about it."

"Cool." I smiled and then pulled her into the camera.

"Say 'Happy Engagement!'"

"Happy engagement!"

We took several photos, and then they were printed out. I used my finger to trace our faces and the shadowiness of the black-and-white images. I never kept pictures of me or even thought of taking them with me when I left home. It seemed insignificant, as our souls are memories of life itself. We carried the memories of every moment. I passed the other six to Jenny and kept one, the weightlessness of the photo and the fresh smell of ink hitting my nose.

I placed the photo in my purse, and she gasped. I glanced at her, puzzled.

"What?"

She gently stroked my purse and said, "Where did you get this? I've been dying to have it."

I sighed with relief and rolled my eyes at her foolishness. "Jenny, I thought you were having some kind of episode. Really?"

"I have an addiction to purses. You know that." She giggled. "And by the way, you look amazing. We were so busy crying that I didn't even think to mention it."

"Aww, well—thank you," I said cheerfully. My hands smoothed down my short red mini long-sleeve flared turtleneck dress, paired with red stockings to conceal the bruises on my legs that I hoped no one would notice.

"Of course! I always love your style, Rhi."

"Um, I can send you the details about the purse later if you'd like."

She clapped her hands. "I would love that." She winked at me. "You have no idea what a favor you're doing me." Her rosy cheeks were glowing.

"No problem. Anything for you." I shrugged and turned more toward her. "Now, tell me more about your grand wedding and loving fiancé." We held hands again.

"Okay! Well, I've been thinking about having it—" A loud knock startled us in the booth, and we both jumped at the sound.

We scowled and asked, "Who is it?"

The heavy curtain was pulled aside, and Leenardo came into view. He wore a casual smile, clearly more relaxed than before. In his hand, he balanced a plate packed with food.

"Yes?"

"I thought you might be hungry." He stood tall, blocking the light that streamed in from the dining room.

I pressed my lips together. "Thanks, I guess," I said, taking the plate from him and setting it on my lap.

"Hi, Jenny."

"Hi," she said, guarded.

He let out a breath. "I need to talk to you."

I looked down at my plate, moving the fork around. "Jenny and I were—"

"It's important."

"Maybe later."

"Yeah, we were discussing something, Leenardo." Jenny side-eyed him. "You can talk afterward."

"I'm sorry, but it's important—please." His face displayed a sense of urgency and, if you looked closely enough, guilt about something.

"Please?"

I rolled my eyes. "I don't know—" I didn't want to talk to him; I missed Jenny. I wanted to forget the past few weeks and pretend we were back on the steps in front of my apartment, complaining about life while also smiling at its joys.

"I—sure," she said quickly but hesitantly. "I have to get back to John. He's probably fallen over by now with all the talking." Her eyes focused on me, concerned, and her feet were hesitant to move.

"No," I whispered. "We're not done talking." My eyes pleaded for a sense of my normalcy from Lee's bipolar emotions.

She managed to smile. "We can talk later—don't worry, okay?" She grasped my hands gently, not wanting to let go but reassuring me that I was safe and she would be nearby. "Besides, it's just wedding stuff." She winked as he made room for her to leave the photo booth, and then he sat beside me.

"I won't be too far. Call if you need me!"

"Love you!" I shouted,

"I love you too!" she replied, happily skipping out the door, her eyes fixed on me as she went.

I played with the food on my plate while he relaxed in the booth. He propped one leg up and kept an eye on the door. I took a bite of broccoli as my stomach growled at the smell.

"Looks like I showed up on time," he chuckled.

"Yep." I swallowed hard. "What did you want to talk to me about?"

"I want to discuss last night."

I looked up at him and sat up straight. "Okay."

"I, um— I know I can have a temper sometimes and wanted to—"

"Apologize?"

"Yes, what you said," he expressed, rubbing his hands roughly against his pants leg.

"Okay, but that only works if you actually say it."

His eyes drifted around before locking onto me. "I'm sorry for how I acted last night. I'll make an effort to be gentler." His voice wavered as if he had never apologized or didn't want to.

I presented the fork to him with a piece of ham on it. "Apology accepted," I said casually, even though I could have screamed at him instead. He scraped his teeth against the fork, removed the ham with his mouth, and smirked as he chewed. His reddish-brown eyes signaled a truce between us, and his golden blonde hair warmed my heart.

I dipped my pinky into the brown gravy and sucked it off. "I guess we're getting along like you wanted."

He nodded in agreement. With a playful smile, he raised his eyebrows and touched my curly French updo. "I love the silence between us," he said.

"Why?" I asked, smirking and perplexed. "I just do. We get along better when we aren't clawing at each other's throats. You know, the beauty between our two identities flows more freely when we don't."

"Beauty— I didn't realize you felt that way." I set down the fork and raised an eyebrow in amazement at his confession. "I think you can be cool sometimes, too."

He laughed and returned his hand to his lap. "Sometimes, I forget we think differently."

"Sorry."

"About what?"

"I'm sorry that we just don't mesh well."

His jaw tightened, showcasing his exquisitely shaped jawline and perfect lips. "Don't be, but I do think you can be sweet too."

"I'm truly flattered," I said with a playful smile, lightly teasing him for the compliment. It was very kind of him to say that if only it could last longer than a few minutes or a day.

"You're welcome, and if you don't mind my asking."

"Mm?"

"Can I have another piece of ham?"

"You sure?"

"Mm-hmm." I stabbed my fork into my plate, picked up another piece of ham, and handed it to him.

He bit into it and said, "This is a good piece of ham." He smiled tightly, chewing the tenderness of the meat.

"It is," I grinned at him. We closed the curtain and basked in the soft glow of the photo booth lights.

I leaned against the wall in the dark, gloomy room, feeling utterly alone. Yet, I could hear the laughter and voices of guests echoing throughout the estate. I was very happy for Jenny; she had found Mr. Right, and I knew in my heart that he would take good care of her. She deserved every blessing that came her way.

For as long as I've known her, she has never harmed anyone—not even a bug—yet she had a fighting spirit within her. I would truly miss her and her striking red hair. My lucky clover would be gone. She was the most optimistic person I knew, which often made me feel sad, especially since she was leaving soon.

The party began to wind down around midnight. I looked at the shimmering wooden floor, which reflected the blue hour of the night, causing shadows to dance across the room. The room's darkness urged me to dance in the moonlight. I wasn't fond of parties, but I endured them for others because they brightened their perception of the world—a small community of people who believed in each other or wanted to be around others. I didn't. I wanted to be home. I slipped into the light coming from the windows and sat on the bare floor, kicking my heels off.

I was lost in my thoughts, surrounded by the emptiness around me. I listened as the dust in the room danced in the wind, and the floors and walls creaked and groaned with the movement of people throughout the house. I could feel the chill rising from the foundation. It moved me to realize that the estate was alive. I longed for a house filled with sounds and history that extended beyond the making of my very soul.

Someone had left a large window open. The wind and curtains fluttered as if the house were haunted. It felt livelier than ever, with people shouting their goodbyes, expressing their love, and stumbling out of the estate drunk. I could only glimpse faint bodies and faces in the yellow, blinding light streaming through the barely cracked door.

I entwined my arms while stretching my back, feeling the cold, damp breeze against my legs. Suddenly, the door creaked loudly upon opening, and the sound of shoes tapping on the wooden floor drew my attention. I lowered my arms and squinted to see who had entered, but the person stopped and hid in the darkness of the room.

I didn't speak, move, or feel afraid. I could never be frightened of people; my fear lay in not being able to roam freely in life. The wind picked up and blew harshly against my face, so I crawled over to it and closed it. I looked back, and the person remained in the same spot, silent.

"Who are you?" I turned my back to the window and stood up slowly, keeping my eyes fixed on the figure. "I know how to fight, and it won't be pretty."

The person laughed and stepped into the light. "I'm up for a challenge," Leenardo winked at me while holding a bottle of wine and two glasses.

I sighed in relief and grabbed a glass from his hands. "Asshole," I said, raising it for him to pour some for me.

"I thought you might enjoy a treat after dinner."

I chuckled. "Yeah, sure, why not?" I winked at him as he poured the most vibrant red wine into my glass, the sweetness wafting up to my nose. "Thanks."

"You're welcome." He placed the bottle on the table by the door and took a sip of wine. "What are you doing in here all by yourself? I searched everywhere for you."

I sighed at the thought of having to explain myself. "I just wanted some time alone. It's nice to be by myself sometimes." I sat back down on the floor, and he joined me. "So—why were you looking for me?"

"I wanted to check if you were ready to go, but I see you're not." I nodded and took a sip of wine, using one hand to lean back a bit on the floor.

"Am I ever?" I smirked. "I wouldn't know."

"No, you wouldn't since the few things we know about each other are hardly anything."

"I agree," he sighed heavily from his chest. "Do you like music?"

"Who doesn't?"

He smiled at me and pulled out his phone. "Pick a song."

"Why?"

"I haven't gotten a dance yet."

"I didn't realize I promised you one," I giggled. "Are you asking me?"

"No. I'm telling you." He smiled and handed the phone to me. "Fine."

I sat up straight and scrolled through the list of songs on his phone. Most of them were either classic or Italian music, except for one—an American classic love song called "Summer Wine" by Nancy Sinatra. I turned up the volume, dashed to the table, and set the phone down. Before playing it, I extended my hand and asked, "Shall we dance?" I smiled as I finished my wine, eager to dance to something other than instrumental music.

He smiled as he stood up, taking my hand and pulling me into the dance quickly, his hand resting on my lower back. I giggled as I wrapped my arms around his neck. We danced in circles while the music blasted, drowning out the noise from the remaining partygoers. I began to sing along with the song, swaying my head back and forth as if I were singing a lullaby for Lee. At first, he just smiled and laughed, but then he joined me in surprising harmony as we sang softly together, moving across the room as much as space allowed us.

Eventually, the music flowed through our bodies as we danced. Then Leenardo stopped to spin me around and dipped me low. He lifted me up, and I burst into laughter as our faces came together. His hands lifted me slightly above the ground as he twirled me around. I let out a small scream when he swung me, and then he gently lowered me back down. We stepped back, and he spun me around again, with my back to him and our arms crossed as we danced.

I sang at the top of my lungs as the song repeated. I slipped out of Leenardo's embrace and danced backward, swaying my hips slowly, bending down, and swirling in circles around the room. My fitted dress couldn't move with the air, but the energy in my body did. He tossed his suit jacket onto the floor while moving his shoulders and arms. I danced as he followed me around, using my finger to beckon him closer as I sang Summer Wine.

The song had stopped, so we played it again, but this time, he sat out the dancing while I swarmed the room with excitement and energy. He lay on the floor sideways, legs crossed, waving his hand as he watched me, his little siren in a cage. I whirled barefoot around the room, wine in hand, swaying to the music, entranced.

He nodded his head to the rhythm and whistled at me. "Rhiannon, ladies and gentlemen!" He chuckled as I bent down and crawled over to him on the floor.

"Are you tired already?"

I tilted my head, tipsy, and said, "Mm—I wanted to see you up close." Everything in the room began to move in ways I couldn't perceive, and what I glimpsed were vibrant rainbows filling the air. I paused, creating a significant gap between us, and knelt on my knees. "I see."

"What do you see?" he laughed, looking around the room. "I just see."

He looked confused. "Okay," he said, gazing at me with a flicker of kindness in his eyes. "I think we should call it a night."

I shook my head as the colors swirled. Placing my hand on my racing heart, I felt no fear. I just laughed hysterically and then glanced at Leenardo. I bit my lip and asked, "Did you ever think you would be in this situation?"

"When you say situation, do you mean us?" I nodded, feeling more relaxed and sensual all over my body. "No." We looked at each other for a moment. "It's fate." I shrugged, feeling a bit silly.

"Fate?"

"That's what this is, Lee. Fate! Why else would we run into each other?" I bit my nail while I dissociated and mumbled, "You're my key to freedom."

"Mm?"

I stole one last glance at his beautiful face, feeling my pulse quicken and a surge of energy flood my body. I stood up. "Rhiannon," he said, his brow furrowed with concern as he sat up. I smiled and dashed through the estate, hearing muffled voices from various rooms and Leenardo calling my name. I noticed the dim lights flashing as I pushed through the back door and stepped outside.

I dashed toward the water, my stockings getting muddy as the wind whipped against my face and back. Breathing heavily, I paused at the water's edge and noticed an old, rotting wooden boat. I laughed, captivated by the vibrant colors dancing in the reflection of the water and the night's light. I quickly undressed, tossed my clothes on the ground, and took a deep breath before diving into the water. I felt like a fish gasping for air. The smoothness of the estate's waterfront caressed my bare body, soothing my scaly skin and easing the heaviness of my tail. The calmness of the water made it easy to swim, refreshing my lungs and cleansing my soul.

It felt like hours had passed before I heard people screaming my name. I rolled my eyes as I emerged from the water, peering at the land and watching the humans search for me. I smiled when I noticed the fear in Leenardo's expression. As I took in the night and the moon's brightness, I floated on my back, drifting far out. It called to me — not to return home but to celebrate. It needed my love, and so I offered it. It saddened me that I had no rock to rest my tail on; it would have made an excellent scratching post for my scales.

The ocean was icy cold, and I felt like an iceberg drifting away from the shore. Looking closely at the moon, one could see baby sirens swimming around in their Luna crates, waiting to find a home. Most sirens were fortunate to be born of the ocean, but being born of the moon was highly regarded, as it governed the ocean's spirits and could destroy any being if it chose. Any siren born under its influence carried a legacy and power beyond anyone's understanding.

I missed home, but no matter how vast the sea was, I realized it could never compare to the one that shaped my very essence. I rolled over and began swimming toward the shore, where I could still see everyone losing their minds over my absence. Thankfully, everyone eventually went back inside the estate, except for Leenardo. He rubbed his temples, looking stressed. I hid behind the old boat, peeking out from its cover, and began singing the song from earlier.

He started to walk away, so I sang louder, my voice echoing in his ears. He paused for a moment, gazing at the waterfront. "Hello!" he shouted, frustrated.

I began singing again, startling him. "Hello!" he shouted again, but I continued singing until he bravely approached the boat, trying to locate the source of the sound. He climbed into the boat and sat there, gazing out at the water. I slyly swam beneath the old boat, tapping it lightly to tease him. "Who's there?" he asked in a hoarse yet friendly voice. He sounded lovely when he spoke softly and caringly, which made him appear livelier. "I'm losing my mind," he whispered.

He closed his eyes and tried to calm his nerves, alone, out in the dark of the night on an old, creaky, and rotten boat. I waited about three seconds before rising from the water, his eyes still closed. I sang lowly, holding onto the dry rot, my hands aching from its roughness. I pulled on the boat's side, rocked it, and continued to sing. He turned his head slowly, his chest breathing heavy, and opened his eyes.

I smiled and said, "You found me, or more like I found you."

He was speechless, shaking his head in disbelief as he glanced back at the estate, where people searched for me with flashlights, calling my name. "You know you scared the hell out of us, especially Jenny," he said, leaning over me. "Well, do you?"

I giggled, feeling playful and carefree about the consequences of my actions.

"Maybe."

"Get out of the water; it's freezing! Everyone should know you're back," he said, rubbing his cold, shivering arms.

"It doesn't bother me," I replied with a carefree shrug.

"Well, it bothers me! Come on out," he whispered, concerned.

"Grouch!"

"You've had enough fun. Please let me help you out of the water."

"You're no fun," I pouted, frowning. "What will you give me if I do?"

He immediately moved closer and asked, "What do you want?"

I giggled. "A moonlight's kiss."

"What is that?"

"It doesn't matter what it is. I want one." He nodded, his breath forming icicles in the cold. "Okay, what do I need to do?" I created the name for fun. Amazingly, he was willing to help me out of the water so he could be seen as the hero rather than the prey.

"Drink the water bathed in moonlight, then kiss a siren beneath the moon, and the seas will bless you."

He frowned, clearly amused. "Are you serious?"

"Mm-hmm." I giggled. "No one is making you do anything."

He sighed and moved to the end of the boat, dipping both hands into the water. He scooped it up, watching the moon's reflection ripple on the surface, drank some, and returned to his spot.

"I assume you are the siren." I nodded with a smile. "Okay, a kiss you shall have," he said as his shaky hands let my wet, tangled hair fall.

I tilted my head back and closed my eyes. The cool breeze brushed against my aching, cold, red lips. At first, I felt nothing, and then a wave of warmth washed over me. He placed his hand behind my head for support as we lingered in the kiss. I expected it to be short and sweet, but it was captivating—a bit feverish, making me feel as if the water were boiling my scales off while my tail reshaped into my legs. The shouts of my name faded away, but the sounds of our lips colliding filled my ears as he practically pulled me out of the water and into the boat, my bare breast scraping against the side of its rotting structure. My feet kicked frantically, and my stomach fluttered with butterflies.

He wrapped his coat around me, and his kisses turned into gentle pecks as he lifted me into his arms and stepped out of the boat onto the grass, shouting, "I found her!"

I knew I was breaking my number one rule, but I had done it plenty of times before. This time, however, the soft sheerness of the clothing didn't come between us. My mind was blank, except for the memory of his lips.

Chapter 12

'Do You See Me?'

"Oh, plunge me deep in love — put out my senses, leave me deaf and blind."

-Sara Teasdale

A scoop of vanilla ice cream, topped with miniature marshmallows and peppermint, was dropped into my hot chocolate as I held out my hands, ready to receive it on another chilly day. The city was as loud as ever, with streets filled with cars passing by and splashing a mixture of dirt and rainwater onto the ground. He stood at the edge of the sidewalk, waiting for me while I grabbed my hot chocolate, blowing on it to cool it down as I stirred.

His black leather glove looked stiff and frozen as he held his hot chocolate. His right foot tapped relentlessly against the cold, wet concrete while his leather jacket flapped in the wind. He lowered his head to sip from his cup, and his eyes glanced over at me.

As I dragged my boots along the pavement, a broad smile spread across my face, the sound akin to stepping on crisp autumn leaves. I savored the aroma of fall rising from my cup as I closed the distance between us. My chunky curls bounced into my face, obscuring my view of Leenardo.

"Hey, stranger!" I shouted playfully. "All by yourself?"

"Depends," he replied, licking hot cocoa off his lips.

"On what?"

"On what you consider to be lonely." A smirk appeared on his face as he sniffled and adjusted his jacket with his free hand.

"It's good that I'm used to lonely strangers."

"Yeah."

"Yeah! I've been around so many that I'm an expert now," I said, gripping my cup tightly and smiling. "What's on the agenda for today?"

He finished his hot chocolate and tossed the cup in the trash. Then, he rested his arms by his sides, cracked his neck, and exhaled slowly. "I have one minor stop today."

I nodded. "Okay. How long will it take? I'm cold and tired."

"I don't know, but you're coming with me so that you won't be bored."

"Bored? When am I not bored?" I chuckled tiredly. "I think we should get hot chocolate more often; this is really good."

"It's hot cocoa, and it's all good."

"No, it isn't." I laughed in the prejudice of being a picky eater and drinker.

"Okay, enlighten me," he said, crossing his arms, prepared for a debate. "No shortcuts, either."

'Shortcuts? Never!" I bit my bottom lip. "Hot chocolate is a very meticulous drink to create. There are only so many ways to make it. If you can't make it even with the same three to two ingredients, it just goes to waste and tastes awful."

"Is that so?"

"Well, yes. I mean, you wouldn't understand." I sipped more hot chocolate. "And why is that?" he asked, moving us away from the edge of the sidewalk.

"You're rich, so you're used to everything being of high quality."

"Bullshit."

"It's not, but it is the truth."

"I don't see how that relates to making hot chocolate."

"It's fifty-fifty. You don't have to be wealthy to enjoy or create the best hot chocolate, although it can sometimes imply having the best resources for it. As I mentioned, it all depends on the situation.

His light brown eyelashes fluttered as he squinted in thought. "You might be right. I can see the possibility of that," he said, chuckling uncertainly, unaware of what my words implied.

"I might be!"

"You might be," he scoffed, pushing his hair back and clenching his jaw. "Okay. Can you make the best hot chocolate?"

"We're not talking about me."

"Oh no! We are, since you're such an expert. I'd love for you to make me hot cocoa sometime."

I shook my hand from side to side in uncertainty. "Eh, I can try, but there's no guarantee it'll be amazing."

"I'll manage."

"It's a date." I winked at him, admiring his stubbornness on the subject. "A date it is. Are you done?"

"I don't know. My lack of funds might need to savor the hot chocolate," I teased him.

"I can believe that."

"Asshole," I said, glaring at him before tossing the cup into the garbage, splattering his leather jacket. "Oops!" I gritted my teeth, on the verge of exploding from my clumsiness.

"It's alright," he replied, attempting to hide his irritation as he looked at his drenched jacket. "My wealth can cover damaged goods." He raised an eyebrow sharply.

"I can believe that," I mimicked, then turned to head toward the limo. "Napkins at the stand!" I hollered back at him.

"Good to know!" he waved his arms, pointing to the hot chocolate that had spilled on him. "This is vintage and something my father passed down to me, just like his father did before him!"

"Sounds like a 'you' problem!" I giggled, but I felt nervous about nearly ruining a family heirloom. It didn't matter that it was just a jacket; it made me feel embarrassed — something I wasn't used to, at least not with him.

I could hear him fussing as he cleaned himself up. "You're going to pay for this!"

"What's new?" I smirked and shouted as I quickly glanced back at him, giving me the finger, before hurrying back to the limo. "Just my luck," I muttered under my breath.

I waited in the hotel bar area. It was dimly lit and somewhat empty, like many places I've visited recently. Everyone spoke in whispers around me. The table was made of metal with a wooden post, and the chair had a leopard print with a small purple lamp on top. The floors were checkered in black and white, and several long, flowing mahogany curtains hung in the doorway. Random artistic pictures were positioned in front of a mirror on the wall above the table, and two large chandeliers in shades of pink and yellow dangled from the ceiling. They resembled teeth placed next to each other, creating a curved effect. The bar was located to the far right, through the doorways next to an exit.

Leenardo was in the lobby talking to the receptionist about getting us a room. He still hadn't explained why we were there, but I assumed he wanted a change of scenery. I couldn't complain; his apartment was beautiful, but I had grown tired of looking at it. The hotel wasn't particularly impressive either; it seemed less extravagant than the last one he had stayed in.

I traced my finger around the glass of water out of boredom. I noticed there were many more men than women in the place. I might have been overthinking it, but it felt strange. I only spotted two women. One seemed to accompany her husband, while the other sat alone, like me. She was young and barely dressed for the weather.

The men were either old or middle-aged, dressed in suits. The air was thick with secrets and melancholy. I wasn't a stranger to it, and it seemed Leenardo wasn't either; otherwise, he wouldn't have chosen this place. I set the glass on the table and noticed Leenardo walking toward me.

I perked up and smiled as he stood before me and asked, "Are you ready?" I nodded and smiled again while grabbing my coat and purse. He held me at the waist as we made our way back into the lobby, passing everyone along the way.

"Can I ask you something?"

"Yes," he said as we stopped in front of the elevator.

"Is this place what I think it is?"

He smirked. "I don't know. What do you think it is?"

I shrugged calmly and said, "A dirty hotel." He drew me nearer. "A place where men meet working girls like me." I watched him, remaining completely still. The elevator dinged and opened.

"Not that it matters, but yes, it is." We stepped inside and pressed the button for the eighth floor. "I told you I had a stop to make."

"I didn't know it was here. We girls had heard about this place, but to see it up close is—"

"Is?" I smirked, removing his hand as I leaned against the elevator wall. "I don't know. It just makes me feel a certain way."

"Okay," he replied, caressing my cheek. "I have a surprise for you when we get to the room."

"You really know how to spoil a girl."

"It's my specialty." He winked as the elevator doors opened to a vast, empty hallway. I stepped out ahead of him, walking down the corridor as if I knew exactly where I was headed and which room I was supposed to enter. After about ten paces, he walked around me and paused at room 21, sliding the key to unlock the door.

He pushed the door open and said, "After you."

"Mm—it's cute." I mocked as I stood in the living room. The walls were a loud, hideous red, with leopard-print furniture and a gold bar with an empty shelf behind them. "It's their best."

"Not really." I chuckled and then sighed. "So, where's the surprise?"

He pointed his head toward the bedroom and said, "In there."

I rolled my eyes and quickly walked over to the door, turning the knob slowly. "In here?" I looked back at Lee. He nodded. "Yes. Are you afraid it's something you won't like?"

"No. I just hate surprises." I smirked and walked into the room. On the bed was a black box. I dropped my coat and purse onto the floor and quickly opened the box. Inside was a dress—a stunning dress.

I hopped onto the bed and pulled it out of the box while Lee stood in the doorway.

"It's gorgeous. You could have told me you wanted some alone time with me," I smiled teasingly.

He put his hands in his pockets. "I didn't want to make a fuss."

I giggled. "Sure. But what am I supposed to do with it?"

"I want you to wear it for me." I ran my fingers over the dress, feeling its softness. "Mm—okay. Give me a few minutes." He nodded and closed the door behind him as he stepped out of the room.

I gently placed it on the bed and undressed. The dress was an exquisite strapless design in pristine white, its sheer fabric whispering against my skin as I slipped it on. The delicate layers of material clung effortlessly to my figure, offering a tempting glimpse of the lacy white lingerie beneath. Each curve was subtly highlighted, creating an elegant silhouette.

As I turned in the soft light, the dress transformed, its wraithlike quality becoming even more pronounced. The way the fabric caught the light gave it a dreamy, luminous effect as if a halo surrounded me. The combination of the airy dress and the delicate lingerie beneath created a harmonious blend, making me feel like a vision in white.

I was surely going to be enchanting tonight. In his eyes, I would be like the moonlight.

I zipped up my black leather boots and wandered into the bathroom, dampening my curls with warm water for a fresh look. As I admired myself in the mirror, I realized that, for the first time, I looked more beautiful than I had ever thought possible. However, I felt a twinge of guilt, knowing this transformation was mainly for Leenardo's pleasure rather than my own.

I gathered my belongings from the floor, placed them on the chair in the room, and opened my purse. I took out my brush and began to style my wet curls. I sank back onto the bed, brushing my hair carefully while observing the purple walls around me, which were made of fabric decorated with images of trees and vast landscapes carved into them. Then, a knock came at the door.

"Yeah!"

He opened the door, and the creaking hinges announced his presence. "I set up the bar. Would you like a drink?"

"Surprise me." I smiled slightly, curious about us being at a hotel; the brim of the brush becoming painful to hold because of my tight grip.

"Okay," he said, nodding. "But don't take too long."

"Does it matter? We're the only two here."

He chuckled. "I know, but still, don't take too long."

"Okay," I said softly, rolling my eyes.

I put my brush back in my purse, sprayed perfume in all the right places, entered the living room, and sat at the mini-bar while he prepared our drinks.

"How long are we going to be here?"

"You like martinis?"

"I've never had one." I bit my nail. "Are you going to answer my question?"

He exhaled. "We'll be here for two days."

"Okay, and what for?"

He carefully picked up the elegant martini glasses, their sleek curves glistening under the soft light.

With a steady hand, he poured the chilled martini into each glass, the liquid swirling gracefully as it filled them. Finally, he reached for the jar of olives, selecting a plump green one and gently dropping it into each glass, allowing it to sink.

"Well, you know I mentioned I had to make a quick stop."

"Mm-hmm," I said, using my pinky to stir my drink.

"I have an old friend who used to be my business partner, and he's coming with a few of his friends. It's his birthday, and this is the only time we could meet to discuss that business. That's why we're here."

"You need two days to discuss business with me tagging along." He swirled the drink in his glass. "No, and yes. I need one day to discuss business and another day just for us. As for you being here, I thought it would help the deal go smoother."

"You mean you want me to flirt and make him feel important."

"Did I mention how great you look?" he smirked. "You really do."

I chuckled. "I'll help you, but I wish you had told me before we left."

"I have a habit of not wanting to explain things too much."

"I know," I said as I gulped down the martini and pushed my glass toward him for another one.

"Jenkins will bring us a fresh set of clothes later tonight, so don't worry about sleeping in that dress." He winked. "Just know you'll be out of it."

I bit my lip. "Mm, is that so?"

"Mm-hmm." He winked again, caressing my chin until a knock came at the door. "Now I understand why you were being so nice to me."

He set his glass down and walked toward the door. "Sure you do." He winked.

A group of three men entered the hotel with a woman who didn't seem like an ordinary person but rather like a working girl. I felt the night would be long and the party lively. I stayed at the bar while the woman joined me. The men hugged and patted each other on the back. They all wore suits reminiscent of Leenardo's; their skin was smooth, their hair slicked back or styled, and they displayed pretentious behavior.

She placed the birthday cake on the counter, removed her jacket, and tossed it across the bar. Leaning forward, she said, "Hi. I'm Cherry."

I tossed an olive into my mouth. "Hi, I'm Rhiannon."

"That's such a beautiful name — very rare." She smiled. "Where are you from?"

"Nowhere around here. How about you?"

"I grew up here," she smiled, showing her gap. "Did they hire you, too?"

"Not exactly. That one hired me," I replied, pointing to Leenardo.

"Mm — well, let the party begin." She turned around and started pouring liquor into several glasses filled with ice. "Yeah," I sighed, feeling a pit in my stomach. I didn't know why, but I had never liked being surrounded by so many men.

Leenardo and his friends sat on the couches, discussing business ideas that Cherry and I found confusing. They didn't mind being overheard since we wouldn't understand their conversation anyway. They joked, debated, and argued passionately over a business deal in just an hour. I started to feel bored, so I decided to focus on watching Cherry as she cut the birthday cake for everyone while still keeping an eye on Leenardo and his enthusiasm for his project out of the corner of my eye.

It was the third time I had seen him so lively and open; however, I was just a prostitute to him, despite his occasional leniency.

"Rhiannon," Lee called, leaning back on the couch with his legs crossed. I turned on the stool and said, "Yes?"

"Come here for a minute." I obliged and walked over to sit by Leenardo. His arm was around me, and his ex-business partner and friends stared at me. "What do you need?" I asked, feeling awkward.

"My friend Peter here wanted to meet you." He glanced at an average-height man with black eyes, pale skin, and brown hair, sporting a birthmark on his cheek.

"Hello, Peter."

"Lee didn't mention how beautiful you are."

"Thanks. I'm very flattered."

"No problem, beautiful," he said with a wink, then spread his legs. "Lee, where have you been hiding her?" he joked mockingly.

Leenardo blushed like a kid with a crush. "Some place you couldn't snatch her up."

"Oh! I would never."

"I mean, you have a habit of stealing Peter." He smirked as his arm tightened around me.

"I don't recall, but if at any time she gets tired of you—" he pulled out a business card and handed it to me. "She can always call me."

I flipped the card over twice and nodded politely. "I heard it was your birthday, so happy birthday," I said sweetly.

He smiled, "Well, thank you." Then he whispered something to the other men, and they laughed.

"Hey Cherry! I think it's time for cake." Peter stared at me with his hollow, dark eyes. "It is my birthday, after all."

Cherry brought the cake, and everyone sang Happy Birthday while getting their drinks refilled. At their command, she turned on some music and began to charm some of the men in the room. I glanced over at Leenardo to see if he wanted me to do the same, but he simply asked, "Do you want some cake?"

"Sure," I said, taking a bite of his cake since I wasn't hungry. Peter shifted to the far end of the couch to distance himself from Cherry and the other two men. It seemed like his focus was on me.

"I don't mean to be rude, but Lee tells me you are a new friend."

I smirked. "You can say that." Leenardo pulled his arm away and leaned forward. "I'm going to the bathroom. I'll be right back." He patted my thigh. "Okay."

I settled back onto the couch and stayed silent. Peter grinned at me eerily, showcasing his square-shaped, overly bleached teeth. He smoothed back his hair, placed his cake on the table, then leaned back, spreading his legs. "How old are you?"

I frowned. "Why do you want to know?"

"You look a bit young for Lee."

"Well, I'm not. We're about the same age." I fiddled with my nails, feeling bored. "I'm twenty-six, in case you're wondering."

"I didn't mean to offend you." He caressed his legs while observing the tightness of my dress and licked his teeth. "You look young for your age."

"My age is indeed a young age." I crossed my arms and noticed Cherry making out with both men across from me, her body being caressed. "Since we're on the subject, how old are you?"

Peter laughed, scratching his nose. "I'm thirty-three."

I leaned forward and motioned for him to come closer. "Want to hear a secret?"

"Yeah."

"You look your age." I winked and smiled, leaning back against the couch pillow behind me. Peter laughed, then moved over to the couch where I was sitting.

"Um—I don't want to seem like a weirdo." He took a sip of his drink. "But Lee said you would grant me a wish for my birthday." I rolled my eyes but agreed to help smooth things over.

I mustered a flirtatious smile and said, "Sure, why not?" He smiled and moved closer. "I have two wishes."

I nodded, and he moved even closer. "I know what you do and who you are. Lee told me."

"Okay." I smiled, slightly annoyed at the obviousness.

"He pays you, right?"

"He does."

He smiled again and eventually sat close to me, his arm resting over the couch. "All right. I want you to sit on my lap."

I giggled. "Is that one of your wishes?" He nodded, a bead of sweat forming on his forehead as his breathing grew heavy. I slowly licked my lips while maintaining eye contact, then gently settled onto his lap. I could feel Peter's bulge as I playfully shifted in his lap. "Is that okay?"

"Yes." I tangled my fingers in his hair while he closed his eyes and inhaled the scent of my neck. "You smell so—good." He brushed soft kisses across my hand and neck.

"Thank you." He gently caressed my legs and stared at me with his lifeless eyes and unsettling smile. He squeezed my ass once or twice. "You are beautiful woman."

"And you are a handsome man." I replied sweetly and routinely. "You feel good, huh?" I asked while shifting in his lap, his bulge growing and his heart racing. "Can I feel them?"

"Feel what, handsome?"

"Your breasts." I nodded, and he grasped my breasts roughly. "God! You're beautiful." I seriously doubt that. I assumed it was his boner talking. "Softer, baby," I said as I guided his hands to move more slowly and kissed his forehead twice.

Cherry and the other two men decided to have their own party, so they said goodbye and left the hotel room, leaving Lee, Peter, and me alone. Peter slid his hands down to my waist as he kissed my neck and breasts, pressing his hips against me.

I ran my fingers through his hair and rolled my eyes. You'd think Leenardo was savvy with deals and wouldn't need a prostitute to sway his clients' decisions. "Yes, baby. Keep it coming," I moaned in a practiced tone.

"Rhiannon." He mumbled against my neck, then stopped. "Can I kiss you?"

I shook my head. "No," I said softly. "It's against my policy, sorry."

"But you have the most luscious lips."

"I know, but no."

Peter looked disappointed. "Will you grant my second wish?"

I sighed and smiled as we looked into each other's eyes. "What is it?"

"Lee pays you, right?"

"Yes, baby, he does. What does that have to do with anything?"

"Nothing. Nothing."

"Well, what is it, baby?"

"You're so sexy when you say that," he smiled, then whispered in my ear. At first, I couldn't hear him until I asked him to repeat it. It was faint but audible. What he asked of me was impossible and insane — it was against my policy, and Leenardo knew that.

"No," I said, attempting to stand up from his lap, but he pulled me back. "Just listen. Please listen!"

"I said NO!" He pushed me back onto the couch and lay down on top of me. "He said you would. Besides, it's your job!"

"I don't care what he said; just let me go!" I shouted as he held me down.

He scoffed. "You think you're too good for me!"

"I mean, if you were bright enough!"

He chuckled in anger and attempted to lift my dress. "NO!" I repeated, but he ignored me, so I kneed him in the balls, and he fell back onto the couch. "LEE! LEE! LEE!" I sprinted out of the living room and into the bedroom, where I found him startled and sitting on the bed.

. "What's wrong?"

"WHAT'S WRONG? WHAT'S WRONG?"

"Calm down, Rhiannon." We could hear Peter whining like a baby on the couch about his precious, disgusting balls. "What did you do?"

"WHAT I HAD TO DO! WHAT THE FUCK DID YOU DO!"

Leenardo peeked out the door and saw Peter, angry and shouting about what I had done. He left me alone in the room and tried to calm him down. I sat on the bed, furious about the deal he had made behind my back. He had no right to try to pawn me off like a mere toy. It was my rules and my way, no matter his contract. I didn't care if his business deal was rock solid; let it be without me.

It was my body. My choice, and he didn't even ask. He was a scumbag, and here I thought he had a shred of human decency left, but I guess not when it comes to prostitutes. I needed to find a way out of this hotel. I couldn't stay here. It was clear he would side with Peter. I felt in my gut that I was in a dangerous position. I should have known he didn't want me to entice him or flirt only.

I listened as Peter screamed at the top of his lungs about respect and the business deal. If Leenardo didn't let him have me, they wouldn't be on good terms afterward. The sound of his annoying, whiny voice echoed throughout the hotel room. I didn't hear a peep from Leenardo. He let Peter rant endlessly until he finally fell quiet. I grabbed my purse, took a knife, and lay on the bed. I prepared myself for the worst as my heart raced, thinking my life was in danger.

I hoped the Moon and the sea would protect me or give me the courage to defend myself. As the door slammed shut with a loud thud, I shot up from the bed, my heart racing. In front of me stood Lee, his jaw clenched and brow furrowed, exuding a palpable sense of frustration and anger. His red eyes seemed to want to set me ablaze.

"It doesn't look good—he's angry."

"I think we both know that."

"Why?"

"Why what?"

"Why did you have to attack him?"

"Mm, let's see, he pinned me to the couch and attempted to rape me! It doesn't get any fucking clearer than that!"

"Lower your FUCKING VOICE!" he smiled tightly.

"I will when you start making sense, LEENARDO!"

He paced back and forth in the room. "Look, I know I told you to flirt with him."

"Yeah, yeah, you did, but it turns out you promised me to him without even asking."

"I know. I know, and I'm sorry, but I need this."

"I think that ship has sailed because you know I take one client at a time, and right now, you are my client!"

He nodded. "I understand, but I made a promise to him. I thought you wouldn't mind since I'm paying you." He smiled. "I need you to do this for me, okay?" He touched my arm, and I flinched.

"I don't care," I said stubbornly about my policy. "You didn't ask, and I don't want to."

"I'll give you a bonus," he winked and pulled out his phone. "How much?"

"No."

"How much?" I shook my head. "HOW MUCH!"

"Are you going to cry now, just like him?" I asked with a giggle.

He nodded again and leaned against the bedroom door. "If you don't do this, I'll tell Jenkins to pack up your stuff and throw it out of my apartment, and I'll take back all the money I've given you. Shit! I'll even make you owe me for the money I spent on you." He put his hands in his pockets, his expression remaining completely emotionless.

"You wouldn't."

"I dare you to try me; I don't beg. I always get what I want."

"This is coercion!"

He shrugged, devoid of any emotion. "It's just for one night." He forced a smile and approached me, squatting down. "It's sex. He's not asking for much."

I searched his eyes, and there was nothing, just like Peter's. They were empty and hollow. "I thought we had an understanding."

He chuckled. "You're a prostitute, we'll never come to an understanding. It's just business, and I'm willing to pay you. One man in one night. It won't kill you."

"You are—"

"What?" he tilted his head. "What am I?"

"You are who I imagined you to be."

"Who am I?"

"Nothing—just nothing."

He patted my leg and stood up. "Okay, I'll head out there to try to calm him down and make some more drinks. You have two choices: either come and apologize or leave and go back to that dump you call a neighborhood." He caressed my cheek. "Think it over."

"I could kill you, right now." I slapped his hand away, unnoticeably wiping his touch off my leg.

"At least wait until afterward," he smirked.

A sudden, sharp pain shot through my back and stomach as I bent over, clutching my abdomen. Flashbacks consumed my mind. I saw Rio sneaking into our apartment at night while we were sleeping. He forced himself on top of me while Bambie was high out of her mind and passed out. His cold, bony body was pressed against mine as I screamed in agony, hoping for it to end. I could hear echoes of his grunts and moans while he forced himself inside me. She was unaware or perhaps ignored it, but he preferred them young and tight.

He would make us have sex with two or three men at a time for quick money. I hated it. Every fiber in my body resisted it. The men were never kind or gentle. We would leave with bruises, fractures, or soreness that lasted for days or even months. Imagine enduring that pain and still having to work the streets. We were treated like cattle, poked, and prodded as if we were nothing more than objects.

After Rio died, I made sure we wouldn't have to go through that again and that we would never face hunger, exploitation, or mistreatment. I felt sick knowing I had the choice to go through that experience again. I needed the money. I couldn't even cry, mainly because the door was open.

It was left open to demonstrate his power. Whether I stayed or left him, he betrayed me. He would feel like a king, a mastermind, and a genius. Sure, he would lose a little money, but I would lose more. I wanted to grab the knife next to me and kill them both for believing I owed them something.

I believed we had an understanding, but we didn't. There was no common ground. I was a prostitute, and he was a businessman. I slowly sank to the floor and stifled the screams that threatened to escape. Most days, I could fend for myself, but I was worn out from fighting the darkness inside me and surrounding me. One day, I felt like a person; the next, I felt like property. I wasn't sure how to feel about Leenardo Sisto, but I knew I wanted to kill him. I wanted to stab him and Peter a hundred times, but I didn't want to end up in prison for it.

I pulled my knees to my chest and rested my head against the bed, listening to my own breathing as I made a decision. I wanted to finalize it before Lee returned to the room. Sometimes, he felt like a devil in disguise. I didn't believe in such things, but a beautiful man like him had to be a fallen angel. Why else would he embody both grotesqueness and beauty?

He was just another Rio, a loose cannon living a miserable existence. He had no soul; he had died a long time ago. All that remained was his darkness—likely a darkness he justified for his wickedness and harsh ways. And I didn't have to obey his demands.

Perhaps going back to square one wouldn't be so bad. I would be in debt, but at least my morals would stay intact. I could spend a few more years with Bambi, but that would mean relying on tricking more than usual. Still, I couldn't repay the thousands of dollars I owed. Bambi wasn't much help; she was also worn out from that lifestyle.

I sank my nails into the carpet as I screamed silently into the suffocating, dry air of the room. I knew he saw me as nothing more than something to be walked over and used for pleasure. But I couldn't understand why I felt so betrayed by him. I could handle his mood swings and dark days, but trying to treat me like an object killed me.

I was naive to believe things would be different. I wanted us to discover common ground where we could eventually respect and confide in each other as equal business partners — where he could find pleasure, and I could receive payment. However, this crossed a line.

A hot tear burned my cheek as I tugged at the carpeted floor. I yearned for freedom, but at what cost? Guilt washed over me as I contemplated his offer — I desperately needed the money. I could hear them whispering and laughing, likely hoping I would change my mind. Uncertain of what to do, I sat on the floor and reflected on my situation.

I knew they would become restless, searching for an answer I was hesitant to give.

Chunks of carpet were in my hand as flashes of the past hour and my life unfolded before me. I wanted to run to the ocean and go home. I wanted to call on the moon to scorch them from this earth and make them burn. I wanted to slap my tail against the roaring sea, rocks singing among my sisters to lure them to their deaths. I wanted to swallow their souls and spit them out into a pit of fire on the ocean floor.

I wanted them to drown so badly that their bodies would float for days bloated. I demanded blood, and with that, I could feel my body becoming translucent as my legs and feet melded together. The room around me blurred, and my eyes glowed a deep, vibrant red. My teeth sharpened, and my nails morphed into claws. My curls turned brittle and unraveled, obscuring my face.

I craved their blood. I demanded that their blood be offered to me as a sacrifice. I didn't care much for Peter and would have happily bitten his head off at the first chance I got. On the other hand, Leenardo was different. He deceived me. He tricked me, and I desired a sea of blood. I demanded it. I would torture him for days until he begged for mercy. I would take pleasure in pulling out his nails one at a time. I aimed to immobilize him so he couldn't escape or defend himself. I desired for him to witness his life slipping away as I drained the life from him. He would serve as a delightful meal for days while the sea echoed my name and the moon beckoned for an eternity of my existence.

It sounded heavenly to my ears as the hotel room grew quiet. There were no more whispers, yelling, or talking. I would be the prey for the night, but without knowledge, they became my prey, and I was their predator. I would drain them dry. My darkness fed not only on me but also on others. I didn't mind sinking my teeth into anyone, whether a person or a man. I didn't belong to anyone and intended to uphold that tradition.

Chapter 13
'You Will Never Be Her'

"Swept by the tempest of your love,
a taper in a rushing wind."

- *Sara Teasdale*

The plush bathroom towel wrapped snugly around me felt constricting, making it difficult to take a deep breath. I could feel the tender rawness of my skin brushing against the cool, soft bed covers beneath me. With trembling hands, I carefully unwrapped a gift with an elegant blue ribbon. As water dripped from my damp hair and trickled down my face, I stared at the mysterious package. Absentmindedly, I played with the end of the ribbon, pondering the identities of the senders, knowing there were only two possibilities.

We were still at the hotel. Peter had left after a pleasurable and entertaining night, while Leenardo wanted us to stay, and I didn't know why. It felt like I was outside my body, observing myself and the events unfolding. I felt dirty as I roughly ran my hands over my arms, hoping to wash away the lingering smell and touch of his friend. I promised myself never to let something like last night happen again. I should have said, "No." I should have pulled out my gun and made a scene to confront such sleaziness. Either way, it would have given me a sense of justice. I planned to go tomorrow instead of leaving at the end of the week. With my savings, I was sure I could still chase my future or attempt to do so.

I pulled the gift out of the box, which rested inside a tied pouch. It wasn't heavy; it felt smooth and was made of glass. When I took it out, I discovered it was a carousel music box. It was an exact replica of the night Lee and I attended his friend's event. It shimmered in the light as I turned the key to play it, and the song that played was "Summer Wine" by Nancy Sinatra and Lee Hazlewood.

I covered my mouth as my heart sank at the sound of the music. It was a cruel gesture for Leenardo to make, especially after what happened last night. Disgust washed over me, clinging tightly as I pushed the music box away. I fell back onto the bed and curled into a ball. The song played on repeat, infuriating me further. I could imagine him thinking it was a victory, a pathetic attempt at a kind gesture for someone like me — a working girl who would never be loved or seen as anything more than a whore.

It was a beautiful gift, or at least I thought so. I was saddened to realize that it would be marked by such a horrific history created in just one day and one night. I could never view it as something precious; instead, it felt more like a punishment.

He was like an owner waving a treat in front of his pet, hoping it would be satisfied after forcing it to obey his whims. But I was a delicate and captivating creature trapped in a cage for his amusement. It was hard to admit, but I was never in control and could never be. I was a prostitute, and he was a wealthy businessman. In society, he held more value than I did.

The carousel spun endlessly as I lay facing it, watching the song loop repeatedly while my eyes grew dry from its blinding white brightness.

✳

As I looked out the window, he took a bite of the heavy, frosted dark chocolate cake. I noticed him staring at me; his presence made me feel ill. He demanded that people respect his boundaries, yet he violated others' boundaries, which made him a heretic. I thought he would be different from other tricks, but I was wrong.

He snapped his fingers to grab my attention. I slowly turned to face him, and he said, "Come down to earth with the rest of us."

"Maybe I don't want to."

He smirked, making me want to stab his charming face. "What's on that pretty mind of yours?"

"Nothing. Should there be something?"

"I don't know, you tell me." He took another bite of the cake. "This is really good. There's enough for both of us; you should try it." He slid the plate toward me.

"I lost my appetite, but please indulge yourself." I slid it back.

"Your loss," he chuckled, appearing at ease. I fiddled with my fork and asked, "What do you see when you look at me?"

Confused, he shrugged and scowled at the question, pausing his meal. He wiped his mouth with a napkin. "I don't know. I haven't thought much about it."

"Mm," I said, unfazed by his egotism.

He rolled his eyes. "If I really have to think about it, I'd say you're a stubborn woman I picked up off the streets, someone I find tolerable and even kind at times."

I nodded in response, licking my teeth and smiling in disbelief at his guts.

"Aren't you going to answer now?"

I shook my head while fiddling with the table napkin. He chuckled and said, "Oh, that's right, you made it very clear from day one that you think I'm an asshole and stupidly rich."

"Your words, not mine." I winked, ready for dinner to be over with and to resign from the contract.

He scoffed. "Did you like the gift?"

"No."

"No?"

I called the waiter for the check. "No, I didn't like it, especially after last night." He received the bill from the waiter, signed it, placed his card down, and handed it back to the waiter.

"I appreciate last night because it secured me a million-dollar business deal." He winked. "Take pride in yourself and what you accomplished for me. I apologize for doing it at the last minute, but it was necessary."

I exhaled, cracking my knuckles, disgusted by his thought process. "You call that an apology?" I said, anger glinting in my tone.

"No, but what's done is done," he said, leaning back in his chair. "I thought the gift would express my appreciation."

"It doesn't! If anything, it only makes me want to kill you even more."

"You're being dramatic."

"Being dramatic would mean slamming it across your fucking face and then against the wall." I laughed ironically. "Read the room, Lee."

"I gave you two choices, and you chose, so don't blame me for your guilty conscience."

I nodded again. "Tell me, do you have a guilty conscience?"

"No. I sleep like a baby." He sipped some water. "If you don't like the reward, consider this." He slid a stack of papers toward me just as the waiter appeared, handing Lee his receipt before leaving. I scanned the pages while flipping through them. It was another long-term employment contract from Lee. I pushed it away. The scent of freshly printed paper and ink lingered in the air.

"What do you think? I mean, you don't have to give me an answer right now." He stared at me, his breath quick with negotiation.

"No, I wanted to talk to you about this. I want to leave."

He shook his head and set his glass on the table. "We have a good thing going. Think it over tonight or in the morning, and we can discuss it. But it's good to strike while the iron is hot!" He clenched his fist as if making a pitch. "I mean ten thousand dollars a year with your own allowance and a place to live. That's a good deal."

"Mm. You make it sound so charming," I said, clasping my hands in mockery.

He laughed. "I know you're mad at me, and that'll last only a day, but don't miss out because I won't wait forever."

"I don't wish for you to."

"I would be happy to." He winked at me again effortlessly. I fell silent, no longer wanting to speak, as I took in the dining room around me. It was beautifully lit and decorated, yet I felt engulfed in darkness with the devil of a man I desperately wanted to escape. I had made up my mind; I would leave tonight, regardless of his charm or good looks.

He rested his forearm on the table and flipped a quarter between his fingers. "You're the bluest woman I've ever met." He chuckled.

"Why do you say that?" I asked, my face contorted in confusion. "You're blue."

I sighed. "Blue?"

He smiled faintly and said, "You may not notice, but in every light, even the faintest, your hair sometimes looks like the darkest of blue, as if the ocean itself lent it to you. That, and you brood more than I do."

"Thanks, I guess," I replied, disgusted, crossing my arms. "Believe me, I don't brood more than you do."

"No need. It's just something I noticed, that's all." He tucked the coin back into his pocket and straightened his dress shirt.

"Are you ready?"

"Yes," I said, lightly tapping the table as I stood up from it.

The door stood wide open as I dragged my suitcase across the carpeted floor, the wheels squeaking in the room's silence. I tossed the bag onto the bed and carefully folded my clothes, placing each item inside. I felt a surge of anticipation about leaving, fueled by my desire for freedom. I owed him nothing, and he owed me nothing in return, so there was no reason for me to stay.

I was tired of him and this dreary, depressing hotel.

I hurriedly packed my belongings, trying to avoid giving him a chance to object since he had gone downstairs. I didn't have much to pack, as Jenkins had provided us with enough for just a night and a day. Out of the corner of my eye, I noticed the music box he had gifted me shining in the light where I had left it. Although it was beautiful, the thought of keeping it made me feel nauseous, knowing it was from Leenardo. I closed my suitcase and zipped it up, planning to leave the box behind since he was its creator.

I felt the hairs on the back of my neck rise as I quickly turned around, and Leenardo stood in the doorway. His hands were in his pockets, and his expression showed no emotion as he entered the room. I slid back onto the bed and sat down, my arms crossed as I held onto my knees. My black lingerie peeked out from under my fitted brown sweater, which I paired with a matching calf-length skirt.

He stood beside the bedroom dresser, crossing his legs, his hands still in his pockets. "Are you going somewhere?"

"Yes. I'm leaving. I realized I don't want to do this anymore."

"Mm-hmm." He bit the side of his lip and placed a free hand on the edge of the dresser. "I thought we discussed that you would think it over tonight or in the morning."

"I thought it over, and I'm saying no," I replied with firm conviction.

"You're so stubborn, you know that?"

"I know."

"I'm a little surprised," he said, shaking his head in disappointment. "I thought we were getting along and that you'd be the first one to jump at extra money in your pockets."

I looked down at the floor, swinging my feet. "Me too, but I guess my morals got the best of me."

He chuckled. "Are you saying I have no morals?"

"I'm saying you crossed the line! I'm saying you don't care about anyone but yourself."

He frowned. "Where is this coming from? Is this still about last night? I apologized for crying out loud!" he waved his hand in annoyance.

I stood up, not too far from him. "It's about everything. It's about how you treat me! It's about every little thing, even the way you carry yourself." I exhaled in frustration. "I mean, Leenardo, even now, you still can't see that what you did and how you act go way beyond an apology; it won't fix anything."

"I'm sorry if I'm confident in who I am and what I want. I thought you understood that."

"Oh, I get it. You want everything to go your way, and if it doesn't, everyone else is just a damn inconvenience."

"You're absolutely right!"

He chuckled again, rubbing his nose. "What do you want me to say?"

"Nothing more. I want to leave this suffocating situation, and I don't want you to find me even more tolerable and stubborn in five years or more."

He crossed his arms and stood tall, his chin held high. "You don't think I find this arrangement suffocating as well. I was being generous, offering you anything past the despicable existence you call a life. When you asked me the question, did you want me to say I admire and love you because I don't? You're a prostitute! I find it pathetic myself. I have to seek a shallow form of intimacy to feel anything other than mourning for my wife. The bitter thought of touching other women besides her kills me!

He shook his head and pushed his hair back.

I rolled my eyes and remarked, "I can't believe the words that just came out of your mouth." I paced around the other side of the bedroom. "I hate fucking for money, and you think I want you to tell me that you love me." I widened my eyes in pure amusement and madness. "How dare you suggest that I'm just some hopeless soul searching for love among a pile of diamonds? Well, I'm not!"

He clapped his hands. "I'm glad to hear that, and this has been settled because if you want to leave, then go ahead. Be my guest. As you mentioned, I have many more valuable women who are much more interesting."

"Is that so?"

"Yes!"

"And that lady in the restaurant when we first met. Did you feel the same way about her? Did you apologize to her for making her feel worthless when you, my sir, are the most messed up person of anyone?" I laughed hysterically. "I mean, poor woman. Any woman, really, who has to deal with a freak like you who uses other women for your wife to live through."

His jaw tensed, and his eyes lowered. "You're pathetic! If it weren't for me, you would still be fucking a hundred men a night just to make the amount I have given you." He wiped his mouth and sniffed. "You—you're just another whore craving attention and love whether you admit it or not."

I nodded, set my suitcase on the floor, and slowly walked over to Lee. "You think I need you? Huh?"

"Did and still do. Let's see how long you can hold on to that money with a junkie roommate and no resources for anything better than the rotten thing between your legs." I blacked out, and rage filled my body.

"Really?"

"Yes," he nodded. "You think I need you," I muttered to myself, puzzled by his delusion. "You think I need you?" I pressed him.

"You think—I NEED YOU!" I pushed him again.

"Stop, Rhiannon," he said, standing still. "NO, TELL ME! YOU THINK I NEED YOU!"

I pushed him again and again, shouting, "YOU THINK I NEED YOU! I DON'T NEED YOU OR YOUR LOVE OR ANYTHING ELSE! I DON'T NEED YOU!" Tears streamed down my face as I stopped pushing him and began to hit him with my small fists, aiming them at the forcefield of his chest.

"STOP! STOP! RHIANNON! STOP!" he shouted back at me, gripping my tiny wrists. "STOP!" he exclaimed for the last time before pushing me so hard that I fell back onto the hotel mirror in the corner, shattering it, with the glass falling to the floor like confetti—though it didn't feel soft like confetti. It felt sharp, thin, and precise as it cut me.

I moaned in agony as I realized what had happened and what he had done. I didn't care if it was unintentional or not; it hurt like hell, especially when I rolled over onto the floor, crouching in pain with cuts on my hands. He couldn't help but make things worse as they went on.

"Rhiannon?" he said, stunned, his hand over his mouth. "I'm so—so sorry. I didn't mean to—I just wanted you to stop hitting me." He seemed genuinely concerned for my well-being. I wasn't hearing any of it. I guess everything in life was pent up inside me because I had an adrenaline rush. As he tried to help me up, I quickly sprang off the floor and slammed him against the wall, hoping to hurt him as he had hurt me.

"How do you like that? Asshole!" I said, catching my breath and touching my sore, bleeding hands. "Bambi was right. You are a fucking weirdo, and I feel sorry for your wife for having to put up with you and your insanity." I walked over to grab my suitcase, but he grabbed my wrist.

"Don't you dare mention my wife again!" he demanded as we both noticed the glimmering darkness surrounding us. "Let go of me!"

"Not until you apologize."

"NO! fuck you and your crazy obsession with ALANA!"

Before I knew it, his grip tightened, and his eyes glowed an even deeper shade of red than before. My suitcase fell to the floor as he dragged me by my arm into the living room and pushed me down. He marched back into the bedroom to retrieve my suitcase, then returned and threw it at my feet.

"Get out!" he demanded forcefully. "You've crossed the line!"

I chuckled and said, "I crossed the line? Just look at who's throwing whom out."

"You wanted to leave, so go ahead."

"What about the last of my money?"

"You didn't finish the week, so—" He shrugged. "Just leave!"

I sighed deeply and stood up, struggling to lift my suitcase. He was cheating me out of my last bit of money. I didn't care how much he had already given me; I stood tall and demanded, "I want my money."

He laughed at me. "I'm not giving you anything." He shoved his hands into his pockets and turned to leave the living room. "The exit is that way; it was nice working with you."

I knew what I had to do, but it would be dangerous. I suddenly realized that I didn't have my purse. "My purse is still in my room," I said, hoping he would go and get it for me. "For your sake, I hope it is."

"And what if it isn't?"

"I won't let you leave this hotel, but I will throw you out."

I rolled my eyes. "I just need my purse."

He glanced at me sideways, walked back into the room, emerged with my purse, dangled it from his pinky finger, and handed it to me. "Goodbye." He gestured for me to leave, and I nodded, rummaging through my purse, my hands raw, sore, and bloody.

"Make sure to see a doctor when you leave."

"Trust me, I will." I braced myself as I approached the door, then turned around with a gun in my hand. Leenardo was startled by the sight and raised his hands instinctively. "I'm sorry, really sorry, but I need that money."

He smirked, agitated yet fearful. "Money? I gave you enough!"

"Not nearly!" I looked at him nervously. "Now go to your suitcase under the bed and hand me what I'm owed. And don't lie about not having it because you do."

He nodded and walked to the bedroom, and I followed behind. He approached the bed and glanced back at me. "Put it on the bed and open it!"

He grabbed the black suitcase from under the bed and opened it, counting the two to three stacks of money. He always kept some on hand just in case of emergencies.

My hands ached from the stinging cuts, but inside, I felt excited about the cash I would soon have. He was a prick, anyway. He deserved it. He stacked the money and placed it on the bed. I slid my suitcase toward him for him to put it in, and he obliged.

"Hurry up!" I pulled back the trigger.

"Okay," he shook his head. "You're crazy; you know that?"

"Maybe I am," I sneered. "But I hope you remember this moment."

"And why is that?" he asked mockingly as he closed and zipped my suitcase. "Because you should never fuck over anyone, especially someone like me."

"A lesson from a prostitute."

"No, a lesson from me," I winked at him. "Slide it over to me."

The suitcase flew toward me, and so did Lee. He charged at me, trying to wrestle the gun from my hands. We struggled throughout the bedroom, crashing into the dressers, closet, and walls. Eventually, I gained the upper hand and struck him over the head with the gun.

He dropped to the floor near the broken mirror glass. "Are you fucking crazy! I have a gun!" I shot at the wall twice. "Do you want to fucking live?"

He groaned, rubbing his head in pain.

"Stupid!" I said, laughing at him.

"I may be that, but you're a thief and a whore."

I shrugged. "Well, remember this WHORE overtook you," I whispered. "And don't fucking follow me!" I pointed the gun at his head.

"Okay, okay."

"Good boy," I whispered harshly.

I walked backward, dragging my suitcase stuffed with cash as I raced out of the hotel room. With a gun in hand, I sprinted toward the elevator, adrenaline coursing through my veins. I was bloodied and desperate to escape. I pressed the elevator button repeatedly, urging it to arrive faster while glancing quickly behind me to make sure I was in the clear.

I felt more scarred than ever before. Everything changed instantly, like a mighty wind sweeping away a house. What made it worse was that I didn't know if the bullets in my gun barrel were old or new—I had kept it for many years. This was the first time I was close to using it on someone. It would break me to see someone die in front of me, but if I had to, I wouldn't shy away from putting a bullet in his arm or leg. It would be too pleasurable to do so.

The elevator door slid open with a soft ding, and I hesitated for a moment before stepping inside. My hands throbbed with every movement, and I winced as I grasped the handle, tossing my heavy suitcase against the wall with a dull thud. As I pressed the lobby button, the sharp pain in my hands reminded me of the fresh cuts that stained them crimson.

Just then, I caught sight of a familiar figure racing down the hallway toward me. It was Leenardo, and his face was a blend of anger and pain as he shouted my name, his voice echoing off the lined walls. His frantic calls pulled me back into the moment, and I felt a rush of adrenaline as I anticipated the race against time.

"Rhiannon!" he yelled, blood trickling down his forehead, his appearance morbid, and his elegant attire ruined. I waved goodbye with a pained smile as the doors closed, leaving him in the dim, shabby hallway of the hotel.

The ship I sought proved to be stronger than I had anticipated. You might assume it had many mighty men, but only one was strong enough to break me so easily. My jewel of tears flowed like a river across my icy, clear skin as I gazed out at the sea of broken ships and sirens that lay lifeless from war. The movement of the waves was as enchanting as ever while everything else bled in its presence.

The scales on my body were pricked. The claws embedded in my hands bore skin and blood underneath. My eyes, once reptilian and sometimes appearing red with anger, have faded to a dull blue, as if they are blind. The dark, wet hair on my head carried the scent of my enemy. The translucent skin on my body began to peel and shed, darkening the flat mountain of rock I lay on and transforming it green.

Buried treasure surrounded me, as did my fallen sisters. I tried to speak to the ocean, but it didn't respond. It simply moved farther away whenever I called out, taking the lovely bright light of the moon with it. They left me in the darkness as it crept closer. I trembled in fear as I struggled to drag my heavy tail across the land, attempting to outrun it.

The skies darkened as gray clouds gathered, rumbling with thunder. Everything around me glowed purple as a massive tornado of black smoke chased me relentlessly. In its wake, it left bubbling black tar that boiled and melted anything in its path.

The thunder roared, almost as if it were screaming. The bodies of my fallen sisters melted into the tar, and the rocks began to crumble. I screeched in pain as my scales scraped against the hot surface of the land. Jewels still filled my eyes as I fought harder to reach somewhere safe, but the smoke crept closer.

I stopped running and raised my voice into the darkness surrounding me. I felt myself rising higher and higher, but nothing happened. Exhausted, bruised, and broken, I collapsed in the spot where I had paused. I allowed the darkness to envelop me as I took my last breath, resigned to the fact that I hadn't won the war.

I closed my eyes as I felt the dark, swirling smoke burn the lower half of my body. I let out a piercing scream, yet my treasure clung to me and offered no protection. I braced myself for the worst as overwhelming waves washed over me. It felt suffocating, but I didn't struggle. I didn't want to fight; I was too tired.

A burst of sparkling light emerged from all around me and from deep within. It obliterated everything in its path and purified my body. At first, it hurt, but gradually, I became numb—so numb that I forgot who I was, what I was, and where I was headed.

It felt like murder, but gentle. It was as gentle as being tucked into the softest bed while unable to move, forced to watch everything around you without any remedy to take away the horrid pain and ambiance filling you at the same time. Come to think of it—it was just like drowning, swallowing everything at once until you surrendered to the serenity of the water, knowing it would bring you home no matter what, without regret and with the assurance that you did your best in life.

Chapter 14
'Passage of Time'

The taxi's tires screeched to a stop in front of my apartment. I continued dialing Bambi's number, but she didn't pick up, and the lights in our apartment were dimmer than usual. This indicated she was either hanging out with someone or sound asleep. I tipped the taxi driver and jiggled the old door handle, feeling the chill in the air as I wrapped my arms around myself to keep warm.

Entering, the frigid apartment, some kids played dice in the shadows near the staircase, while Amy argued with a tenant about her late rent. Everything was just as it usually was. The old stairs creaked beneath me as I passed by, feeling like a forgotten ghost. The dusky pink of my fur coat swished in the wind as I dragged my suitcase noisily up the steps to the same life I desperately hoped to leave behind.

The building was quieter than usual, and the silence put me on edge as if something were wrong. Typically, there would be a party or two at this time, along with the sounds of people using drugs and fights breaking out like wildcats. As I reached my floor, I noticed that many of our neighbors had been evicted, their doors marked with prominent red notices.

The night felt even cloudier than I had anticipated. I had hoped the nightlife would offer one last thrill before I left it behind forever. I strolled down the dark hallway, preparing myself as I passed each door. The weight in my heart made me acutely aware of my uncertain future.

I took a deep breath and paused in front of our apartment door before gently knocking. My mind was unsettled, knowing that Bambi would likely lecture me and joke about my expenses. I knocked again and called for Bambi to open the door, but was met only with silence. Assuming she was gone, I rummaged through my purse and found a pin.

A gust of wind slammed against the door of an abandoned apartment, startling me as I shivered from the cold. I noticed the window was left open, likely by drug users or other working girls. I let out a small chuckle as I inserted my pin into the keyhole, twisting and turning it to unlock the door.

Finally, I heard a click and jumped with joy. I took the pin out and put it back in my purse before opening the door. Outside, it was dark and freezing; I could see my breath in the air. Inside, I couldn't see much except for a dingy old lamp in the corner, which was broken and lying on the floor.

I flipped the light switch twice, but the lights were out. "Great," I muttered, feeling overwhelmed by everything I had experienced. Now, I would have to change a light bulb before I could wash away all the blood and pain.

I quickly grabbed my suitcase from outside the apartment, walked into the room, and set it on the bed. I made my way to the kitchen, tossed my fur coat onto the table, and then turned back to close the door. Keeping my hand close to the wall, I navigated through the darkness. The smell of the apartment reeked like something had died. As I reached for the handle, my boots slipped out from under me, and I fell beside something hard. I also felt wetness underneath me; it was lukewarm and formed a large pool.

I sat up in distress after realizing what I had tripped over. When I poked it, I felt that it was warm and made of flesh. I rolled my eyes as everything suddenly clicked into place. It had to be Bambi, drunk out of her mind, and I was lying in her vomit. I couldn't help but chuckle a bit because I realized I had made it home.

"Bambi!" I tried to wake her up, but she didn't respond; she was completely unconscious. I managed to stand and walk to the bathroom, slapping my hands against the wall for support. I turned on the light, which flickered and shone brightly, giving me a sense of clarity. I smiled and stepped into the light, only to notice my hands were covered in blood. I couldn't remember having fought Leenardo that hard. I turned on the water and began washing my hands, only to see more blood in my hair and on my body.

I was completely soaked as I spun around. Worry settled in my chest and stomach, but reality struck my heart as I ran out of the bathroom. I dropped to the floor and dragged Bambi toward the light streaming in from the window. The soreness of my cuts throbbed as I collapsed against the dry, crunchy wall on the far side of the room. I gently smacked her face and called her name to wake her up. I laid her flat over my lap with all my strength as I examined her body until I felt a cut on her arm, so I placed both of them over her chest, bringing them into the light to see that her wrists were slit.

I began to panic as I checked her pulse on her deeply cut wrists and neck, then listened for her heart, but it was empty. Nothing inside her beat as fiercely as before; she was silent within as if she had never existed at all. I rocked back and forth, trying to wake her again, calling her name as she lay there like a ragged doll, lifeless and pale.

I hit her face with such force that it felt like the bones in my hands cracked as I shouted, "Come on, baby! Wake up for me, please! Please, Bambi!"

My eyes were blurry, and my mouth ached from all the yelling. "I love *YOU*," I said softly. "Moe," I whispered. "Moe," I repeated. "I can't do this without you, so please wake up. We promised not to leave each other, remember? Together forever!"

"I *LOVE YOU*! PLEASE GET UP!" I held her hand. "I *LOVE* you!"

I didn't know what to do, so I tore the sleeves off my sweater and wrapped them around her wrists to stop the bleeding. But it didn't matter; she became ice cold. I held her close as the twilight enveloped us, and when I looked up, the moon shone brightly in the sky once more.

I shook my head as tears streamed down my cheeks, falling onto her chest. I placed my hand where her heart should be and asked in disbelief, "Do you want to leave?"

I swallowed hard. "We can, okay?" I stared into her cold, lifeless gray eyes, wide open. "You can tell from the expression on my face that I'm not lying this time. I need you to get up so we can leave this hellhole once and for all." I smiled, teetering on the edge of insanity, trying to shake her awake. "M—Moe!" I shouted at the top of my lungs as I moved her to the bed and wrapped her in our sheets.

"It's okay. You're okay now," I whispered as I closed her eyes and kissed her on the cheek. I sat beside her body, the apartment door still open. For about five minutes, I stayed there, feeling the weight of the moment and suddenly very small. I looked around the room, absorbing its emptiness and abandoned memories.

I lost control of my emotions and my body as I fell to my knees, unleashing a wave of sounds that reverberated through the building, causing objects to crash to the floor. The windows shattered as I hyperventilated, crying out for anyone who could hear me. My eyes turned completely white as I felt them roll back, and I began to tremble and foam at the mouth. My back arched painfully, forming spikes as I collapsed onto the floor, wailing like a banshee seeking vengeance for lost love.

I could hear Amy's faint voice shouting from the stairway, but it didn't matter because the pain was unbearable. I kept wailing, feeling the emptiness of the air as if my voice were trapped in the room. My throat gasped for air, struggling to catch the sound.

I pressed my bloodied fingers into the floor, my cries swallowed by the silence of the room as I felt fragile. The precious life I tried to hold onto had already slipped away, deepening the darkness I had thoughtlessly chosen to embrace.

A wave of lightheadedness overtook me, causing me to lose consciousness. Silent tears from my dark brown eyes blended with the pool of blood beneath me. Everything faded in and out, and I could see Moe's feet dangling above me while Amy rushed into the room in total shock, horrified as she bombarded me with questions.

Nothing seemed important as I became deaf—deaf to her pleas, deaf to her questions, and deaf to the world I was born into. All I could see were little black-and-white spots before I closed my eyes.

The sound of the ocean is indescribable; it can only be heard underwater as muffled echoes, distant and unreachable to your ears. It felt like losing Moe all over again, knowing she was no longer with me. She was gone, and this time, I couldn't save her from the brink of death. The reality of it all seemed so unreal. How could she take her own life? She had her episodes, but I could always bring her back to see the light in a gray world that resembled her eyes.

I couldn't say much about Moe except that she felt like family to me— a sister, and I loved her deeply. We looked out for each other. Deep down, I knew our time together wouldn't last and that we would eventually go our separate ways, but not through death, at least not yet. I believed we would share normalcy and independence together.

I had become so accustomed to caring for others that sometimes I forgot they were individuals with their own existences, not just responsibilities to manage. I didn't want to dwell on past arguments, sly comments, and judgments we had made toward each other. We had been only human, after all. She had been only human, and she had had her limits.

I tried not to blame myself for it, but seeing your loved one so cold, lifeless, and bloody, killed something inside you. You didn't know the specific spot it targeted, but it was a wound. A deep wound that would never heal. I trusted her to care for herself, but she couldn't even manage that. After just a couple of weeks without me, she ended up a corpse buried in the ground, reduced to a memory that humans clung to, even as the world forgot.

It sickened me to imagine her rotting in that box, where maggots would eat away at her body until only a skeleton in clothes remained. I felt crushed as I saw Jenny and Tigress at her funeral. While most cultures view funerals as a celebration of life, for us, it was a time of profound sadness. It wasn't a celebration; instead, it felt like a deep wound that throbbed and faded until it eventually became normal to mention her name and cherish our memories of her.

She had more of a chance at life than I did, yet she didn't take it. I typically didn't hate people, but I felt hatred toward Moe for how she made me feel, and I loathed myself for thinking her death would impact me this much for a life so poorly lived. I longed for freedom, not her death.

I simply felt sad.

"Did she leave a note?" I asked, counting the raindrops on the limo window.

"No," Jenny replied, placing her hand empathetically on my knee, but I didn't want to look her in the eye. It would only make me feel worse.

"Classic Moe."

"Yeah, it's just like her to leave this world with a dramatic exit."

"I'll miss her."

"Same here."

"Me too."

Tigress tossed her sunglasses onto the seat and leaned over to grab a miniature bottle of vodka, opening it and taking a sip.

"How are you holding up?"

I remained silent.

"Yeah, how are you?" Jenny repeated.

"I'm alive."

Tigress leaned back in her seat. "That's not an answer."

I exhaled, removed Jenny's hand from my knee, and replied, "It is for today."

"We don't want to fight. We want to make sure you're okay. We loved Moe just as much as you did and are—" she paused for a moment. "—in as much pain as you are."

I sat back quickly and folded my hands. "I know that. Don't you think I know that?"

"We do," Tigress said, tossing the bottle into the can. "But it doesn't hurt to double-check," she added, her eyes stark red from crying and her appearance drab.

"I'm sorry." I rubbed my temple. "I love you guys. It's just that I can't shake the feeling that I'm to blame for leaving her alone."

"Don't be!" Jenny moved to the other end of the limo. "It was only a matter of time, and we all knew it. From the day Rio died, she was on a path with no return, so don't you dare feel like it's your fault."

"I know she was a lost cause."

"We all did, but still hoped it would get better."

"Yeah, well, we were wrong about that." I glanced quickly at both of them before turning my gaze back to the window. "You know she would have driven herself to her own funeral if it meant being the center of attention." I chuckled softly, tinged with sadness. "She would have loved it."

"Moe would tell us that we had more to live for than crying over her, but if it suited us, then why not?" We all laughed.

"This is her goodbye party," we all smiled. "Yeah." Tigress grabbed another small bottle of alcohol and raised it in the air. "To Bambi, the firecracker!"

"To Moe!" we all shouted as we passed the bottle around, taking drinks from it. "And most importantly, let's pray for her."

My smile faded, and I glanced at Jenny. "What the hell do you mean by 'pray' for her?" My heart started to race.

"Leave me out of it." Tigress waved her hands in surrender and shrugged.

Jenny smiled nervously and said, "I mean, that is what she would have wanted us to do, and you know we all grew up in religious homes."

"I know, but Moe wasn't religious at all. She would have laughed in your face at what you just said." I gripped my dress tightly, feeling tense.

"I didn't mean any harm. I just wanted to pray for her soul so she could go to heaven."

I rolled my eyes. "Heaven? So you think she's in hell?"

"She didn't say that, but I don't really believe in it."

"You told us to leave you out of it." I shot a glare at Tigress before turning to face Jenny. "I don't buy into that, and you know Moe didn't either."

She sighed and said, "In some ways, she did."

"She never told me anything."

"Well, that's because you didn't believe in it; I just wanted to pray for her. It's a sign of respect."

I chuckled, a bit annoyed. "Go ahead and do it by yourself; she isn't in hell."

Jenny crossed her legs and placed her hands on her knees, clearly frustrated with me. "What do you believe?"

"I believe that for prostitutes, religion should be thrown out the window. Don't you think?"

"No. I mean, we have sinned, but God forgives. Jesus walked among whores and thieves, didn't he?"

"Yeah, and look where that got him."

"She would have wanted me to; it would make me feel better."

I laughed in her face, feeling both anger and sadness. I brushed some hair away from my face. "I mean, pray. Pray?" I whispered. "She's not in hell; she's lost—lost somewhere she must pull herself out from. It's a place that only she can escape, on her own."

"Mm-hmm. Where's that?"

"Death," I nodded, replying. "It's a soul's damnation based on their perspective on life. It's like a crawl space that she must struggle to escape from. But yes, do pray for her, even though lying in the coffin won't help her at all." I took a long breath. "But then again, she might just be at peace somewhere. Who the hell knows?"

"Okay, thanks for clarifying. I just wanted to help." Her expression was sorrowful, and her eyes glistened with tears.

Tigress clapped her hands and laughed. "So grim! Can we change the subject now?"

"Not a problem." Jenny wiped away her tears, and Tigress added, "Rhiannon, if you don't mind, please stop hurting my sister's feelings. You're not the only one who's angry and hurt today."

"I didn't seek that intention."

"It's okay."

"Stop. Okay," Tigress said, giving me a sharp look.

"Sorry." I held Jenny's hand and kissed her cheek. "Sorry, red." I winked as I returned to my respectful corner of the limo. "I love you both, and thank you for the wreath for Bambi. She would have loved it."

"I love you, too."

"I love you," we all smiled at one another. "And you're welcome, but John and I didn't buy it."

I looked puzzled and asked, "What do you mean, if not, who?" I fixed my gaze on Tigress.

"Don't look at me."

Jenny looked down at the floor and sighed. "It was so beautiful—um, but none of us bought it. It was a gift from Leenardo."

"What? Why didn't anyone tell me?" I said, disgust written on my face. I never wanted to hear that name again. "Geez—I touched it and even took a picture with it. Really!"

"We couldn't say no; otherwise, there wouldn't be a wreath."

I buried my face in my hands and sighed. "Yeah, I get it. It was for our sister, so I get it."

"What happened between you two? You never explained how you got those cuts on your hands?"

"Nothing happened."

"I doubt that."

"That's the only answer I can give you."

Tigress scoffed and said, "You'll have to tell us sooner or later."

"Yeah."

"Well, not on this day of all days. Not today, okay?"

"Okay," they both responded. "What are you going to do now?"

The limo sped through the city streets. The trees swayed in the wind while cars and pedestrians moved briskly along the busy avenues, and life continued at its usual pace. Rain poured down harder than on any other day, making the atmosphere gloomy and cold. Inside, the limo had a brand-new smell, creaking slightly as it navigated the road. Jenny and Tigress stared at me expectantly as if I had all the answers.

I pulled my hand away from my face, tears streaming down, and said, "I don't know. I didn't know what to do when she was here, and I definitely don't know now; she's really gone."

I was furious. She left me alone, breaking the promises we made to each other. I felt a whirlwind of emotions; it seemed almost surreal. I always believed she would live to be at least ninety years old. She had always fought against life's challenges, but this time, she gave up, and I don't understand why. She had me, and I had her. I don't see how that wasn't enough.

I kept blaming myself because it hurt to think that my heart had shattered into pieces over her. I cared for her, but at the same time, she felt like a burden. I was sad that she was gone, yet relieved to be free from the responsibility of caring for someone who reminded me of my mother.

It was distressing to see the moon rise on the night of her death, a symbol of freedom, yet also a reminder that I would have to grapple with its meaning for the rest of my life. Yes, she was gone, but I was still here. It felt like a rush of unfamiliarity.

I felt incomplete as if a part of me was missing, and I sought the wholeness I once had.

"Are you sure there was no note?" I asked again, knowing they were lying. I didn't care if they wanted to spare me from the pain I felt right now. I needed to know what my friend had said in her final moments. Fiddling with my nails, I added, "Please tell the truth this time, no lies."

"Just give her the note, Jenny."

"Tigress!"

"Give her the note, little sis."

I smiled faintly and closed my eyes, extending my bandaged hands. A cold, metal-smelling, bloody piece of paper was placed in my palm, and reopened my eyes. "Thank you," I whispered, kissing the paper. Then, she took out a beaded rosary that had belonged to Bambi. She laid it atop the note in my hand, and I clenched my fingers tightly, anticipating it would leave a mark on my skin.

"She addressed all of us, but you more than anyone else. I wanted to wait until after the funeral." Jenny smiled tightly, holding back tears. "She really loved you." She hugged me tightly, her arms pinning mine down.

"I'm content to know that."

"You should be." She let go of me, and I rested in her arms. "It'll be okay. We will be okay," she said gently, caressing my hair.

"It's pouring like fucking crazy," Tigress said worriedly. "I hope we don't get drenched."

"I hope not because I can't catch a cold. John and I are having dinner later tonight."

"Of course, Prince Charming, and you have even more adventures."

Jenny rolled her eyes. "I'll be happy when you start to like him again."

"Never!" she replied with a cocky smile. "Let's just weather the rain, and then we can talk about the future."

"Okay."

"OKAY," Tigress mocked her sister.

I inhaled the scent of the limo, closed my eyes, and held Moe's note to my chest. Since Moe died, a gaping hole had taken over my life, but knowing she had at least one more say in it comforted me. She didn't leave this world selfishly; rather, she made a courageous decision that led to a dramatic ending, but I knew it was more than her death that affected me that night and in this moment.

Chapter 15

'Never Ending Story'

The subway tunnel presented a stark black-and-white contrast reminiscent of classic films. Two men hurried past me and a few others as if attempting to outrun time, even though it didn't actually exist. The light shining from the stairs above cast shadows of their fleeting figures. The brick walls, concrete floor, and benches all appeared gray under the harsh underground lights, with only a few dim bulbs illuminating small areas where objects or people passed.

I stood near the edge of the platform, with my suitcases next to me and my hands tucked into my black leather jacket. The sunglasses on my face hid my heavy under-eye bags, while the dark cherry lipstick kept my frown in check. It wasn't that I was unhappy to be leaving the Lower East Side; rather, the scent of urine from the subway and the trash blowing through the air made me feel grimy.

I cracked my neck as I stood there and looked out at the empty train tracks, waiting for the ride that would lead to bliss and freedom. It was eerily quiet, with only two other people and me waiting for the train. The lights flickered inconsistently, startling me, and I glanced up at the ceiling, noticing gnats swarming above.

I grew tired of standing, so I dragged my suitcases behind me and gently sat on the bench. My hands were still sore from the cuts I received four days ago. Jenny and Tigress wanted to see me off, but Jenny had a wedding to plan and a marriage to prepare for, so I declined their offer. Instead, I decided to take in the city through the dingy windows of the New York train.

A sense of relaxation washed over me as I realized there was no need to rush. I had all the made-up time in the world to reach my destination, and it felt good to be in a position where I didn't have to look back at the past but could focus on the new horizon ahead.

When I removed my sunglasses, everything around me suddenly

turned bright green. I slipped them into my jacket pocket, letting my bangs fall across my face. Then I leaned forward, opened my purse, and pulled out Moe's rosary. I wrapped it around my wrist, feeling as if she were joining me on the ride to freedom. Even though she wasn't truly beside me, a part of her would be with me in a sense.

I glanced at the two people who, like me, were waiting, pondering their destinations and their lives. Their average appearances overshadowed the questions I had no answers for. I faced forward again, tapping my foot on the concrete platform, willing the train to arrive sooner.

Unfortunately, that didn't happen, but it did attract a small visitor that was furry, flexible, and had tiny, cute paws. I felt it brush against my legs and sneakers. I gently petted the kitten without hesitation, then confidently picked it up and placed it on my lap. "Hello," I whispered as I continued to stroke the kitten. Its fur was completely black, with one white patch on its head. "What's your name, huh?"

It was small and felt boneless, resembling a delicate statue. I contemplated keeping it since I had the money to do so, and while I loved the idea of being alone, I wouldn't mind having another roommate to distract me from the grief in my heart and the chaos that consumed my life. "How about I keep you, huh? Would you like that?" I asked the tiny kitten as it meowed sweetly, making me smile, though only for a moment.

In a quick flash, the train arrived, and a crowd surged onto the platform, bustling like ants building a hill. I gently cradled the kitten in one arm as I boarded the train. Pausing in one of the aisles, I pulled out my phone to find my seat, then tucked it back into my pocket. I carefully made my way to my seat, trying not to disturb the kitten in my arms.

I put the kitten down, stretched my arm, and then placed my suitcases in the overhead compartment. I crossed over, hopped into my seat next to the kitten, and continued petting it. I decided to make it my new companion, but I was unsure about what to name it.

I watched as it took shallow, slow breaths, resting its pretty little eyes. Knowing that I could comfort something living and breathing made me feel connected. I focused on the white spot on top of its head, which seemed to be its weak point. I quickly removed my coat and placed it over the kitten, just enough to ensure it couldn't suffocate, and I wouldn't get in trouble for having it on board without a carry-on and not paying.

I admit I wanted to take this journey alone — I felt it was something I needed to do alone. However, it turned out I wouldn't be alone after all. As difficult as it was, I found myself feeling isolated while traveling without friends or Bambi from a place filled with so many memories, a place that partly shaped who I was.

The scariest and most exciting part of this journey was that I would be alone, very much alone. So many events unfolded over a couple of weeks, and it made me feel reborn. I felt numb at this point in the journey and in the new life I would have.

I peeked beneath the coat to check on the kitten and felt relieved to see it still breathing. I smiled and said, "You'll be with me from now on." I leaned in closer. "I will love and protect you. I will name you Bambi. It's the most cherished name I know, and it belongs to a dear friend of mine, so that makes you family."

I felt my eyes well up with tears, so I dropped the coat and leaned back in the seat. I noticed the ticket collector approaching to check everyone's tickets. I shut my eyes and took a slow, deep breath.

"Are you okay?"

My eyes flew open, and I responded, "Yes?"

"I asked if you were alright, ma'am."

I nodded, swallowing hard, nervous about my newfound freedom. "Oh, yeah, I'm fine." I forced a smile as the collector checked my ticket on my phone. "Okay, you're all set. Have a great day."

"Thank you." I forced a smile once more, exhaled with relief, and glanced behind me to make sure I was clear. Turning back, I felt content that my kitten had not been discovered.

I stared out the window as the train began to move, and with it, my life did, too. I placed earbuds in my ears to block out the silence, but I noticed everything around me from the corner of my eye. The passengers were scattered throughout the train, and the attendants helped with bags and served food, all while the city's scenery and the vast body of water flowed past me.

I shifted in my seat as the tender cuts on my hands irritated me. I didn't expect much, but for once, I hoped the cuts wouldn't scar so that I wouldn't be reminded of him, with his sun-kissed wavy hair and beautiful golden skin. I tried not to think about him too much, but it wasn't easy.

The fight between us was intense. It shouldn't have happened, but life is full of surprises. I knew he could be heartless, and I could be stubborn, but I never thought we would end up hurting one another. Honestly, the fight was just as much my fault as his. No matter how angry he made me, I shouldn't have provoked him. When the events of that night replayed in my mind, they hurt me even more.

I tried to shake him from my mind, but it only made me feel worse. I realized that the pain from that night affected me more than I had initially thought. He had hurt me more than I wanted to admit. I wished it wasn't true, but deep down, I had a soft spot for him that I was reluctant to acknowledge. I wanted to be like stone — unmoved and unyielding. I desperately wished it wasn't true, so I pretended he didn't exist for a while. However, the truth was right in front of me: he existed, and he would always haunt me.

My heart swelled at the reality of it all. It made me cry even more as I faced the window, the loud music blasting in my ears. I struggled to suppress the thought of us being more than what we were to each other. It didn't excuse his behavior towards me or how he treated me like I was nothing. He was so hot and cold, and sometimes it drove me mad, but I never thought it would go so far as to make me feel something for him.

There was supposed to be common ground between us, but we drove a knife into that. I even contemplated long-term employment with a decent man who could steal your heart with just one look. I was naive, kind, and too understanding toward someone who couldn't do the same for me. Even now, I wanted him to understand me and the situation, but he was just as stubborn as I was.

The look on his face when the elevator doors closed hit me hard, especially when I realized that I was just as bruised as he was. In the end, it didn't matter; we wouldn't see each other again, and that hurt even more. I burst into silent tears as I held my heart, thinking about leaving not just him but everything I knew behind.

I was curious about how he was doing and whether his scars would heal at the same rate as mine or even faster by the time he started seeing another girl. There was only one person who held his heart, no matter who came along. Maybe I did want something from him; I just didn't know what it was. I tried to wipe away the tears, but they flowed like a river.

The music began to annoy me, so I took off the earbuds and put them back in my coat pocket. It was refreshing to hear the silence again. I wiped my face with my hands and noticed trickles of water outside the window. As I looked closer, I realized it wasn't rain but faint reflections of the ocean, even though the train was nowhere near the water.

I heard the soft sounds of splashing and felt a surge of happiness as I realized it was the spirits of the sea calling to me. I smiled through my tears, feeling a deep connection. They knew I needed them. I wasn't alone. They wanted to rescue me, and I wanted to be saved. It felt good to be heard again.

I closed my eyes and rested my head on the seat, feeling my body rise into the air before landing on my rock. The scent of grass, salt water, and sea air comforted me. With awareness, I could sense the weight of my shimmering tail, my claws' sharpness, and my skin's smoothness. It made me smile. I was back where I belonged and felt safe.

With a single note, I sang out to the ocean to express my gratitude and to the moon in its slumber, for they did not abandon me in my time of need. I was going home, knowing they would guide me. I was going home—